House of Quietus

Christine Holt

A CIP catalogue record for this title is available from the British Library.

ISBN 978-1-7391961-2-7 (Paperback)

ISBN 978-1-7391961-3-4 (Kindle)

First published 2023

Dedicated to the loving memory of Kenny,
Ruth, Richard and Deborah Holt

How do you murder someone?
By enjoying every delicious moment ...

CHAPTER ONE

Theresa Franks was exhausted. Her hollowed eyes, her gaunt cheeks and her dull complexion were like the worn fabric of her clothes. The bairns drained her soul. They were always complaining about something: lack of money, bland food, holes in their shoes, the cold, ill-fitting clothes. They never stopped moaning. Times were hard and she was desperate. Maybe this weekend away would give her some space and time to reflect on what had happened.

She wasn't a bad person; the circumstances had driven her to it. It had all happened so quickly, there had been no plan, no intent, it was through desperation. Her children were always hungry. Seven mouths to feed, eight including herself, it was an impossible task to keep everyone satisfied.

Theresa Franks had no idea who JF and CF were, but the chance to get away - she felt guilty for abandoning the bairns but also thankful for the respite from them.

The invite had promised exquisite dining, fine spirits and entertainment. Her parched tongue ran over her cracked lips at the thought of enticing smells and delicious food. Her tummy rumbled.

She had nearly fainted when the invite stated she would be awarded a thousand pounds for attending the wedding. There must have been a mistake. JF & CF must have confused her with someone else, but a grand would be a life changing sum of money.

Thanking God that it wasn't snowing, she had layered her tatty clothes to protect herself from the biting cold and had left Penrith at nine o'clock that morning. Her feet were already blistered having been walking for almost five hours, but she didn't want to be late. The pain would be it worth for a thousand pounds.

With a bit of wheeling and dealing, Harold Arnold had managed to cadge a few rides off dodgy acquaintances to get from Wigton to Keswick. The first horse was a bit of a donkey but better than walking and his mate had dropped him off at the barren heights of Caldbeck Common. From there, he had a slightly more luxurious ride on a rotting trap for two to the north east edges of Bassenthwaite Lake. Harry then had to walk to St Bega's Church, where he had brokered another deal to get him to Keswick.

The old shire horse made slow progress as it pulled the laden cart. Harry scratched at his shaved head and re-adjusted the flat cap to distract himself from his numb arse. He pumped his right hand three times, feeling the tension in his muscular forearms, and bulging biceps. The journey had been tediously slow, but bloody hell, he'd do anything to get to that island! He would have sold his soul to the devil for a thousand quid. With that kind of money, he could disappear. At 32 years old, he was young enough to make a fresh start and get away from her, get away from everyone. Escape the embarrassment of what had happened. Inbred locals, the bastards. He'd have the last laugh.

Eliza Hart stepped off the train and onto the platform at Keswick Railway Station. The journey had been sufficiently comfortable from Cockermouth, but now she had to find the accommodating young man to carry her oversized trunk to the carriage and take her to the rendezvous point at the lake.

Dressed to perfection in rose pink and navy blue, she stood under the glass veranda by the entrance door to the waiting room and posed. Her dark hair was silky smooth, and her hat was pinned at an angle for elegance. Her hazel eyes were mesmerising, and her warm skin tone always attracted attention. She wasn't vain, it was simply a fact that men were always eager to express their thoughts and enquire as to her exotic roots. Women less so.

Eliza smiled as a couple walked past her. The handsome

gentleman returned her smile and tipped his top hat out of respect whilst his wife glared and grabbed hold of his elbow, wrapping her forearm through his. Eliza always found amusement in the actions of jealous wives, but she would behave herself this weekend.

The bride and groom were a mystery, their initials not provoking any sort of familiarity. Anyway, with a gift of one thousand pounds, the weekend was promising to be interesting. Maybe she would finally find a suitable husband. The bride and groom were obviously rich, high society maybe, aristocracy possibly. Whoever they were, a wedding would distract her from the issues back home.

Cornelius Binks admired the grand houses as he made his way by black cab through Grasmere. The houses in the village were too expensive and the ones overlooking the lake were astronomically priced. His cottage was quaint, detached and set within a third of an acre of land, but he craved the manor house on the hill with the stunning fell views or the uninterrupted lakeside vista that only the wealthy could afford. From what he had heard, those houses were inherited, passed down through subsequent generations. He was new money and impressive properties like that were hard to buy.

Orphaned at the age of two, he had no recollection of his parents. With his chiselled chin, blue eyes and black hair speckled with grey, he had always imagined his parents to be young lovers. Handsome and beguiling, they had found love and had adored the two years spent with their precious son. In reality, he had no idea who they were or what had happened to them.

In the company of others, Cornelius was charming, with a natural ability to change his level of engagement depending on the intellect of his opponent. However, solitude was his preference, and his next goal was to create a library in the cottage with a secret hidey hole to which he could escape.

He checked his tailored suit for imperfections.

The wooden wheels of the cab trundled along the dirt tracks. Having lived in the Lake District for almost three years, he was still unsure of the hills, fells or mountains, or whatever they were called. He had heard of Helvellyn, he knew that was somewhere on his right and he knew Skiddaw was somewhere to the north of Keswick, but climbing hills, all that hard effort, toiling away for no reward, what was the purpose in doing that? No, he had other hills to climb, bigger hills, mountains. He wanted to ascend and would stop at nothing to fulfil his dreams of wealth and success. He was obviously gaining recognition, being asked to attend a wedding of people who were stinking rich. Who in their right mind gives away a thousand pounds as a gift? The bride and groom must be mad and wallowing in money.

Cornelius was thankful for the invite. The gesture had settled his nerves somewhat, that word had obviously not spread about his recent misdemeanours and run in with the police. Anyway, that was old news, he had learned his lesson, there was no way he was doing that again. His gaze ascended to the snow-capped mountain on his right and he shivered. Onwards and upwards as they say.

Vivienne Kry had tears in her eyes, how appropriate. Her surname was officially Kraj which should sound like Kry, but everyone pronounced it as if rhyming with Madge. Therefore, she had started changing her name on documents, for the mispronunciation and spelling errors grated the core of her bones. A slight change to her name may also misdirect those who had heard the story. Distance her somewhat from the whole sorry saga.

Not an ideal time to be invited to a wedding. She hoped she would not break down at seeing the happy couple marry, whoever they were. This was not the time to be joyous in romance and love, with everything that had recently transpired, but for a thousand pounds she would pretend.

She had lived in Keswick all her life, but she could not determine the identities of JF & CF. John Franklin was already married, unless he was considering bigamy. James Farmer was betrothed but his fiancée was Mary Jefferson. JF, JF – John, Joseph,

James, Jeremiah - oh there was Jeremiah from the church, but his surname was Smith or Smythe, something like that. Not one for surprises, Vivienne continued to rack her brain for who the couple may be.

Looking in the mirror, she tied her golden hair into a messy bun and pinned a simple blue hat over the top. Her amber eyes and creamy skin were deliciously warm and in stark contrast to her aloof manner. She locked her front door. Living in an isolated location close to Castlerigg Stone Circle, she set off after lunch, giving herself plenty of time to walk into the market town of Keswick. Her heart was already pining for home.

Someone would have to die for George Jones not to be smiling. As usual, he had a grin on his face as he rode the train from Carlisle to Penrith. His brown hair was flecked with golden tones and his brown eyes were like chocolate bejewelled with cinder toffee. He was boyish rather than handsome and had the vibrancy of a child seeing the many wonders of the world.

There were people from all walks of life milling around the platform as he waited for his connecting train to Keswick. People watching was fascinating: fancy folk in quality clothes, workers caked in dirt, ragamuffins selling their mudlark wares.

George flicked a penny in the air. A scrawny little boy, wearing a girl's dress and sporting hobnail boots on his feet, noticed the movement and grabbed the coin. The boy's eyes teared by the kind gesture, "Thank you, sir. Good luck to you on this fine day." He ran as best he could with his clown feet towards a food stall outside the station.

George sighed, happy to have made someone smile. He delighted in witnessing joy. Why be sad? He couldn't understand miserable people - the moaners, the groaners, the depressed - just be happy, think positive thoughts and life, luck, fate would be kind to you. Well maybe not always, there had been a few problems to deal with recently, but he had sorted that out and was free again to enjoy the fruits of his labour.

Cliff Dacosta's striking looks had always roused curious stares off the locals. Tall, broad and toned, he was an imposing presence. Even though he was born in England, was well spoken and wore clean clothes that fitted well, his dark skin and blue eyes made folk wary and they kept their distance. He had learned not to trust. He had to be suspicious of everyone and everything. Self-reliance was the key. Independence was paramount in this world. Don't ask for anything, don't rely on anyone and take responsibility for yourself. Can't blame anyone else then. He glanced sideways at his travelling companions in the carriage. They were quiet: reading, sleeping or admiring the scenery.

Cliff had never been to Keswick. He had never really left Whitehaven before. This weekend was going to be interesting. Hopefully, the start of something new, something better. He had principles though, and although the money was certainly the main incentive, he would never lower himself to do anything for it. He had already been goaded into doing things he didn't want to do and that hadn't ended well. Never again, he had to remain strong, stay true to his principles, find another way to prove himself, prove himself worthy of respect and he would win. He would show them, one way or another.

Bernard Pratt loved to indulge, so the promise of exquisite food was probably more of an incentive than the money. He laughed to himself, his belly wobbling, knowing fine well that statement was not true. Maybe he could open a shop, a bakery or a confectionery, something pretty, selling colourful sweet temptations, things people could not resist. Food so utterly scrumptious that they would work all week just to buy his delicious chocolates and pastries. His mouth watered at the thought. Kendal was a bit boring, functional compared to its prettier neighbours. He wanted the quaint, the pretty, the twee – he laughed again but with a tinge of sadness – his mother had once said he could not say sweet when he was little and would say twee. He truly missed her. The sweetness of life had soured the day she died. Life had never been the same. Bernard had never forgiven himself for the part he had played in her downward spiral, but this business idea, he would turn his life around and make her proud.

Sarah Silver was having the time of her life. She had no idea who JF & CF were, but weddings were always such fun. Sadly, she felt too old to find love at the age of 72. Her husband had died years ago, and she had lived on her own ever since. A few old, dithery characters had asked for her hand in marriage over the years but she had now spent too much time on her own and enjoyed the freedom this provided.

Since receiving the invite, she had imagined what she would do with the money. There were too many choices, but she would have to give some of it to her children and grandchildren and her first great grandchild was on its way! How exciting! The money would certainly help make life easier for them. As for the rest, she intended on enjoying herself. She had always been so prim and proper growing up. Following rules, doing as she was told, trying not to break the law, she was now too old to be dictated to.

Her white hair was baby soft, and her skin had a gentle rose hue. People always commented how well she looked for her age. With what had happened recently, she no longer cared about what people thought anyway. Life was for living and she intended on going out with a bang.

CHAPTER TWO

The ice-cold lake rippled as the four occupants of the rowing boat inched their way closer to the island. Everyone was silent, listening to the rhythmical sounds of the creaking wooden oars straining against the metal holder as the boat headed towards their isolated destination.

In the fading light, the surrounding fells were menacing layers of dark shadows. Like lurking monsters, they were crawling over each other to watch proceedings as strangers gathered on Vicar Island. From the boat and shoreline, the abode could not be seen, but the monsters were familiar with Derwent Isle House, they had an all-seeing perspective from their vantage point. They had presided over this stretch of water for thousands of years. They knew its secrets.

The invite had instructed the guests to rendezvous on the shingle shoreline of Derwentwater, at the end of Lake Road, Keswick. The weekend's events sounded intriguing, with grand accommodation in which to reside, delicious food and beverages in which to partake and a generous gift of one thousand pounds for attending a wedding, even though no-one knew with certainty who was getting married. However, a thousand pounds was too much of a temptation to resist and would see each of the bewildered guests blessed with a small fortune, a life changing sum of money.

Three strangers had gathered on the shore, and the old man, now doing the rowing, had checked their names against a list. The strangers wondered if he was mute for he had failed to utter a single word but he had guided them as best he could with his actions: a subtle movement of his eyes, a nod of his head, pointing, or simply just demonstrating what he wanted them to do.

The lake was dark grey as the subtle waves lapped against the bow. On approaching the island, the old man lifted the oars into the boat, allowing momentum to carry them the last few inches into a covered boat house with four empty moorings. He grabbed the rope which was lying in the boat like a dead water snake. Carefully, he stood on the central wooden seat, synchronised his balance with the gentle sway, then stepped onto the slats of the small jetty. He securely tied the rope to a metal ring, then steadied the boat for the three occupants. They took it in turn to disembark, feeling strange at the still sensation of being on land.

Thomas Montgomery had dark shadows under his eyes as if sleep evaded him. His skin was deathly pale in the waning light. His moustache hair was darker than the grey and white tufts of his beard. Ferret like, he was tall, thin and slightly stooped, probably from rowing to and from the shoreline.

After adjusting his flat cap, he held aloft his lantern and guided the three nervous guests around to the right, past a quaint church, through the grounds and up to the house whose main entrance was on the south side. The surrounding fells had now captured the sun and in the deepening darkness the house appeared grand but mysterious, like a classical Roman villa on Lake Como.

Having climbed the steps to the main entrance, Thomas Montgomery opened the door and stepped aside to welcome the guests inside. A central staircase rose with grandeur to a galleried landing. Displayed in elaborate frames were paintings of rich and beautiful people in colourful attire. White marble statues decorated classical niches, and urns with impressive plants softened the architectural design, giving the impression of a Mediterranean orangery.

Luke Notts appeared from an archway on the right. His dark hair was slicked to the side, his creamy skin glowed and his intense blue eyes shimmered in the candlelight. His chubby face was youthful, but he looked confident and professional in his black and white butler uniform. On his command, the group deposited their luggage in the hallway, and he respectfully took their coats. "Please, this way," he said as he walked across the hall and through an arch on the left. They were soon greeted by chatter and laughter from six other guests.

Decorated in a floral design, the room felt cosy despite its grandeur and the fire was blazing, providing much needed warmth. There were various seating arrangements within the room such as two armchairs either side of a small table, two sofas opposite each other with a low table equally placed between them and in the grand bay window were four sumptuous armchairs positioned around a table.

Luke Notts informed the three latest guests to help themselves to the indulgences on offer. He pointed to a table laden with numerous drinks and canapés. With stealth like grace, he then mingled between the other six guests to check on their welfare and needs before standing by the doorway.

"Guests, may I please have your attention. Since you are now all here, your hosts would like me to welcome you to Derwent Isle House. They will soon join you for dinner, to personally welcome you to the island and to offer their sincere thanks for you attending this most special weekend of celebration.

"This evening's events will entail a delightful three-course meal, created by our very own cook, Mr Thomas Montgomery, who you have already met, and dinner will be served by me, Mr Luke Notts. I will be at your beck and call for the entirety of your stay, so please do not hesitate to ask me any questions or request any items or services." He raised a cheeky eyebrow.

"Before dinner, you will be called individually to take part in the first event of the weekend. This will be to have your fortune told by our talented tarot card reader, Daphne De'Ath, who is well respected in the world of divination. The cards will be noted and their meanings passed to our hosts but all other information discussed between yourselves and Madame De'Ath will be strictly confidential. It is up to you whether you divulge this information to other guests. After the reading, I will personally escort you to your room.

"Dinner will be served for seven thirty precisely and following that you are then free to socialise or sleep, for everyone here appreciates it has been a long day of travel and suspense for your fellow participants. Thank you for your time. Oh, and whatever happens these next few days, please just have fun and enjoy the hospitality offered by your hosts." Mr Notts bowed his head and left the room.

Eliza Hart dared to speak to the men she had shared the boat with, "Well, I'm not sure about you, gentlemen, but I'm desperate for a drink." She swayed over to the table and perused the items on offer. She decided to take a gamble on a green concoction in a crystal punch bowl. In the subtle light, her dark hair was shimmering, her skin tone warm and there was a glint in her hazel eyes.

Mesmerised by her assertive confidence, George Jones smiled, "Then I shall join you, for I need some courage." He was dressed in a tailored suit if a little worn in places.

"Well, if you two are having one then so shall I." Bernard Pratt loved food and wine. In truth, he didn't need an excuse, he could quite happily indulge all day long. His increasing roundness was evidence of his passion. He tried to bring together the straining buttons on his waistcoat.

Eliza Hart seductively drank the green concoction from the crystal glass. Closing her eyes, she savoured the fruity taste of melon, licking her rosy red lips then sighing with pleasure. She opened her eyes to the two men staring at her, so she held up her glass to make a toast, "Cheers, everyone. Health, wealth and happiness."

They clinked glasses and repeated the toast.

"And to our generous hosts," said Bernard Pratt, who then took a large gulp of the green liquid.

"How are you two gentlemen acquainted with the bride and groom?" Eliza's hazel eyes perused the room.

The men confirmed they were unsure who JF & CF were.

"Do you know *anyone* here?" asked George Jones. He directed his question more to the stunning Eliza Hart than to Bernard Pratt.

"No one even vaguely familiar," offered Bernard, his mouth full of choux pastry, fragments spraying into the air as he talked.

Eliza confirmed she did not recognise anyone either. "That means we are unlikely to be family, which leads me to conclude we must be acquainted through friends."

"We could be neighbours I suppose. I'm from Kendal. Where you both from?" asked Bernard.

"Cockermouth," said Eliza.

"Carlisle," replied George. "But if we were neighbours, again we would recognise each other."

Eliza and Bernard agreed.

George shrugged his shoulders. "Could be through work or business associates?"

"I doubt that. Rich and poor gathered here, too strange a collection of people through entrepreneurial routes." Eliza once again sipped from her glass.

"Could be the rich employ the poor ones in their service?" offered George.

"Perhaps," said Eliza. A pause as they scanned the room, searching for possible links. "Were you two offered money?"

George and Bernard could not hide their excitement, their eyes brightening at the fortune promised. They nodded their heads in synchronisation, then confirmed the gifted amount.

"Do you think we'll be offered it?" asked George.

"Not sure, seems too good to be true," said Bernard. "A thousand pounds! It can't possibly be real, but I really do hope it is."

Eliza sipped her drink, then after a moment replied, "I'm not convinced either, but I'm damned well going to insist on it." In a surprise move, she knocked back her drink in one swift action, slammed her glass on the table, then sauntered away.

George and Bernard grimaced at each other. Eliza Hart was a stunning but scary lady.

CHAPTER THREE

As the alcohol helped to settled nerves, everyone was becoming acquainted. The nine guests were beginning to smile and relax with the forced situation. Mr Notts, the butler, stood in the doorway and asked for their attention, "Madame De'Ath would like to see Miss Vivienne Kry. Vivienne, if you would like to follow me."

Vivienne's heart went into panic mode. She had hoped someone else would be called first and tell everyone what had happened. Never mind, too late now, she followed Mr Notts out of the room and across the entrance hallway. She wore a functional navy-blue skirt and light-blue blouse. Her hair was like strands of melting gold, smooth and glistening, but simply tied back into a messy bun, leaving a few shorter curls to soften her serious face. Her eyes were amber and her lips blood-red. Vivienne wondered how accurate Madame De'Ath would be with her predictions.

Her heart was fluttering like a butterfly, too fragile in such an enclosed space, missing beats of the drum. This was not a good sign. Mr Notts stopped outside of a closed doorway and Vivienne abruptly halted behind him. She had been caught in the momentum. Not wanting to stop, not wanting to face the truth.

"Good luck, Vivienne. I hope you have a positive reading." Mr Notts smiled at her. He knocked, then waited for the prompt to open the door.

Reluctantly, Miss Vivienne Kry took one cautious step at a time into the unknown. The room was shadowed, with only a handful of candles flickering in the darkness. Madame De'Ath was sitting behind a small, round table which was covered with a large square of white cotton. On top of the tablecloth was a smaller square of purple silk. Tarot cards lay at the centre, face down, detailing a symmetrical swirly pattern in red, pink and white.

"Vivienne, welcome, I am Madame De'Ath. Please, sit down and make yourself comfortable. I can see that you are nervous, but do not be afraid. My spirit guides are lovely, seven-year-old twins, a boy and girl, from the Zia Pueblo, New Mexico. I can't hear them, but they occasionally show me things. They will protect us from any evil spirits and will prevent demons from attaching themselves to us."

A cold shiver permeated through Vivienne's already trembling body. Talking about dead children, evil spirits and demons was not helping her to relax.

Madame De'Ath was still smiling but her eyes were now closed, she seemed to be channelling some sort of energy. Her dress was an iridescent green. Her hair was the shade of copper; the top half loosely tied-up, leaving perfect waves cascading over her neckline. The green stone in her pendant seemed to swirl like mist in the flickering candlelight. Her skin was flawless, peppered by faint freckles over the bridge of her nose. Vivienne was avoiding her obvious thoughts but there was no way of denying it. Madame De'Ath was a dwarf. Thankfully, her ruminations were curtailed when the lady opened her eyes.

"Vivienne, the time has come. If you would be so kind as to pick up the cards and shuffle them in any way you want for as long as you want. When you are happy, please place them back on the silk. Face down."

Doing as she was told, Vivienne slowly reached across the table and picked up the cards. She was shaking. The size of the pack too large for her petite hands. She shuffled the cards awkwardly, scared she would drop them and send them tumbling over the table.

Madame De'Ath said, "When you are ready, I will turn over the top three cards. The first will indicate your past, and events that have been. The second card represents your present, the here and now, and those factors influencing your current circumstances."

Vivienne now regretted her thoughts about Madame De'Ath being a dwarf.

"The third card will give us insight into your future. The future may change, depending on your life choices but will be an indication of how your life may progress if you continue on this particular path."

Vivienne shuffled the cards for approximately thirty seconds more. She placed the pack face down on the silk as requested. She tried to steady her breathing but was failing.

Madame De'Ath turned over the first card, placed it on the table and smiled. "The Two of Cups. This card represents your past. I associate this card with happiness, pure friendships, love and marriage. A positive card, you have experienced lovely times."

Vivienne was reluctant to engage. She didn't want to give anything away, but she had been happy and in love. She had considered marriage, but sadly, it was not meant to be.

"The next card you have drawn is the Four of Batons. This card represents your present circumstances, what is happening now. On the surface another positive card. You are content, you have found tranquillity and peace. You have this idyllic haven, this refuge from life in which you hide away. You feel safe there and are reluctant to leave the confines of this haven you and your loved one have created."

Keep still, stay calm, don't give anything away, was all Vivienne could think of.

The third card was revealed as the Three of Swords. "I'm very sorry to say but the future currently suggests separation but I'm unsure if this means from your present situation, or separation from your loved one. There is a sorrow, loneliness, something missing, something important which is absent from your life. The twins are showing me a lock and key. They may be suggesting don't lock yourself away. Engage with others, enjoy life, be free. It may be a haven, but don't imprison yourself in a fortress of your own making."

Was that it? Was it over with? Could she go now? Vivienne was desperate to leave.

"Do you have any questions?" asked Madame De'Ath.

"Only to ask if I may go now, if that is agreeable?"

"Why yes of course. Before you leave, I would just like to

confirm that the cards you have chosen, and their meanings, will be forwarded to our hosts. Otherwise, the choice is yours as to whether you tell the other guests about your reading. Good luck, Vivienne. It has been a pleasure meeting you."

"And you, Madame. Thank you for reading my cards." Vivienne rose from her chair and walked out of the room. She closed the door behind her then momentarily froze. What was she doing here? A thousand pounds would be a life changing amount of money but was it worth all this? Did Madame De'Ath know her secret? She had to find a way off the island, but Mr Notts suddenly appeared with her trunk to show her to her room.

CHAPTER FOUR

Madame De'Ath was spiritually exhausted. She had now read the cards of all nine guests, and she was desperate for respite. However, Jeremy Fisher had insisted she come to his suite to divulge each reading immediately after the session. Ascending the grand staircase with difficulty, she waddled down the corridor and headed to the master bedroom on the second floor. She knocked on his door.

Catherine Fawcett answered, "Daphne, please come in."

She sat down as indicated on an Italian Renaissance chair, upholstered in red and gold.

Jeremy Fisher asked, "Do you have the list?"

"Yes, here are all the readings, each card, past, present and future and then a brief overview of the meaning." Daphne passed him three pieces of paper on which she had scribed each reading.

After a quick perusal, Jeremy asked, "Any that were particularly interesting?"

"Nothing of any real interest, however, I was saddened by the fact that not one of them currently has a happy ending. As it stands, each and every one of them picked cards that held negative connotations."

"Let's go through each one."

Daphne sighed discreetly. She had hoped the detailed written explanations of each card would have been sufficient. Undertaking readings was a tiring exercise. As much as her spirit guides tried to protect her, she always felt drained after concentrating for so long.

Jeremy returned her papers and Daphne went through each

reading.

"Vivienne Kry is a beautiful young woman, with gorgeous, golden hair but portrays herself as so very plain and dowdy. She has an aura of grey. She holds herself so perfectly still. She seems aloof, but I think she has a nervous disposition. There were tremors in her hands and at times in her voice, though she barely spoke. She seemed distant, quiet, unsure, so very cautious. She didn't ask any questions, just asked if she could leave." She read from her notes and detailed each card.

"Next," demanded Jeremy.

"Eliza Hart chose Justice, The Magician and Judgement. If my memory serves me right, I think she was the only guest to pick three major arcana cards. A fair past, she was raised in a harmonious environment with good intentions, a virtuous outlook on life and a sincere desire to do the right thing. However, the balance of power changes and she becomes confident, holds strong beliefs and has the willpower to get whatever she desires. The cards say she is manipulative, deceptive and will use trickery and ill means to fulfil those desires. Because of her actions she will face judgement in the end."

"Sounds like my kind of woman. Describe her physically," commanded Jeremy.

"She's beautiful and oozes confidence. Hazel-coloured eyes, olive skin, there's definitely a touch of foreign blood in those veins, I had the sense of spices, maybe India, somewhere exotic that like. Slim but curves in all the right places and elegant, she gives the impression of not caring. Maybe she does, maybe she doesn't, she's hard to read, gives little away."

Jeremy sneered over at his fiancée, "Sadly, Catherine, you too give very little away."

Catherine rolled her eyes and sighed.

"Then I read Cornelius Binks. His cards were The World, Two of Batons and Three of Swords. His past was one of perfection, success, things were triumphant and favourable. His present is one of maturity, he's a natural leader, building on his success and attaining great heights professionally. Then a change, there's sorrow and strife in his future.

"Cornelius is handsome and clever, but he knows it. His maturity gives him time. He absorbs information, ponders before rushing into decisions, waits for the right opportunity."

"Sounds like my type of man." Catherine sneered at Jeremy.

"I quite agree, he sounds attractive in many ways." Jeremy sneered back at her.

Sensing tension, Daphne continued, desperate for some solitude before dinner. "Bernard Pratt was next. He chose Ace of Cups, The Tower and Queen of Swords. Basically, he had a happy childhood home and an abundant lifestyle, but he is currently going through turmoil, everything is collapsing around him, there's chaos, ruin and misery. And although he appears to be funny and happy and light-hearted, beneath that jovial exterior he really is lonely and sad."

"I bet he's the fat one, isn't he?" asked Jeremy. "The one who wobbled up the path. The one who nearly capsized the boat."

"Don't be so rude," said Catherine.

"Honestly, woman, he can't bloody hear me, he's downstairs, probably stuffing his face right now."

Catherine tutted at his obnoxious attitude, "But there really is no need to be so offensive."

Jeremy was just about to give a cutting retort when Daphne De'Ath intervened, "Then Sarah Silver, she's a funny wee soul, I really like her, but her cards make me cautious. Nine of Pentacles, Queen of Pentacles and The Moon. Her past seems to be one of prudence, being vigilant and safe, no risk taking, which seems to link nicely with her current situation of well-being, prosperity, and security. Yet her future is The Moon which is one of scandals, deception, caution and insincerity. She's a bad influence and has unknown enemies."

"Describe her." In his throne like chair, Jeremy shifted his weight to the left and crossed his legs.

"Sweet, likeable, cheeky eyes, petite, tiny hands but long, artistic fingers. Late sixties, early seventies, perhaps. Shocking white hair that looks so soft."

"I bet you'll lust after her, too." Catherine looked away with her nose in the air.

"Who's being rude now? Are you judging her on her age? She sounds full of life, a bit of a closet goer if you ask me, she could be fun."

Catherine and Jeremy continued bickering about the guests. Daphne tried to stifle a yawn but failed to stop her face from contorting. She tried to get her hosts back on track, but they were now arguing about the wedding.

"Shall I continue?" asked Daphne.

Catherine replied, "Yes, of course, please do, I apologise for our behaviour."

"Apologise for yourself, you started it with your jealousy."

If stares could kill, Jeremy would now be dead.

Desperately wanting to avoid more arguments, Daphne read the remaining names from her list. "Cliff Dacosta picked Six of Cups, Seven of Batons and The Moon. He seemed obsessed by his past, for some reason reluctant to move on. He's faced obstacles and challenges, but he's surmounted them. He's strong and generally successful. But The Moon, Sarah Silver picked the same card for her future, there's a scandal, some sort of deception or trickery about to take place."

Not wanting to give Jeremy or Catherine a chance to argue again, she went on to describe him without being asked. "Cliff is tall, broad, a goliath of a man, maybe in his fifties. He reminds me of an aloof cat, watching proceedings with disdain and mistrust. He's got a sun-kissed cast to his skin. The twins showed me somewhere exotic, like a palm-fringed Caribbean island, but he has blue eyes, an intriguing combination. He's got the bushy mutton chops going on, sprinkled with grey.

"Theresa Franks, Four of Coins, Justice and Five of Cups. Been a bit of a hoarder in her past, a bit of a miser too, loved material things. She has seven children. This seemed to be the change to her present day. Lives a more fair and balanced life now. Seems a bit more reasonable, a bit easier to live with. Sad to say I think her husband may leave her though. A case of too little too late. There's a break-up of the marriage, or if they do stay together there is no love. She looks haggard, older than her years, tired with life's ongoing challenges. She could easily just disappear from the world. Worn clothes, shabby shoes, holes, so many things missing in her life." Daphne continued quickly.

"Two more to go. George Jones is adorable, smiley eyes, lovely white teeth, and genuinely a sweetheart. His hair is warm, light brown with lovely streaks of gold, I could feel positivity oozing from him. Lovely chap in my opinion. He picked The Lovers, Wheel of Fortune and Two of Swords. His past has been about love, infatuation, seeing beauty everywhere but he's rather naïve when it comes to matters of the heart. But he falls on his feet, whether destiny or fate or luck, whatever you want to call it, he drifts through life and just enjoys each moment. In the future he meets his nemesis. This will stifle his creativity, suppress his adoration and oppose his actions.

"Last one. Harold Arnold, but he said he prefers Harry. Of short, stocky build, he's a strong lad. Works in a sawmill, lugging tree trunks around. Big muscles, he can't move very easily, his clothes bulge when he flexes, he moves with an awkward sway. A bit rough around the edges, he often says the wrong things which ends up insulting people."

Catherine looked over at Jeremy and raised her eyebrows. He ignored her.

"Harry chose Seven of Coins, Five of Cups and Judgement. Basically, everything he has ever done has been through physical hard work, probably mental hard work too. But at the moment, I believe he is estranged from his wife. He wouldn't open up to explain why but the twins were crying. His wife seems sad and distraught. His future card is Judgement which represents repenting of sins. I'm not sure what he has done to her, but he needs to apologise and atone for his actions. Maybe then he can be forgiven and move on with his life without this burden hanging over him."

Daphne sighed, she really needed to lie down. She was struggling to keep her eyes open as she looked at Jeremy and then to Catherine.

Jeremy was the first to speak, "So no one picked The Devil or Death?" Daphne shook her head. "How utterly boring. As to the readings, if I'm being honest, I have forgotten everything you have said." With some difficulty, he stood from the chair and stretched his spine. "But leave me your scribblings as a reminder. Thank you, Daphne, you may go."

She thanked them both then left the room.

"What do you make of the readings?" asked Catherine.

Jeremy did not immediately reply. Leaning on his cane, he paced the room before saying, "All very interesting. Good to have a reference point and see how things change over the course of the weekend. But for now, let's get ready and head downstairs for dinner and become acquainted with our guests. I'm wondering if they have sussed why they are here yet."

A shiver trickled down Catherine's spine.

PRESENT DAY

The fire was roaring, but the mane of red, orange and gold flames failed to warm the persistent chill in the air. Fernleigh was a detached Victorian villa. Built in 1845, the house had been abandoned over a hundred years ago and Jack wanted to know the gory details as to why.

Fernleigh had two downstairs reception rooms. From the entrance hall, on the left was *the ballroom* which was a total over exaggeration. At 32 by 22 feet, the room identified as grand, with beautiful wooden flooring, an impressive marble fireplace, a stunning chandelier and ornate plaster mouldings on the ceiling and walls.

Perpendicular to the fireplace were two huge sofas and between them stood a glass coffee table. In the middle of the room was a dining table for six. At the far end of the room were two chaise longues on which to lounge and admire the garden through the double glass doors. Millie had given the room its name, her impression on seeing it for the first time. He missed his wife. The house seemed empty without her.

From the impressive hallway, the room on the right was *the cosy room*. A total misnomer. Smaller than its sibling, the dimensions were 16 by 16 feet. There was a simple fireplace surrounded by the original colourful tiles. Each tile was individual but together they formed flowers either side of the hearth. There was a two seater sofa, a small round dining table and a dresser. The room faced north and always felt cold and dark. They had soon come to realise the room would never ever feel cosy.

Jack sat on the sofa in the ballroom. Despite the heat from the fire, a shiver spasmed through his body, creating goosebumps. Maybe he was coming down with something, although he felt well enough, just a little tired from work that day.

He had lost count of the number of messages he had formulated on his phone then deleted. There was so much to say but he did not want to give anything away. When the message was detailed, he sounded like a nutter. When the message was brief, he sounded menacing. Maybe he should just ring her and see what happens.

His heart was racing, jeez, he was only making a phone call so why did he feel so nervous? He shivered again but this time a rush of blood made him flush. He was sweating. Maybe he *was* ill. Hot and cold chills were not normal. He wiped his sweaty palms on his jeans. December was the time of year when viruses would suddenly appear out of nowhere. He felt invaded.

As a delay tactic, he put the phone down on the coffee table and went across the hall to the kitchen. He made himself a cup of tea and traipsed back through to the ballroom. Tea had to be boiling hot, so he quickly downed the fluid and prepared to make the call. Beads of perspiration formed on his forehead.

At the fourth attempt, he plucked up the courage to press the call button on his phone … and waited.

"Hello." A sweet feminine voice, accented.

"Hi, is that Soo-Min?"

"Yes, speaking."

"Hi, my name's Jack, and I'm so sorry to bother you, but I was wondering, if you wouldn't mind that is, doing a reading." He was aware he was waffling, a nervous speed to his words.

"Is for you?"

"Not really, well, yes and no. Kind of." *Come on Jack, you sound like a muppet, get a grip.*

"Just tell me what's on your mind. I sure I heard it before."

She sounded so young, almost childlike, could she really be so exposed to life's weirdness?

"I was given your number by a friend. She said you're a medium and do readings for people."

"I an extra small, actually," she laughed, "but yes, I do readings."

Jack wondered why she was laughing but then he got the joke. She sounded lovely and he was thankful she was trying to put him at ease. "This may sound strange, but I'm not actually after a reading for someone. I'm after a reading for … something."

"Go on, Mr Jack, this sound intriguing."

A deep breath, "My wife thinks our house is haunted and she won't live here anymore." He exhaled. At this stage he did not want to admit she had been in a mental hospital where the doctors and nurses had deemed her delusional and paranoid, some sort of psychosis. He panicked, what if Soo-Min could read his thoughts?

"And you like me to visit your home and investigate?"

Jack sighed with relief. This was all he wanted, "Yes, please, if you don't mind."

"Where you live?"

"Scotby."

"I check which bus I need, and the times, and get back to you. How about Friday afternoon? I have no classes then."

"Classes? What is it you do?"

"I at the university on Fusehill Street. Studying criminology with forensic investigation."

"Oh, that sounds interesting."

"It very good, yes. In my final year."

"Great. I look forward to hearing from you about the time, unless you want me to pick you up?" Now he sounded like an axe murderer, offering to pick up a stranger, a young student, foreign by the sounds of it, and bring her to his home.

"That okay, I like getting bus. Just text me your address and I let you know my E. T. A."

"E. T. A?"

"Expected time of arrival."

"Oh, yes, yes of course it is." *Jeez, what a plonker he was.* He'd seen loads of police procedural films and shows over the years.

"See you on Friday."

"See you then, thank you, bye."

He puffed out his cheeks and sighed. What had he let himself in for?

CHAPTER FIVE

Mr Notts requested the nine guests through for dinner. Like the rest of Derwent Isle House, the dining room did not disappoint. Decorated in a classical Italian design, the statues and columns made them believe they were truly in Rome. With hanging planters and oversized urns, one could swear they were near the Mediterranean Sea.

There were twelve place settings, five either side of the table and one at either end. Each guest found their name place and nervously sat down at the table.

Mr Notts cleared his throat, "Please, if I could have your attention." He waited a few moments for complete silence to fall upon the room.

"Although darkness has now fallen upon us, tomorrow you will see the magnificent landscape surrounding this island. We are residing in an 18th century home, set in over seven acres of a private island estate and the views are nothing short of spectacular. You will see the glistening lake in all its glory, feast on the layers of fells, of which the higher ones are snow capped at present, and you will hear nothing but bird song and the gentle lapping of the water.

"But I guess you are really wanting to meet your hosts, to wish them well for their upcoming nuptials and finally hear what is expected of you over the next couple of days.

"Therefore, if you would be so kind to put your hands together." Mr Notts started clapping.

The guests reciprocated in a reserved fashion.

"May I introduce Jeremy Fisher and Catherine Fawcett." Notts abducted his arm, then put his hands together once more, clapping with joyful animation. Cornelius Binks was the first to rise from his chair on seeing their hosts enter the room. Harold Arnold was the last.

Jeremy Fisher had long, greying hair tied back into what looked like a horse's limp tail. He bore weight through a black cane, his nails like talons gripping the silver handle. Of average height, he appeared gaunt, and had scabs around the edges of his mouth. His jacket was sapphire blue, his waistcoat and trousers cool grey and his unbuttoned shirt jet black. He wore no tie. With his unconventional flair, he had an air of authority, an air of superiority. He peered down his upturned nose as his eyes scanned the room. He raised an eyebrow and smiled.

Gliding into the ostentatious room, Catherine Fawcett was elegantly dressed in a cream ensemble with shimmering, elytra embroidery. There were eight layers of frills to the skirt of her dress, suggesting extravagance and wealth. Her neckline was framed by the delicate intricacies of her bodice, with further beetle wing detailing. Contrasting beautifully with her cream dress, her auburn hair was softly tied up and pinned with diamond encrusted butterflies. Despite her maturing beauty, she appeared meek in comparison to Jeremy's arrogance and she sat daintily on the throne-like chair at the opposite end of the table to her intended.

After studying Jeremy and Catherine, the guests sneakily glanced at each other as they sat down. All had vacant looks, each instinctively knowing what the other person was thinking. No one recognised Jeremy Fisher or Catherine Fawcett as family, friend or foe. Neither were they work colleagues, neighbours or acquaintances. There was no flicker of familiarity at all.

Jeremy Fisher commanded the room, "You were each sent an invite, offering you the chance to stay at this luxurious villa, feast on exotic food and indulge in intoxicating beverages at my expense. You were even offered a gift, or as you may come to think of it, payment for your time. A reward of one thousand pounds if you remain here until Sunday afternoon to witness my wedding …" he glanced over to Catherine and was met with a glare, "until after *our* wedding, when Thomas will then escort you back to the mainland by boat.

"But there is a price you must pay, tasks you must complete and games you must play." His beady eyes surveyed the room, everyone appeared nervous. "You must engage in a number of experiments, which will be revealed throughout the weekend. You have already been given a taster, by having your fortune told by the delectable Madame De'Ath, who sends her apologies for this evening's non-attendance." He flicked his hand to the empty chair on his right-hand side. "Drained I believe from reading tarot cards." He tutted and raised an eyebrow. "You may keep the results a secret or tell your new-found friends of your destiny. That choice is yours. Any questions so far?"

The group was initially silent, then a thin woman reluctantly raised her hand, "I think there has been a mistake with the invite. I apologise for my ignorance if I'm wrong, but I don't think I know you. I don't think I should be here." Her whole demeanour was shades of grey, from her tatty clothes to her ragged hair and chapped skin. Mrs Theresa Franks was a mother of seven, only in her forties the demands of family life and poverty had expedited the aging process.

"Theresa Franks, I presume?" asked Jeremy. She nodded her head. "You may not be acquainted with me or recognise my handsome looks, but I know you very well. The invite is correct and was intended for you. I want you here. The promise of one thousand pounds is for the taking if you'd like to stay, to see me marry by beloved Catherine.

"I have wealth beyond the most vivid of imaginations. I cannot even count how much money I have. I have properties everywhere. I am renowned in the field of architecture and design. I have worked with my peers on royal projects and government buildings. I feel special, yet I am unhappy. The woman I love has refused to marry me on numerous occasions. I have everything I could possibly want and need but happiness eludes me. Love evades me. Yet she is there, so near and yet so far. Catherine Fawcett is my desire. I believe I will be happy when she marries me. I ask you all to put pressure on her this weekend, tell her how wonderful I am, how she must be mad, deranged, for denying herself my riches. I implore you to help me fulfil my dream of marrying her."

The group felt immediate sympathy for Jeremy. He had instantly won them over by playing the victim and made Catherine seem uncaring. Her auburn curls were perfectly in place but two of the pins were digging into her scalp and pulling on her hair. She felt uncomfortable. She wanted to scratch her head and alleviate the annoyance, but she refrained, enduring the discomfort in more ways than one.

"Theresa, to allay your worries, the weekend is about love and happiness. What makes us happy? Why is happiness only fleeting? Why do we crave more? Why are we never satisfied with our lot in life? Why do we do the things we do in pursuit of joy and contentment? What is the key to a happy and fulling life?" Jeremy gulped from his glass. Irish whiskey warmed his insides. "Any other questions?"

"When do we get the money?" asked Harold Arnold. His shaved head was too severe a look and his nose suggested he had been no stranger to fights. He flexed and extended the fingers of his right hand, bulking his muscles gained from the hard labour of lugging tree trunks.

Jeremy confirmed, "The money is already counted and placed in envelopes addressed to each of you. Mr Notts will personally hand you the envelope as you leave the house, any time after one o'clock on Sunday afternoon. Like your arrival, you will be escorted in small groups by our excellent cook, Mr Thomas Montgomery, to the boat where he will drop you off on the mainland shore. You will then be free to go your own way but blessed with a small fortune."

As a defensive mechanism, Cliff Dacosta was always suspicious of others' agendas and wanted further clarification. His deep blue eyes locked onto Jeremy, "And the money is definite? No excuses, no reneging, no backing out?"

"I'm not sure what you are implying but I give you my most sincere word, yes, the money is definitely yours. If you participate in each of the tasks, games, events, whatever you want to call them, and you walk away from this house on Sunday afternoon, then yes, you will get the money. If you fail to cooperate, for whatever reason, with the planned tasks or leave the island of your own free will before one o'clock on Sunday, then you will not be entitled to the gift."

The group started separate conversations amongst themselves until another gentleman put up his hand and interrupted. "But a thousand pounds for each of us, that's … a mind-blowing amount. I just can't get my head around that much money. What can we possibly give you, to justify such an amazing sum?"

"Cornelius Binks, I'm guessing?" asked Jeremy.

The gentleman nodded his head. In his mid-forties, he was still handsome, with strong defined features. His clothes were tailored, and he presented himself well, as if money shouldn't be a problem anyway.

"What can each of you possibly give to explain our generosity?" Jeremy tapped his index finger to his lips. "Time. Information. Insight. Wisdom. And of course, the pleasure of your company on Sunday to witness the declaring of our marriage vows."

Catherine Fawcett had remained silent throughout the charade but could not contain her annoyance anymore. With a smile she said, "Jeremy, darling, you have forgotten to add subservience, domination through fear, entrapment through pleasures and luxuries—"

Her fiancé interrupted, "Catherine, my darling, everyone is here of their own free will and as a matter of course will be richly rewarded for their time."

"We will see who is correct when the clock strikes one on Sunday." Catherine smiled sweetly.

"Darling, have you taken your medication? I cannot risk you being re-admitted to the lunatic asylum so close to the wedding."

Catherine stood from her chair; her fingers spread wide on the dining table for support. Her face was flushed with embarrassment. Aware that everyone was staring at her with their mouths hanging open like hungry fish, she kept her thoughts to herself and walked out of the room. Feeding them information would only enrage Jeremy.

"Women," Jeremy tutted, "I'll never understand them, a complete mystery to me as to what goes through their minds. You give them everything they want and still they are not happy." With difficulty, he raised from his chair and left the room to go in search of Catherine.

The nine guests were silent once more, bewildered by what they had witnessed and had learned so far. The weekend certainly promised to be entertaining, if not a little chilling.

CHAPTER SIX

The food was exquisite with a vegetable soup to start, accompanied by honeyed bread. The main course was a raized pie, which Mr Notts had great pleasure in explaining was supposedly a favourite dish served in Queen Victoria's court. The pie consisted of mushrooms stuffed inside a quail, which was placed inside a chicken, then squashed into the eviscerated cavity of a turkey. For an unknown reason, there was no pastry to justify its name.

Everyone complemented Mr Montgomery on his culinary skills. Everything was cooked to perfection. Even Bernard Pratt was overwhelmed by the quantity of dishes on offer, with centrally placed servings of roasted potatoes, mashed carrots and honey-glazed parsnips. The jus was too thin for Bernard, he preferred thick gravy with the consistency of treacle.

Pudding was an exotic fruit cocktail, of which no expense had been spared, and the guests were amazed by delicious fruits they had never tasted before. Then the drinks started to flow.

Beavering away in the background, Mr Notts discreetly tidied everything away and listened in to the guests' conversations.

Sarah Silver and Cornelius Binks were talking about what they would do with the money.

Vivienne Kry and George Jones were trying to decipher how they were acquainted with Jeremy Fisher and Catherine Fawcett.

Theresa Franks and Harold Arnold were perplexed by the apparent awkward relationship of the soon to be bride and groom and felt uncomfortable at the upcoming proceedings. Theresa did not reveal her feelings to Harold, but she was particularly disturbed by Jeremy admitting he knew everything about her.

Eliza Hart and Cliff Dacosta had numerous reservations about the bizarre and forced situation they were in, but the allure of a thousand pounds at the end of this peculiar affair was worth the inconvenience of pretending to celebrate with 'the happy couple'.

Bernard Pratt was disappointed that all the food had been taken away. He would have been happy nibbling on the delicacies throughout the evening as he made more space in his stomach.

Mr Notts interrupted the group once more. "On behalf of your hosts, I would like to thank you for making this evening pleasurable by the presence of your company. Please feel free to explore any of the downstairs rooms that are not marked *Private*. The communal rooms are there for your use and your comfort. Alternatively, you are free to retire for the evening if you prefer. Beverages are still available in the lounge area. Anyone requiring a simple supper or a hot drink, I will be around until midnight. Otherwise, I wish you a pleasant evening." Notts left the room.

Conversation started amongst the guests once more and for a while, they stayed in the dining room, reluctant to move. Harold Arnold was the first to leave when all the bottles of wine had been consumed. He headed through to the lounge area. Sarah Silver and Theresa Franks wished everyone a goodnight as they were the first to retire to their bedrooms. Eliza Hart raised from her chair with a view to exploring the house. George Jones and Cornelius Binks both stood to attention, offering to accompany her on the grand tour. Bernard Pratt, Vivienne Kry and Cliff Dacosta remained seated, unsure on what to do and where to go.

By ten thirty, everyone had gone to bed other than Eliza and Cornelius. For another couple of hours, they continued to experiment with the variety of beverages on offer, making up silly names for the cocktails they were creating. Their favourite name but worst concoction was the Rumbling Rum Flux which would give you explosive diarrhoea if more than a couple of mouthfuls were consumed.

Now in a stupor, and literally laughing at anything, they decided to retire for the night. They checked the downstairs rooms they had access to, ensuring lamps and candles were extinguished, and fires were covered by their protective screen. Even blowing out a candle was hilarious, as Eliza tried three times to blow out a rather large flame. She ended up spitting everywhere, her lips struggling to stay together as she was laughing so intensely. Cornelius tried to open a door, but his hand slipped off the handle and he fell sideways, hitting his nose on the decorative architrave. By the time they had secured downstairs, their stomachs were aching with laughter.

Each holding a lamp to take to their room, they ascended the grand stairs, leaving a deepening darkness in the entrance hall.

Half way up, they heard three bangs on the front door. They stopped and stared at each other, probably wondering if they had each heard the sound.

"Is that someone at the door?" asked Eliza.

Cornelius checked his pocket watch, "It's after one in the morning and we're on an island. Surely not."

"Should we answer it?"

"What do you think?" asked Cornelius.

"What's the worst that could happen?"

Cornelius blew out his cheeks, "Could be a ghost, could be a mad monk, Germans perhaps." He winked.

Eliza pushed him away on his shoulder, "You've had too much to drink, Mr Binks, you're talking gibberish."

"Don't push me in my inebriated state, I might have fallen down the stairs."

They leaned into each other and started laughing.

"You go and answer the door then," suggested Cornelius with a playful smirk on his face. "Could be the bloody butcher with his polished machete and some sausages for you."

"No, you go." Eliza placed her hand on his chest. "I don't want *his* sausages."

"No, you go." Cornelius placed his hand on hers. "I'm not interested in another man's sausage."

Eliza was just about to repeat, *no, you go*, when there was urgent hammering on the door once more.

The teasing had gone, and they sobered quickly.

"Stay here, I'll go and investigate." Cornelius trotted down the stairs, his lamp held aloft.

"We'll both go," said Eliza, as she cautiously descended the grand staircase in her flowing gown.

Cornelius turned the key and opened the heavy door. No one was there.

Eliza collapsed on a chair in the hallway. Aware of the fire hazard in her tipsy state, she carefully placed the lamp she was holding on the small table next to her. "Is the pounding in my head? Are we really that inebriated?"

Cornelius visually searched the grounds once more before closing the door and turning the key. He placed his lamp next to hers and the flames flickered in unison. Offering her his hand, Eliza accepted, and he assisted her up out of the chair. Cornelius took her in his arms, then twirled her around as if they were dancing a Viennese waltz to sweet music. They giggled at the fumbled steps.

"You're a bad influence, Mr Binks."

"I do hope so, Miss Hart."

They stood in the shadows of the grand hallway and swayed in time. Cornelius kissed the top of her head and they both sighed with contentment.

Exhausted by the night's events, they ascended the stairs for the second time, when there was banging on the front door once more and a menacing growl.

With a serious tone, Cornelius said, "I mean it this time, stay here." He galloped down the stairs and opened the door. Again, no one was there. Eliza was standing a third of the way up the stairs when she saw a shadow of a man appear at the hallway window. His ghostly hands were flat against the pane. When he heard her screams, he disappeared.

DIARY

The wedding is on Sunday and I am once again questioning my sanity. I am deliriously tired, yet I cannot sleep due to my troubled mind playing tricks on me. The way he treats me, especially in front of others, is intolerable. I love and loathe him in equal measures. Why does he make loving him so hard and hating him so easy? Sadly, I am questioning if I can go through with the ceremony. To see everyone there, witnessing this lifelong commitment. Can I really go through with this? To protest would truly break his heart. No, I must endure this emotional pain for his sake. His health continues to deteriorate, and I bear witness to the physical pain he endures daily yet his mind remains so sharp. No one has ever captured my heart in this way, a cruel master who dominates and teases, yet he is so kind and forgiving and exciting and adventurous, full of surprises and at times extremely thoughtful. He messes with my mind so frequently that I feel dizzy in his presence. Jeremy is the cross I must bear and I have promised to be by his side until his dying day. I must be strong for Sunday.

CHAPTER SEVEN

Two o'clock in the morning and nearly everyone was gathered downstairs. Only Eliza Hart and Cornelius Binks were dressed appropriately having been socialising to the early hours of the morning. The others wore various states of nightwear: long white gowns, silk pyjamas, dressing robes, nightcaps, bed socks, slippers.

Eliza's screams had created a state of panic and the pandemonium that ensued had roused the guests and staff from their beds.

They were arguing about the best course of action. Cornelius Binks insisted the men get dressed into more suitable attire and search the island for the intruder but the night was bleak and the island swamped in darkness.

George Jones tried to maintain his happy persona but at this time in the morning it was challenging. Movement caught his eye, and he was thankful to see flakes of snow fluttering past the hallway window. He drew their attention to the inclement weather and suggested postponing the search until dawn.

Cliff Dacosta tried to compromise by suggesting they at least have a wander around the outside of the house and check over the moorings to see if anyone had arrived by boat. Arguments continued between the guests as they failed to reach an agreement.

Vivienne Kry directed her question towards Luke Notts who was standing next to her, "And you are sure there is no-one else on the island, no gardeners or servants or chambermaids?"

Mr Notts replied, "I can assure you that there are only myself, Mr Montgomery and Madame De'Ath who are employed here on the island. There are normally other staff, but Mr Fisher wanted to keep things to a minimum for this weekend."

Sarah Silver's long white hair was tied into a plait. She stifled a yawn, "Sorry, but if it's agreeable with yourselves, I might leave you to sort this out. I'm too old to go chasing after men," she did a mischievous wink. "So, nighty night, everyone."

"Night, Sarah, sweet dreams," said Jeremy. "Just ask if you need anything." He grinned at Catherine then winked. She did not rise to his pathetic attempts to goad her.

Everyone wished Sarah a good night.

"I don't think I can sleep knowing someone's prowling around outside," said Theresa Franks. "What if he comes back?"

Harry Arnold yawned, not making the slightest attempt to cover his open mouth. Two teeth were missing. "Then how about we all stay down here and keep watch. If we hear anything, we can respond immediately and catch him."

With travelling fair distances to get to the island and with the excitement of the day, the hosts, staff and guests agreed to this option and quietly dispersed, finding a comfortable sofa or an armchair in which to lounge.

With the guests weary, Mr Notts and Mr Worthington disappeared along the hallway and promised to return with a few pots of tea and some spare pillows and blankets.

Everyone was starting to doze when Jeremy suddenly realised someone was missing. "Where's Bernard Pratt? Has anyone seen him?"

"He went to bed same time as me, around ten ish," said Cliff. His cerulean blue eyes searching the tired faces in the room.

"And has anyone seen Bernard since?" asked Jeremy as he poured himself a whisky.

Heads were shaking.

Catherine commented, "I don't recall him being in the corridor when we all came out of our bedrooms on hearing the screams."

"You're right, he wasn't, as his room is next to mine," said Cliff. He scratched at his black and speckled grey mutton chops.

"Why would Bernard be tapping on windows and banging on doors though?" asked George Jones.

"He was knocking to get back in after he had walked off all the food and drink he's consumed this evening," said Harry sarcastically.

Cornelius smirked, "I didn't think he was ever going to stop eating."

"I thought he was going to burst," said George. "Did you see the strain on his waistcoat buttons?"

Some of the guests tried to refrain from smiling.

Catherine's forehead furrowed. "Cliff, since you know his room, would you mind going upstairs and checking if he is there, please?"

"Of course, Miss Fawcett." Cliff bowed his head and left the room.

A few minutes later he returned. "I knocked first but there was no answer. The door was closed but unlocked. He's not in his room but his covers are messy, as if he had been in bed. His shoes and coat are missing though. Maybe it was him knocking on the door, wanting to get back into the house."

Jeremy stood from his chair, annoyed by the revelation. "The stupid fool. Why would anyone walk around in the freezing cold in the dead of night?" His question was rhetorical. "Goodnight, everyone."

"But Jeremy, why would he knock on the door to be let in, then disappear? Something's not right." Catherine had an uneasy feeling.

"True, he would have knocked and waited, or shouted to be let in," said Eliza. "But don't forget the growl. The sound was menacing, guttural, threatening."

"Was it definitely Bernard you saw at the window?" asked Catherine.

"I cannot say with certainty. It was too dark. All I saw was a shadowed shape, an outline of a man, but his hands looked so pale, almost ghostly in their appearance."

Jeremy laughed, "Like I said, he's stupid. His hands were pale because he's been foolish enough to wander in this bitterly cold weather. He'll have frost bite. Enough of this nonsense. Come on, let's go to bed." Jeremy held out his arm for Catherine to hold but they jumped with fright when there was pounding on the door, followed by the moans of something evil.

Without thinking, Cornelius, Cliff and Harry ran to the door. With a couple of seconds delay to prepare for the unexpected, Harry opened the door. "There's nobody there." He rhythmically descended the external stone steps and looked around the grounds. "We were here within what, ten seconds? How could he get away so fast?"

"That statement proves it's not Bernard then," said George. Expecting to hear laughter, he was shocked to hear another scream.

Eliza Hart was squealing, "There, in the shadows, something running round the corner. That way!" She circumducted her arm in a clockwise direction.

The guests closest to the right-hand window peered outside but by now there was nothing to see.

Without being asked, Cornelius, Harry and Cliff offered to explore the grounds. George felt pressured to go with the men but quickly thought of an excuse, "I'll stay here and protect the others."

The three men disappeared round the corner of the house.

Mr Notts closed the door and locked it. He ushered everyone back into the main lounge area then he sat in the chair by the hallway window so he would be ready to let the men back in.

No one could sleep.

George subtly studied Eliza. Her hazel eyes were captivating and he loved how every glance appeared seductive as she fluttered her long, dark eyelashes. Her green evening dress flaunted every womanly curve of her body. She was chatting with Vivienne who wore a long, shapeless, white nightdress and a blue dressing gown. Vivienne was beautiful too, if a little serious, but her golden hair was like rays of sunshine. Eliza's darkness, Vivienne's brightness, he'd be happy and content with either, or both. A cheeky smile emerged from the corner of his mouth.

Movement brought his attention to the door as Madame De'Ath shuffled into the room. She had obviously just got out of bed as her eyes were sleepy and not really focusing. Even with a deadly name, there was a cuteness about her, with her messy, copper hair and cute freckles. He'd never properly met a dwarf before, only observed one in a freak show when he was dallying with a married woman in Penrith. Madame De'Ath caught him staring at her as she tightened the cord of her dressing gown. He diverted his eyes, wondering if she knew what he was thinking.

During his reading earlier that evening, she had introduced him to her twin spirit guides. That was a weird experience, sending tingles down his arms. He recalled the tarot cards he had picked. The Lovers had made him smile; he couldn't have picked a more appropriate card to describe his past. The Wheel of Fortune had sounded promising, that luck and destiny was on his side, but then the Two of Swords had seemed like a battle.

Madame De'Ath had said The Lovers represented love, beauty, physical connection, an attraction, but can leave one blinded by infatuation and obsession. She had warned him not to be oblivious to the consequences of his actions. He had gulped at that statement, that was his past.

For his present she had said the Wheel of Fortune could be good or bad, depending on nearby cards. Destiny, fate, luck, she hoped it was all positive.

His future wasn't necessarily about fighting, the Two of Swords often represented a stalemate, like opposing factors, cancelling each other out, stagnation. A struggle, yet not really getting anywhere. He had been disappointed to hear that outcome.

George Jones continued observing the ladies in the room. Catherine Fawcett, the bride to be, she was beautiful too but somehow haunted. Her eyes were heavy, and she certainly did not appear to be in love with her intended. George had seen her roll her eyes several times at Jeremy's comments, and sigh with frustration at some of his actions. In fact, her eyes were dead, grey and cloudy whenever she spoke with Jeremy. He was still perplexed as to why they had invited him to their wedding.

Suddenly, there was banging on the front door. Mr Notts had momentarily fallen asleep and had missed the movement by the window. Everyone who was brave enough once again gathered in the hallway. Cornelius was shouting for the door to be opened. Mr

Notts turned the key and then the handle. Cautiously, he opened the door. Cliff and Harry were holding onto a thin, young man with straggly hair and ragged clothes that were far too short for his long limbs. Some sort of bull terrier trembled at his heels.

Jeremy pushed his way through the group. He looked the intruder up and down and could not hide his displeasure at the man's filthy appearance. "And you are?" he asked with disdain.

"Daniel Watters, sir."

CHAPTER EIGHT

"You absolute idiot! You've scared us to death!" cried out Theresa Franks, wrapping her tatty old shawl over her bony shoulders.

The young man looked horrified.

"You've been terrifying us!" stated Eliza Hart. Her olive skin a shade paler than normal.

Daniel Watters was squirming like an eel as he tried to escape the grabbing hands of his captors.

"Explain yourself, now!" shouted Cornelius.

The young man was shaking, his eyes wide with fear, his legs buckling. Harry and Cliff desperately clung on to him.

"Can you speak? Have you lost your tongue?" asked Jeremy.

The young man started crying, his nose running, his limbs now limp with exhaustion.

"Bloody idiot," said Jeremy, then he turned to peruse the crowd. "Mr Montgomery, I appreciate it is late but are you in a fit state to escort this weirdo to the mainland?"

"But it's three in the morning, sir." His voice cracking from little use.

"And your point is?" Jeremy raised an eyebrow.

Thomas Montgomery sighed, "Forgive me, sir. Of course I'll row him over to the shore."

Catherine could see everyone's distress, including the captive. "Daniel, your name sounds familiar. Do we know you?"

He nodded his head, "I'm not too sure, miss. I think so. I was invited to a wedding."

Jeremy intervened, "Let go of the man, now!"

Cliff and Harry released their hold on his skinny forearms.

Daniel slumped to the floor in a cross-legged position and started to rock backwards and forwards. He repeatedly rubbed the skin on his bruised forearms to distract from the pain. The little dog lay down beside him and crawled on its belly to snuggle in.

"My name is Catherine Fawcett. This is Jeremy Fisher." She gazed across to her intended and with her eyes, pleaded for calmness. "I do believe Jeremy sent you an invite to our wedding."

"Well, why didn't the fool respond to the invitation. It clearly stated to reply by the 27th of November." Jeremy tutted his disgust.

The man stroked his little dog as he replied, "I cannot read or write and have no paper."

"Then how did you know you were invited to a wedding and to arrive on this day?" Jeremy did not have the patience to suffer imbeciles.

Catherine intervened on seeing Daniel's distress. She knelt beside him and asked him if she could pat the little dog. He nodded. She gently stroked the softness of its head then proceeded to tickle the dog behind its ears. The dog rolled over and Catherine tickled its tummy. "What's she called?"

"Lily."

"She's adorable."

"She's my only friend."

Catherine's heart faltered at the sad admission, but she could see the calming influence on Daniel as they talked about Lily. "What's her breed?"

"A Staffordshire Bull Terrier. She's a little bluey. She was the runt of a litter of six. I raised her by hand. Fed her milk. I love the little white heart on her forehead."

Catherine desperately wanted to stay there, chatting with Daniel and petting Lily, but her lower limbs were feeling numb, so reluctantly she got back to her feet. Little Lily rolled over and cuddled into Daniel once more. "As she's so sweet, she's invited to the wedding."

"Thank you, miss."

"And may I take this opportunity to say how very sorry we are for how you've been treated. Being on such a remote island, we were just a little shocked to have someone banging on the door at this time of night. I apologise for our behaviour towards you. Please know it was only because we were a little scared." Catherine made subtle gestures to the fellow guests to disperse. "Mr Notts, if you could be so kind as to run Mr Watters a bath to help him warm up, and please find him some appropriate clothing. Mr Montgomery, if you would be so kind as to rustle up something warm for Daniel and Lily to eat. Madame De'Ath, if you could pour Daniel a stiff drink then escort him to the Helm Crag bedroom and wait with him until Mr Notts arrives. Thank you."

Jeremy could not resist interfering, "And Daphne, read his bloody cards whilst you're there."

Everyone finally dispersed.

As Madame De'Ath led him up the stairs, she asked, "How did you get here?"

"By boat."

"On Mr Montgomery's boat?"

Daniel shook his head.

"Your boat?"

He nodded his head.

"And where have you come from?"

He pointed in the direction of Catbells.

"You live somewhere over there, and you've rowed here?"

He nodded once more. Daphne quickly realised this was going to be a long night.

CHAPTER NINE

Mr Montgomery was the first to rise, just after six thirty, and his old bones had taken over an hour to loosen up. From the staff quarters, he made his way to the kitchen to prepare food for fifteen, sixteen including the dog.

Mr Notts made his way downstairs just before seven thirty and proceeded to open the curtains throughout the lower ground floor. He was surprised the snow hadn't laid during the night as the temperature had surely dropped. A shiver cascaded down his back at the thought of the chilling atmosphere. Candles were still required at this time of the morning in December. He lit the main fires in the communal rooms then proceeded to prepare the dining room for breakfast under the glow of warming flames.

A pale morning sun was now stretching its weak limbs over a sleepy island within a misty lake.

The guests had been instructed to gather for breakfast later than planned due to the distressing events of last night. Sarah Silver was the first to arrive downstairs and she sat in blissful peace admiring the beautiful views over Derwentwater and towards the fells. Snow capped the highest heights.

The remaining guests arrived in dribs and drabs and by nine o'clock, the agreed time, there was still an empty chair. "Has anyone seen Bernard since last night?" asked Catherine.

No one had seen him. With all the commotion, everyone had forgotten about Bernard.

"Would you like me to check his room again?" asked Cliff Dacosta.

"Thank you, you are most kind," said Catherine.

Cornelius raised from his chair. "I'll come with you."

"Thank you, both," said Catherine.

On her insistence, the guests were asked to start breakfast so the food did not go cold. Daniel Watters wolfed down his scrambled eggs. Harry Arnold enjoyed the meatier dishes on offer. Vivienne nibbled on some fruit. Theresa Franks enjoyed two boiled eggs. Sarah Silver enjoyed buttered bread and cold ham.

Jeremy sat at the far end of the table and remained silent, preferring to observe and listen to the separate conversations around the room. Everyone was being polite, mainly small talk.

Minutes later, Cornelius and Cliff returned to the dining room.

"He's not there. Messy bed, and shoes and coat still missing, just as last night," said Cliff.

"There really must be a problem as we know the fat bastard wouldn't miss breakfast." Harry Arnold laughed at his own joke. Everyone ignored the distasteful remark.

Jeremy directed his question to Daniel Watters. "You were running around the grounds like a lunatic last night. Did you see Bernard, a rather rotund gentleman?"

"Who me?" asked Daniel, looking scared witless as all eyes descended on him.

"Unless I have somehow become cross-eyed during the night, then yes, I'm looking at you." Jeremy tutted. "Did you see Bernard in the grounds last night, or anyone else for that matter?"

"No sir, I didn't see anyone. I wanted to come in last night which is why I knocked on the door but when I see people or hear voices I just panic and run away. People make me nervous."

Jeremy muttered to himself, *bloody idiot.*

"Who's up for a brisk morning walk through the grounds after breakfast? We can explore the island, appreciate the spectacular fell views and admire the exterior of the house whilst searching for Bernard." Cornelius perused the room for takers.

Sarah Silver, Harry Arnold, Cliff Dacosta and Eliza Hart all agreed to join the search party.

The grounds were bleak being that it was December, but the views were still spectacular, with three hundred and sixty degrees of natural perfection. The lake was gently rippling, and the morning mist was starting to clear as the sun gained height.

To get their bearings, they retraced their steps from yesterday and headed towards the boat house and small jetty. The boat was still there as well as a smaller rowing boat. They quickly concluded Daniel Watters was the owner of the second vessel.

"At least we know Bernard hasn't left the island then," said Sarah Silver. Her white hair was neatly tidied in a low bun and her bonnet perfectly framed her wrinkled face.

"Who's up for venturing inside the church?" asked Cliff Dacosta. His dark skin and blue eyes mesmerising in the daylight.

"Are we allowed in there? It's maybe supposed to be a surprise, and all set up for the wedding," suggested Sarah.

"How about we try the door. If it's locked, fair enough, but if it's open then let's go in," said Harry Arnold. What he lacked in height, at around five foot five, he made up for in girth. His muscles bulging through his clothes.

"I agree," said Eliza. "More fool them if they didn't lock the door on their surprise."

With agreement, they made their way to the church.

The main structure was rectangular with a square tower, and the church was of a simple, functional design. The wooden doors were defensive, rather than artistic, with heavy wrought iron detailing.

Cornelius tried the handle, "It's locked."

"Oh well, that answers that question," said Eliza.

"What if Bernard has locked himself inside?" asked Sarah.

"Why would he do that?" asked Cliff.

"Maybe he's squirreling away all the food." Harry was oblivious to the other guests' annoyed reactions. The joke had worn thin.

"Knock on the door, Cornelius. See if anyone answers." Cliff was standing at the back of the group, keeping an eye on the whole situation.

There were no obvious sounds from inside.

Sarah had an idea. "Can we see through any of the windows? Maybe he's lying on the floor, injured or out cold."

They each picked a window, but the stained glass distorted their view.

For the next hour they walked through the grounds of the seven-acre estate. There were numerous pathways in which to enjoy the splendid views. The fells were majestic, tall and curvaceous, descending in layers, protectively wrapping themselves around the lake, feeding the pool with fresh, mountain water. The air was biting, and with the cloudless blue sky, they all agreed it would be icy later that evening.

As they continued their exploration of the grounds, the guests stumbled upon a folly, built like a medieval tower. The door opened to a rustic room with a cold fireplace and rectangular table surrounded by four chairs. A wooden dresser displayed pretty white and blue crockery.

They climbed the spiral, stone steps to the upper floor. There was a small landing, enough to house two people and the only door was closed. Cornelius twisted the wrought iron circular handle and pushed open the door. The room was decorated to a gothic theme, with dark panelling, exposed brickwork and impressive beams in a conical roof space. Set around a rectangular table were four throne-like chairs on which to sit and admire the views down Derwentwater. There was no place for Bernard to hide in there.

With the grounds too vast to cover inch by inch, they agreed to head back to the main house, each looking forward to a nice cup of tea. The return gave a different perspective. In tones of grey and brown, the house was imposing by size, rather than grandeur, but had an inviting balconied terrace on the upper floor. They concluded this was Jeremy Fisher's suite.

As they approached the more formal gardens close to the house, they happened upon a maze. "Oh, I love mazes," said Sarah. "I wonder how complex it is?"

"We could have a look now, if you'd like?" asked Cornelius.

Sarah shook her head, "I'd be scared of getting lost. How about we head inside and ask Mr Notts about it? Find out what's in the centre so we know what we are looking for." As much as she had set her mind on experiencing new things, there was always the element of doubt inside her head. The inherent caution in any of her decisions.

"Can you smell something odd?" asked Cliff, his eyebrows low, his nose raised.

"It's not a trick question, is it?" asked Harry. "To make us sniff your farts." He laughed.

They all looked at Harry with disdain.

"Now you mention it, my nose is a little irritated," said Eliza. She removed a handkerchief from her purse and covered her nose at the displeasure.

"It's more than just rotting leaves," offered Cliff.

Sarah placed her aged hands over her nose and mouth.

With nothing obvious to see, but with their sense of smell heightened, Cornelius, Cliff and Harry disappeared out of view into the evergreen shrubbery of the maze. Eliza and Sarah heard one of them squeal. The men came rushing out.

"We've found Bernard."

CHAPTER TEN

Sarah Silver and Eliza Hart hurried back to the house to call for assistance whilst Cornelius, Harry and Cliff pulled Bernard out of the shrubbery. The straggly branches scratched their faces and limbs, and the putrid smell was burning their noses, but with a struggle they managed to get Bernard Pratt out into the open air. By then, a crowd had gathered to help with the recovery.

Theresa Franks was approaching fifty years of age and with seven children to care for she had prematurely aged. Even in the winter sun, her hair, skin and clothes were a monotonous grey. She gazed upon Bernard's lifeless body, "Is he dead?"

"I think so, judging by his colour," stated Vivienne Kry. Her golden hair shimmered in the sun's rays and the chill in the air gave her cheeks a rosy hue.

"Did anyone bring a blanket or something in which we can wrap him up so we can carry him back to house?" asked Cornelius.

"Sorry, we thought we were summoning people to help him. We didn't realise he had died," said Mr Notts. "I'll go back and bring something appropriate. God bless his soul." He forged the sign of the cross over his head and chest before leaving the group.

"Does anyone know what happened?" asked Theresa, her thin frame shaking with shock. She pulled her tatty shawl around her bony shoulders.

Cliff Dacosta responded, "There was a strange smell which made us stop and search around here. Seems he's gone into the maze to be sick, as if he's tried to hide away. He's been sick numerous times by the number of puddles of vomit splattered on the ground."

Sarah Silver covered her wrinkled mouth, trying to stop herself from regurgitating her breakfast.

"The poor man, how dreadful to suffer on his own in this way." Theresa turned away. She could no longer stomach the proceedings.

Jeremy and Catherine were walking along the terrace, their pace dictated by Jeremy's infirmity. The crowd stopped talking when they reached the body.

"Oh, my goodness," said Catherine, as she gazed upon Bernard's spreadeagled body. "I was not expecting this outcome. Do we know how he died?" As she lifted her gaze, she caught Vivienne's amber eyes.

Vivienne remained composed, her tone serious. "I've been thinking about that. Possible theories are he's overindulged on the food, felt nauseous, came out here to be sick, hid in the maze away from prying eyes, then choked on his vomit. Simply a tragic situation. Or, he's been poisoned. Whether this was accidental or deliberate, who knows?"

Gasps of shock were heard.

Cornelius tried to settle people's nerves, "But please remember, we are all well, and we have consumed the same drinks and foods as Bernard. Surely that rules out poisoning."

"What if he was targeted?" asked Cliff.

"Why would anyone want to poison Bernard? He was a lovely, happy, chatty, gentle soul," stated Sarah.

Cliff shrugged his broad shoulders.

Catherine edged closer to the supine body. Bernard's brown check jacket and waistcoat were unbuttoned, as if he had loosened the fabric to ease his pain. The top three buttons of his blue shirt were undone and the fabric stained with vomit, like a novice cartographer had been practising his trade, mapping out islands in the sea. Catherine bent down on one knee to gain a visual advantage. White foam was visible around his mouth, like the edges of a stagnant pond. Petechiae were evident under his skin, as if an invading army of red ants had crawled over his chubby face. Respectfully, she lifted his eyelid, his stubby lashes barely visible. Staring into oblivion, his iris was a barren island in a pool of blood.

"For goodness' sake don't touch him," commanded Jeremy, "you could catch something."

"But I'm wearing gloves." Catherine reverted to an upright stance.

"I don't care. You're not an undertaker anymore. Just leave him. There's a cold storage room round the side of the house. For now, we'll put him in there until we have time to discuss what to do."

Tears formed in Sarah's eyes. "That seems so sad, so … disrespectful. Can we not place him in his room?"

Jeremy replied, "He'll contaminate the house and foul the sheets and mattress. And why run the risk of hurting yourself carrying that weight up the stairs."

The crowd remained silent.

Madame De'Ath and Mr Notts appeared along the terrace, carrying some sheets and blankets. Jeremy whispered to Catherine, "She's bloody useless, isn't she. You'd think she would have seen this coming, especially as she's supposed to have twin spirit guides. All three of them are bloody incompetent."

"I don't think it works like that. I think you have to open yourself up and allow the spirits in, and as for the cards, well you have to be asking a certain question."

Jeremy tutted his annoyance. He stood with a wide stance, both hands on his cane, watching proceedings.

The men wrapped Bernard's body in the thinner sheets which was a harder task than they had anticipated. Rolling him side to side on hard, uneven ground took effort. Once the stronger blankets were underneath the body, they carried him a few steps at a time before having to lay him back down on the ground to rest. They flexed their fingers to bring colour back to their hands. Time and again, they lifted the body and managed a few steps, the fabric straining with the dead weight as they persevered in carrying Bernard round the side of the building to place him in the stone outhouse.

On returning to the main house, everyone gathered in the sitting room and although they barely knew Bernard, they were sharing the few stories he had told them since the lake crossing.

The tales soon ran out and a solemn silence settled among the guests.

Eliza's hazel eyes surveyed the faces in the room as she said, "How about we take Bernard's body back to the mainland and try and contact his family?"

There were mumbles of agreement.

"And I suppose we should contact the police," said Vivienne.

There were mumbles of a different sort.

Jeremy considered his response, "Do we have any volunteers to escort Bernard back to shore? Please remember that you will forfeit your gift by leaving the island and you will be disqualified from returning."

Everyone paused, taking the time to consider the consequences of their decisions.

"I don't mind taking him over to the shore," said Vivienne. "I've had enough of this."

Nobody commented.

"But can I at least have some volunteers to carry him to the boat?"

The usual three of Cornelius, Cliff and Harry offered their services. George reluctantly volunteered as eyes fell upon him to even up the numbers. He forced a smile.

"Once you leave, there will no return, and no money," reiterated Jeremy as he stared at Vivienne.

"I acknowledge the terms." She stood from the chair and straightened her blue woollen skirt. "Please excuse me as I'm going to pack my bag. I'll leave immediately after." She headed towards the door.

"Vivienne, please reconsider. It's bitterly cold outside. Bernard will be pretty much preserved out there in these temperatures and being winter it will soon be dark. He said he was from Kendal. You couldn't possibly do anything constructive at this time of day on your own." Sarah walked over to Vivienne and held her hand. "Please, wait until Sunday then I will help you in contacting his family."

"Thank you, but I've made up my mind, I'm leaving."

Jeremy responded, "Then so be it. I'll task Mr Notts with

packing Bernard's belongings. Cornelius, Cliff, Harry and George, you four make a start on carrying Bernard to the jetty. I will collect Bernard's address from the master suite and pass on the information to Vivienne. I will ask Mr Montgomery to row you both over to the shore and he will depart as soon as Bernard's body is on firm ground. There'll only be the two of you, so you'll just have to drag him out of the boat the best you can. Unless you're lucky and there are people there to help. Once on the mainland, Vivienne, can you let the police know what has happened? She nodded. "Then go and pack your belongings."

The group scattered in silence, shocked by what had happened. Theresa, Sarah and Eliza followed Vivienne up the stairs, and tried once more to make her reconsider her decision. They reminded her that one thousand pounds was a life changing fortune and to persevere with staying for the weekend, participating in the wedding and being rich by Sunday afternoon. However, Vivienne was adamant she was leaving and the other women left her to pack her belongings.

The winter sun was close to setting behind the mountains as she said her goodbyes to everyone. She thanked Jeremy and Catherine for the invite and wished them well for their wedded future. Mr Montgomery offered to carry Vivienne's bag, but she insisted on completing the task herself. Mr Notts carried Bernard's bag. As they made their way through the grounds towards the jetty, they saw the four men struggling along the path with the wrapped body. Their hearts sank when they arrived at the jetty.

"Where's me boat?" asked Mr Montgomery. His hunched shoulders slumped further and his head protracted on realising his pride and joy was missing.

Placing her bag on the ground, Vivienne asked, "Are you sure you moored it properly?"

"What a bloody cheek. Of course I moored it properly. I'm seventy-seven this year and never has me boat come undone before. Someone has deliberately untethered it. You can't trust anyone nowadays. I wish I'd locked the boat house doors."

"Please accept my apologies, Mr Montgomery, I did not mean to offend you, it's just that I'm desperate to get off this island. I can't stay here a moment longer." Vivienne looked close to crying. Her amber eyes and golden hair failed to warm her cold persona.

"Lass, if you've learned anything from this experience then think about how your words can hurt others." Thomas Montgomery stormed off, his spindly bowed legs making his balance seem precarious.

Vivienne's demeanour shrank.

Sensing the atmosphere, Cliff diverted their attention by asking, "And where's Daniel's boat? It was here earlier this morning when we were searching for Bernard."

"You're right. His boat was tied there." Harry pointed to the last bay.

"Are there any back up plans for emergencies?" asked Cornelius who was emerging as the natural leader of the group.

Mr Notts shook his head, "Like Mr Montgomery said, we've never lost the boat before."

"Can we somehow raise an alarm to those on the mainland. Light a fire or fire a gun?" suggested Cliff.

"There are no guns on the island and a fire … mmm … I'm not sure the master will agree to that. Too much of a risk on an island surrounded by ancient trees."

"But we are surrounded by water. We could easily put out the flames once we've summoned help." Cliff was not letting this go. "Or we could try sending smoke signals from the fire in the reception room. It's a large fireplace. We could communicate with the mainland, like the red Indians did."

"I guess so, but do you know how to create the signals and would residents in this area know what they mean?" asked Mr Notts.

Silence ensued.

"Could we swim across the lake?" asked George. His warm brown eyes surveying the distance from the island to the shore.

"At a guess, I would estimate a twenty-minute swim, but in these near freezing temperatures, I would not recommend it." Mr Notts was receiving the brunt of people's frustrations.

"Is there enough food for us all, I mean, we were only supposed to be staying until Sunday afternoon. We could be here for days, weeks, months if no one comes to rescue us." Harry took off his flat cap and scratched the emerging dark stubble on his head.

"There is plenty of food to sustain us. We always get a delivery of food by boat on a Monday morning, so we'll be rescued then."

There were sighs of relief all round.

"Why didn't you tell us this at the start?" asked George. "You could see we were worried."

In desperation, Vivienne stated, "I cannot wait until Monday. I need to get off this island today. I cannot tolerate this claustrophobic atmosphere any longer. Could we perhaps use a mirror to catch the remaining rays of sunlight, to try and get attention from the mainland?"

"But there are no houses nearby. If we can't see them, they can't see us," said Mr Notts. As they continued to thrash out ideas, the sun said its final goodbyes on the day.

Mr Notts suggested, "Let's go back to the house before we are plunged into total darkness and decide what to do from there."

There were nods all round. Vivienne and George were now visibly shivering, the bleakness of the island and their situation adding to their discomfort.

"Who agrees that we leave Bernard here? I know it's not ideal but there's no way I'm lugging him back to the house," said Harry.

"I'm ashamed to say I agree." George rubbed his arms with his hands to generate warmth. He was all out of smiles.

"Then can we at least move him, so he is under the shelter of the boathouse roof?" asked Vivienne.

Cliff, Cornelius, Harry and George nodded their heads in synchronisation and proceeded to carry Bernard's blanketed remains to the end bay so he was protected by the overhang of the roof and the bushes flanking the water's edge.

Little Lily suddenly appeared, darting round the corner and down the path as if she was being chased by a much bigger dog. Without hesitation she leapt off the jetty and splashed into the cold, dark water. She paddled for a minute then circled back through the bushes to climb onto dry land. Her body rippled in coordinated shakes and the water sprayed everyone close by. They turned or used their hands as a shield to protect their faces from the icy droplets. Little Lily ran around between their feet, jumped in the water again, paddled for a few seconds then came ashore.

"I think it's safe to say the water is too cold to swim across to shore," said Mr Notts.

"What's she doing?" asked Cliff. "There she goes again, back in the water."

"She's having a little mad half hour," said Harry with a smile on his face. He squatted, his muscular thighs straining his trousers, as he coaxed the dog out of the freezing water.

Lily once again shook herself dry. She was shivering and seemed distressed, taking it in turns to approach each person, but running away as each went to stroke her head. The dog was wide eyed, yawning and making strange noises.

Vivienne gasped and suddenly turned away, covering her mouth with her hands. The only words she said were, "Over there." She pointed. A body was floating face down in the lake.

CHAPTER ELEVEN

Daniel Watters was dead. They had been unable to retrieve the prone body, but Daniel was recognised by his long, straggly hair and by the clothes he had been given. The flow of the water had taken him away from the island. Cornelius Binks had attempted to wade out, but he soon realised the lake was too deep. He had then attempted to swim but the cold water had taken his breath away. He had quickly admitted defeat.

Since spotting the dead body in the water, Vivienne Kry had not muttered a word. Her amber eyes stared into oblivion and her slim arms hung limply by her sides as she stood in the bay of the window.

Sarah Silver was shivering as she huddled by the fire, warming her aged hands by the flames, "I think he's wanted to escape the island. He had already stated he tends to run away when he sees people or hears voices. I think he's panicked and attempted to leave. When he's seen his boat missing, he's tried to swim but he's got into difficulties."

Leaning against the mantlepiece, Cornelius confirmed, "The temperature of that water was deadly. Nobody could have survived for more than a few minutes in those icy waters."

"The poor boy. I know he was technically a man but mentally he was just a bairn. What an absolute tragedy."

Theresa Franks was close to tears, thinking about her own children, hoping they were safe and sound.

"At this rate, there'll be none of us left by Sunday." As was becoming the norm, everyone ignored Harry's inappropriate remark.

Jeremy was interrogating Madame De'Ath in the master suite. "What are your thoughts about the boy?"

"An absolutely devastating turn of events, sir." She interlocked her petite fingers.

"Did you not predict this? I hired you for your world-renowned skills."

"I apologise profusely for not informing you sooner of his tarot card reading as I—"

Jeremy held up his flattened palm and turned away from her with a look of disdain, "Too late for excuses, just tell me what the cards divulged."

Madame De'Ath recalled Daniel's reading from when she had escorted the young man to his room in the early hours of the morning. The first card he had chosen was The Hermit. Daphne had thought this was the perfect card to describe the poor boy. His past had been one of isolation, withdrawing from society and being cautious of strangers. He had always struggled to face facts, preferring to hide away, fearful of the unknown.

The second card drawn was the Eight of Cups. Daphne explained to Jeremy that this card represented Daniel's present circumstances. She had interpreted this as him withdrawing further from society and dwelling in his own little world. He could not tolerate any sort of intrusion or change into his personal life or space. With help from her spirit guides, the twins had shown her that his father had died, resulting in his mother being unable to cope and had recently been in and out of the lunatic asylum for bouts of profound melancholy. This fitted with Daniel's dishevelled appearance and scrawny limbs. The twins had shown Daniel's mother reading the wedding invite and sending him on his way to the island for the money.

The Valet of Swords was the last card drawn. Daphne had thought this strange at the time as Daniel was no knight of the realm. The meaning alluded to perception, vigilance, and delving into the unknown. Daniel had heightened senses to noise and movement, and he was certainly vigilant of his surroundings, but the final part did not make sense. With his social avoidance, why would Daniel delve into the unknown? With the gift of hindsight, maybe the card had predicted his death, as Daniel had ventured onto the island, not knowing what to expect, and had then delved into the unknown depths of Derwentwater. A true valet, Daniel must have had immense mental strength and courage to do what he did.

Jeremy lit a cigar and puffed smoke into the air. "Why didn't the twins warn you of his death?"

"They only show me what has transpired. They cannot tell me the future. The person has to choose their own fate."

"There is a tarot card specifically called Death. Why didn't Daniel pick this card?"

Daphne stroked her red hair out of her eyes. Her voice a little tentative, "It doesn't quite work like that. Perhaps Daniel wasn't choosing death, he was choosing to escape the island. The valet of swords was predicting his fight to be free."

Jeremy's mouth puckered to the side, obviously unimpressed by the art of divination.

"What was Bernard Pratt's last card? Do you recall?"

"I don't sir, but I still have my notes if you would like me to retrieve the information?"

"Yes, that would be interesting." Jeremy gulped his Irish whiskey. "One more thing, I would like you to read my cards, and Catherine's if she's agreeable. Maybe I will finally be able to understand that bloody woman."

Conversation in the main reception room was becoming more interesting as the alcoholic beverages flowed.

"Has anyone fathomed why we are here yet?" asked Cornelius Binks. In his forties and with distinguished good looks, he was young enough to appeal to the younger guests but mature enough to be taken seriously by the older guests.

"Are we not here for a wedding?"

Surprised by George's answer, Cornelius said, "Really? Everyone, ask yourself this question, why me?"

"What do you mean?" Harry Arnold asked.

Cornelius sighed. "Why would Jeremy and Catherine ask you, me, Sarah, Eliza, George etcetera to their wedding? We have already ascertained that none of us know them, but Jeremy has intimated that he knows us, or at least he said he knows Theresa very well."

Theresa wrapped her shawl tighter around her shoulders. "I must admit, that comment chilled me to the bone."

"I'm still not sure what you are getting at." Harry walked over to the drinks cabinet and poured himself another whiskey.

Cornelius thought of some examples. "We have already ascertained we are not family, friends, colleagues, neighbours or even acquaintances, so what exactly are we? Have we been randomly selected or is there a link?"

"I see what you mean," said George. He fingered the cleft in his chin. "Do you have a theory?"

Cornelius offered, "We all live within a certain radius from here."

"That's maybe just for convenience though. I live in Carlisle and that was hard enough getting here," said George.

"Same for me, I had to walk from Penrith. Couldn't afford the train or cab fairs. Don't have a horse or friends with carts," said Theresa.

"It's not that then. Any other ideas?" asked Cornelius.

"Maybe we are related, long lost cousins, nephews, sisters, branches of the family we knew nothing about," suggested George.

"It's a possibility I suppose but I doubt it," said Eliza. She compared skin tones with Cliff. "My father was from India and if I recall correctly, Cliff's father was from Jamaica."

Cliff nodded.

"Jeremy mentioned happiness at dinner yesterday. He said he wanted to learn from us. Gain some insight into what makes us happy." George's smile was starting to return. "Maybe that's the clue."

"We could certainly do with some cheering up," said Sarah. "Go on then, you start. Tell us what makes you happy."

George thought for a moment. "Women: I love their hair, their soft skin, their smell, their smile, their touch. The love of a good woman would make me happy."

"Women are the bane of my life," said Harry. "Well one in particular. It's all very sweet at first when they are interested in you, but once you marry them, they turn into something demonic. They scream, shout, moan, the mood swings. Nothing you do is ever good enough. Look at the mother-in-law, that's how your misses will turn out." He made a fist, tensing his biceps, as if he was imagining punching her in the face.

"That's why I'm never getting married," said Cornelius, "not worth all the grief. That's why I'm going grey." He touched his temples.

"That's why I've got no hair," said Harry. "A receding hairline from all the bloody stress so I shave it off, and I'm only thirty-two."

There were a few titters. Theresa continued the conversation, "It would be wonderful to find true love, but if we are talking about current spouses then mine was bloody useless, a totally lazy git. I'm better off without him."

Eliza Hart, Vivienne Kry and Sarah Silver were noticeably quiet during the conversation about spouses. Cliff Dacosta admitted that he loved women too and would quite happily settle down if he found the right one, but no one would have him. Around Whitehaven, his name had become synonymous with warfare.

There were sighs of sympathy around the room.

"You're a true gentleman, Cliff. Strong, yet reserved, with a quiet intelligence. You really are the tall, dark and handsome stranger. I'd have you if I was twenty years younger." Sarah Silver put her hand over her mouth and giggled. Everyone laughed.

Even Cliff was on the verge of smiling, "Thank you, Sarah. I'm honoured." He bowed his head.

As the conversation on that topic waned, everyone naturally looked to George's left, as if going clockwise round the group.

"I take it it's my turn," said Theresa. She coughed nervously. "I love my children, they make me happy, but they also make me sad. When they're happy, I'm happy. When they are hungry, or need new clothes or are poorly, then it breaks my heart. I just want to be able to provide for them. Enough money to feed them so they will grow to be healthy and happy. Enough money to give them proper beds to sleep on. I'd love a bigger house too, with money to buy new things, keep things clean, make a lovely home."

"So rather than your children making you happy, it's money that would make you happy?" asked Cornelius. His striking blue eyes cool against his black and speckled grey hair.

Theresa thought for a moment before answering, "Yes and no. The children do make me happy, so I can be happy even without money. But I guess what I'm concluding is more money would make me happier."

The guests discussed children and money as a source of happiness. Everyone agreed that more money would make them happier. There was less agreement when it came to children.

"I don't have any children, or none that I'm aware of," said Harry with a twinkle in his eye. The guests were unsure if he was joking.

Only when asked directly, Vivienne and Eliza admitted they did not have children and were unsure as to whether they wanted any.

"It all sounds very much like hard work," said Eliza. "As long as my husband was rich and we could afford a nanny and maids, then I may contemplate children. However, they do say your figure changes for the worse after childbirth and the thought of pushing that out of there terrifies me." Eliza grimaced. "And women have died during the childbirth process." She stood up and sauntered over to the drinks table, holding her hand in the air as if waving the idea goodbye.

Their attention moved to Vivienne to clarify her meaning on the topic. "It's just never been the right time." Despite further questions, Vivienne refused to expand on her thoughts and feelings.

They looked at Sarah Silver for the next topic. "Now it's my turn … yikes … it's hard isn't it … what makes me happy?" A pause. "I'll be honest and say I am here for the money, of course I am, but that's not the main reason. I'm not rich by any means, but I have sufficient money put by to live a fairly comfortable life. Over the years, I think happiness for me is doing the right thing. Having everything in order. Being organised. Being clean.

Anticipating friction. Avoiding conflict. Not allowing problems to develop. I guess what I'm saying is I like everything being planned and orderly. My happiness comes from expecting the unexpected which calms me. To sum up, I hate surprises and love routine."

"And how do you feel being here?" asked Cliff.

"I'm a wreck if the truth be told." She held out her trembling hands for them all to see. "I'm seventy-two and when I received the wedding invite through the post, I was intrigued. It made me reflect on how mundane my life had become and I wanted a little adventure, a little bit of excitement in my life, a little chaos, but this has confirmed I'm happy being at home, content within my own little world with my routines."

"Fair play to you, each to their own," said Cliff.

Everyone then discussed if home, routines and doing the right things made them happy. As with the other suggestions, there were opposing arguments.

"Routine would bore me to tears," said Eliza as she gracefully sat back down in the armchair.

"Me too," said Cornelius, "surely everyone needs a little excitement in their life." He smiled at the dazzling Miss Hart with her warm skin tone and dark hair.

She responded with a seductive look, "Exploring, experiencing new things, excitement, ecstasy, events that thrill or shock, everything that makes your heart race with pleasure. That makes me happy."

The other guests tried to hide their amusement.

"So, I guess it's me next," said Cliff, trying to fill the awkward silence of the room. "To be honest, I've had a few run ins recently, some money troubles, so for me, money would definitely make me happier. And as for routine, I would have said it sounds boring, but with everything I've been through, maybe a sense of stability would make me happy. I've had to hide away, avoid people, lie, fight to survive, and run away, so for me I just want some peace and quiet. The freedom to be me and not worry about anyone or anything else. To know I'm safe from harm. To have that security in order to properly rest and relax and be happy. Having a comfortable home with a walled garden and big metal gates that I can lock, that would be perfect."

"Thanks for your honesty, Cliff. Must have taken a lot of courage to admit that." Cornelius got out of his chair and offered his hand to Cliff. They shook hands and everyone did a little clap. Sarah patted Cliff's shoulder.

For the first time, everyone agreed that feeling safe from harm and being yourself were important factors in attaining happiness. However, the topics of a comfortable home and more money were still important factors in most people's attempts at finding happiness.

The next chair was empty. "Since Harry has left the room, Eliza, do you want to go next?" suggested Cliff.

"I have already given some insight into what makes me happy," she once again smiled at Cornelius, "but if I must pick one thing then I'd have to say more money because of course you can buy happiness. And I don't mean just sufficient amounts to get by, scraping a few pennies together to buy a morsel of food. I want luxuries, beautiful dresses, a manor house in the country, servants, the ability to travel, exquisite foods. I could go on but I need another drink." She rose from the chair. "Anyone else want one?"

There was a prolonged break as everyone refilled their glasses and conversations went off topic until Cliff brought everyone together. "Seems like Harry's not coming back and now Cornelius is missing. Bet they've left so they don't have to answer the question."

George yawned, then stretched before heading over to the bay window. "I must admit, I'm none the wiser for our conversation. I can't believe Jeremy and Catherine would pay us each one thousand pounds just to hear what makes us happy."

Sarah replied, "And we can't even agree on that: love, money, excitement, routine, surprises, security, children, no children, spouse, no spouse, freedom, peace. I would add another one. Hope. Hope that things will get better, hope that things will work out, hope that love will conquer all, hope that our children and love ones will also find happiness, hope that we will live in peace and be pain free."

"That's lovely, Sarah, but hope is just wishful thinking. I have hoped for many things but have been bitterly disappointed. Hope has failed me and resulted in resentment." Vivienne rose from her chair. "Excuse me." She left the room with tears in her eyes.

"Oh I hope I haven't offended her." Sarah put her thumb and index finger to her lips in contemplation.

"Don't worry. With everything that has happened I think Vivienne just needs some space and time in which to reflect," said Cliff. "She's barely said a word since finding Daniel Watters face down in the water."

George broke the silence. "There's got to be more to the invite than us talking about happiness. We are missing something, we are linked somehow, just can't think what it may be."

Theresa hesitated before stating, "I think I may know but I don't want to say in case I'm wrong."

CHAPTER TWELVE

Theresa Franks burst into tears and hurried out of the room, knocking into Cornelius and Harry in the hallway. Her worn leather boots were supple as she scurried up the stairs.

Cornelius dared to enquire, "Theresa, are you well?"

She was too upset to respond.

Wiping away her tears with her threadbare shawl, Theresa was unlocking her bedroom door when Catherine and Madame De'Ath rounded into the hallway. The women saw her distress and immediately headed towards her, but Theresa managed to open the door and hurried inside. The key turning in the lock was audible.

"What on earth has happened? Can I help you in anyway?" Catherine listened intently, but all she could hear was sobbing. "Please, let me in, I'm worried about you, I cannot leave you on your own, knowing you are distraught and hurting." She listened once more, there were sniffs and sighs. "Please, open the door, I'm not leaving, even if it means sleeping in the corridor all night, I'll wait here so you know you have someone close by who cares." Catherine indicated for Madame De'Ath to go. The woman nodded and headed along the corridor, turning right at the end. Once she was out of sight, Catherine lowered herself onto the floorboards and leaned back against the wall. The sobbing from the room was abating and the sighs less frequent. Eventually, Catherine heard footsteps approaching the door and the key turned in the lock. Theresa opened the door a few inches.

"I'm only letting you in because this is your home. I feel you deserve respect for your kind hospitality." Her eyes were swollen and red, matching her nose. She searched for a dry section of handkerchief.

Catherine smiled, "Sadly, this isn't our house. We are only renting the property. A month of self-imposed solitary confinement." She smiled, trying to lighten the sombre mood. "One of Jeremy's many acquaintances owns the place."

Theresa's body slumped, exhausted by the outpouring of sadness.

"I'm not going to pry. I can see you are upset, and I genuinely hope this is only a temporary state of unease. However, if I can get you anything, some tea, or something to eat perhaps? I can certainly get you a dry handkerchief." She smiled again, hoping Theresa would see the funny side, which she did.

"A clean handkerchief would be lovely, thank you."

Within a few minutes, Catherine returned with a pristine white handkerchief embroidered with pink roses in the corners. Theresa was grateful for the kind gesture.

"I'm sorry for getting upset. It's your wedding tomorrow and we should be celebrating. I'm lowering the mood, I'm like a dark cloud raining down on everything. And with Bernard and then Daniel, I'm …" her voice tailed off.

"But they were not your fault. There was nothing we could do. Tragic accidents by the look of things. Please do not place any blame on yourself."

"We were talking before, about why we are here. We were talking about happiness. We were discussing why *we* were here. Why us specifically." The sobbing had long since stopped but she paused to compose herself. A silent tear contoured down her face.

"Why are you here?" asked Catherine.

"For the money, for the bairns, for respite. I'm weary. I've had enough. I don't want to be here anymore."

"You only have until tomorrow then you are free to leave the island, with all the money owed."

"I'm not meaning that. I mean … I don't want to be here. Here, this world, I've had enough, I'm exhausted, I just bring misery to those around me."

"Theresa, please don't say those things. Your family, your

husband, they surely love you, they—"

"My husband left me. The bairns, they try their best, God bless their souls, but I can't cope anymore. I'm … I'm …"

"You sound so strong. I do believe you walked all the way from Penrith to get here. That is no mean feat in this weather. You will get through this."

Tears burst through the dam once more, "I know why I'm here. It's a punishment for what I did."

"What did you do?"

"I nearly killed a man."

Catherine took a while to respond, thinking the worst. "Your husband?"

"Good God no, even though I'd love to get me hands round his scrawny neck. No, it was an accident, honestly it was. I was out one evening. I was trying to pinch food for the bairns. There was this house, it was dark, seven ish, and there was no light from inside. I thought the house was empty and I was desperate for food. The sash window was slightly ajar, I pushed it up, climbed inside. I pocketed food: bread, cheese, a jar of preserve. Then I got brave. Started looking around for other things, something of value I could sell. Then he walked in, an old man bless him. I hid in the corner, tried to stop breathing but me heart seemed so loud. It was dark, he was shuffling, his bald head was catching the tiny bit of light from outside, he had a cane. His knees were bent outwards, in fact he was bent everywhere, his back, his hips. Then he saw me and panicked, then hit me with his stick. I didn't mean to hurt him. I was thinking of me brood. I just wanted to get away."

"Oh no, how awful, but you were desperate, starving, people will understand if they hear the full story."

"They don't understand though, there was a knife on the bench. He was hitting me with his stick, it was a reaction, I had to stop him, I was hurting." She buried her head in her hands. "He fell to the floor."

Catherine moved closer and wrapped her arms around the woman's trembling body. "You stabbed him?"

"Truly, I thought I'd killed him. Me nerves have been so bad ever since. I've barely left the house, sending the children out for food as I'm terrified to venture anywhere. I've since heard the old man survived but went downhill. Mentally ill. Screaming out in the night, crying, scared of being alone. He ended up in the asylum. No one knew who attacked him or why and he cannot recall what happened. Since that day I've been a nervous wreck, waiting for the day the police come to arrest me. Coming here, it's the first time I've left the house in months. Is it a punishment, and we are all here to die for our sins? Bernard? Daniel? Me?" Sobbing, she tried to calm her breathing through pursed lips.

Unsure what to say or do, Catherine could only answer from the heart. "Being honest, I really do not know the reasons why you have been invited here. Jeremy arranged everything. He has not confided in me as to his reasons, telling me he wants our wedding day to be a surprise. Unfortunately, I cannot confirm or deny anything, but Jeremy is at heart a good man. He appears abrupt and cruel at times but he truly is kind. Caring for waifs and strays, funding orphanages, hospitals and asylums. He is so driven to improve health, wealth and happiness. He dreams of a wonderful world where everyone is happy." She paused. "As we are being honest, he did not actually say that. His exact words were, 'I don't want to lay eyes on the grubby people. I want the world to be beautiful." The women managed to smile at the insult. "I admit, his strategies are strange, but he truly means well by everything he does."

Theresa sighed, depleted of a will to argue. She stared vaguely at the pretty, flowery picture on the wall of her room. Catherine spoke but Theresa was oblivious to her words, in a sort of protective trance, blocking any further trauma or stress.

Catherine squeezed Theresa's hand but elicited no response. Feeling the time was right to leave, she made her way over to the door. "I'll call on you later, see if you need anything."

Theresa continued staring at the picture. The pink and purple flowers pretty against the green leaves and grass. As quietly as possible, Catherine closed the door behind her and went in search of peace and quiet.

A while later, Catherine found Jeremy interrogating everyone in the main reception room about happiness. Catherine could see the discomfort amongst the guests. Eliza Hart appeared bored; her arms folded across her bosom. Cornelius Binks seemed uncomfortable, fidgeting in his chair. Sarah Silver was pretending to be interested but her smile appeared forced. Harold Arnold was slumped in his armchair, trying to maintain his focus but his eyes often drifting into sleep. Cliff Dacosta was … hmm …hard to read. He was staring at Jeremy, almost like he hated him, barely a blink to distract him from his thoughts. Vivienne Kry was formal, closed. George Jones was the only person to be genuinely smiling.

"My dear Catherine, how good of you to join us." Everyone smiled, welcoming the distraction. "We have each declared what makes us happy and the conclusion is money does not necessarily in itself make us happy, but is the gateway to achieving happiness, whether that be for a house, clothes, food, horses, excitement, travel etcetera." Jeremy got up out of the chair and gave himself a few moments to stretch, before limping across the room to greet Catherine with a kiss on each cheek.

"As you all know by now, I have considerable wealth. I have travelled the world, experienced so many delicacies, have been entertained in various ways, own numerous abodes and have found the love of my life, but I am still unhappy. I crave more, I search for thrills, I am never satisfied, always on the lookout for the 'holy grail', that elusive chalice that promises so much. I can categorically confirm that none of the things you crave will make you happy. I truly believe that happiness can only ever be a fleeting emotion. You will become bored with that new dress, you will tire of your spouses jokes, you will become irritated by your child's constant demands, travelling will become a chore, etcetera, etcetera."

The room remained silent as Jeremy walked back to his chair. "Establishing that money would make you happy was a totally predictable response, so, in order to delve deeper and truly find out the key to happiness, we will now discuss death. As you are lying on your death bed, what would you crave? Is it your family, friends, food, pets, a loved one? I doubt your dying wish would be to see or spend time with your money. Are memories important? Is a hug or kiss desired? Holding a loved one's hand, knowing they are close as you pass away? What would be important to you? What would you say to someone as you were dying?"

Catherine interjected, "I think we need to give our guests a break from all these questions. And with Bernard and Daniel only just passing, maybe you should reconsider discussing—"

"Don't tell me what I can and can't do. The weekend's events are planned, and everyone agreed to partake in the tasks and will be richly rewarding for their time and insights."

Everyone glanced at each other, sensing the discomfort.

"Please forgive me, Jeremy, I did not mean to suggest—"

"Just get me a drink, woman, and be quick about it."

Catherine could feel the flush of embarrassment spread across her face. He had been so cruel to her of late. Over the last three years he had been kind and considerate, giving her everything she wanted yet for the last few weeks he had been callous and short-tempered, scolding her for the slightest annoyance.

"If I may be so bold, I do believe we would all welcome a break." Cliff tried to catch everyone's eye and the nods were reassuring.

Jeremy sighed, annoyed by the lack of resilience to being questioned. "Then for goodness' sake, be back here for ..." he looked at the clock on the mantlepiece, "six, then we have an hour and a half before we are called through for dinner." He got out of the chair on the second attempt and stormed out of the room with a look of disdain.

"Are you alright?" Sarah Silver placed her hand on Catherine's forearm.

"Please do not fret. Sadly, I have become accustomed to his ways."

"Don't allow any man, or woman for that matter, to treat you like a stray dog. Draw the boundaries now otherwise you'll be forever at his beck and call."

"Honestly, I'm fine. But if I may ask a small favour?"

Sarah nodded, "Go on."

Catherine asked if she would be so kind as to check on Theresa.

"Why yes of course. I'll take her up a pot of tea."

Vivienne had overheard the conversation. "You go on up. I'll ask Mr Notts for the tea and bring it up as soon as it's ready."

"I really do appreciate your help, ladies." Catherine excused herself and exited the room.

Unsure as to what would greet her, Catherine knocked on the door to Jeremy's suite and waited for him to respond before entering the room. Cautiously, she turned the handle and pushed open the door. Jeremy's elbows were on the desk, his head in his hands, he was swearing under his breath.

"Can I help in any way or would you prefer solitude?" Nervously, she waited by the door for an answer.

He raised his head out of his hands but did not lay his eyes upon her, preferring to look straight ahead at the wall. "Sit." With an upturned palm, he indicated for her to sit on the armchair by the fire. "I must apologise for before. Do you forgive me?"

"Of course I do, but you are worrying me." She straightened her skirts.

"This bloody curse is killing me. Pocks are ravaging my body and pain riddles my entire being. I even have sores around my anus, I'm in perpetual agony, and yet the guests cannot even tolerate being questioned." He tutted.

Through all the years she had known him, tact and diplomacy were never his forte. "Then maybe we should try something else. There must be a cure, there must be something we can do." Catherine rose from the chair and was heading over to the medical books on the bookshelf.

"Save me your pity. You and I both know we have tried every tincture, infusion and elixir we know of, but no one has the cure for syphilis. We have employed the best doctors, alchemists and priests in their field. This is God, making me suffer for the sins of my past. Retribution for the pain I have inflicted on others over the years. For the fornication, the lust, the misery I have caused, the satanic allegiance in self-gratification and a hedonistic lifestyle. Punishing me, making me suffer, for the wrongs I need to put right." He gulped a large dose of a golden fluid from a crystal glass.

"God does not punish. You are scolding yourself. In all the years I have known you, you have never indulged in self-pity. Everyone has admired you, for your generosity, your positivity, your drive to succeed. You are admired within so many professions and have amassed an impressive fortune."

"Stop now, for I know you are only trying to cheer me up. Do you still love me, Catherine? Are you willing to marry me, knowing about this curse? Knowing I will surely die someday?" He coughed. "Will you look after me, in sickness and in health?"

"You know I have my reservations. You know I will forever stand by you and that I cannot understand why we have to be married to confirm this. We have agreed that intimacy is not an option open to us because of this infliction. And you know I still love Solomon."

"For goodness' sake, shut up about that blasted ragamuffin! He's a bloody lunatic!"

"You know fine well he is incarcerated in that asylum against his will because you accused him of insanity. You know he is completely of sound mind. You just wanted him out of the way. Solomon will never divulge your secrets. He is a man of his word. You can trust him."

"I know you still care about him, but I cannot for the life of me understand why you still have feelings for a useless pauper." Jeremy got out of the chair and hobbled around the room, obviously in pain, his face distorting with the discomfort he was experiencing.

"Anyway, our secret is safe only because he is locked away from society."

"You are impossible to argue with." Catherine made to leave.

"One more thing, since you raised the topic of secrets and locations. Do you want to know why we are here?"

"You want to know the secret to a happy life, something that has eluded you despite your wealth and critical acclaim in the field of architecture and design. You want insight into people's last wishes before they die to see if this correlates with what would have made them happy in life. Or something along those lines."

"True, but do you know why we are here, on this particular island?"

"I thought it was because you knew the owner and because of its isolated location, so no interruptions, less interference for your studies into happiness."

"There is another reason." Jeremy limped over to the fire, preferring the comfy armchair to the harder captain's chair by the desk. He sat down with a wince.

Intrigued, Catherine sat down in the matching armchair next to him.

"Previous occupants of this island have alluded to hidden biblical treasure."

Wearily, Catherine sighed. *Not again.* "What is this new treasure you seek?"

"I haven't a bloody clue. My research has brought me to this island but I have failed in my quest to find anything here."

"Are you admitting defeat and asking for my assistance?" A wry smile formed on her face.

"Please do not tell a soul." For the first time in a while, they smiled at each other with warmth.

"Then tell me what you know."

"You don't need to know all the details, but I have recently happened upon information alluding to ancient treasure hidden on the island.

"In the 16th century, at the request of Queen Elizabeth, German miners were invited to Keswick to explore the nearby fells. Renowned for their expertise, the queen created a charter, a Company of Mines Royal, allowing them to mine deep into the landscape.

"The locals detested this influx of migrant workers. Over weeks, months and years, the foreigners courted local women and paraded their newly acquired wealth from the profits of their finds. Having whipped up so much hatred from the local men, the Germans were forced to seek refuge on Derwent Isle, to escape the baying crowds and to hide their wares. For decades, the miners quarried deep within the surrounding fells, finding lead, copper, silver and graphite amongst other things.

"Moving on through the centuries, the information is suspiciously scant, but the island is then renamed Vicar Island and comes under ownership of the monks from Fountains Abbey, in Yorkshire. St Benedict, whoever he was, supposedly said, 'Idleness is the enemy of the soul, and that manual labour and sacred reading should occupy the brethren,' or words to that effect. The monks became known as lay brothers which over time became labourers. They worked hard on wool production, breeding of animals, quarrying of slate and stone and of course mining the fells, just like the Germans did many years ago."

"I think I'm following this but what exactly are you alluding to? What is the treasure?"

Jeremy rose from his chair and stretched his back. He hobbled over to the fire and stood with a wide stance trying to ease his pain. "There is treasure here, I just know it. Miners of Royal appointment quarry the lands for years. The information is scant, but I have evidence to suggest the Romans also mined these fells. Then the monks suddenly appear, and the miners disappear. There must be something biblical hidden here."

"But you don't know what or where exactly?" Catherine stood from her chair and wandered around the suite, gazing upon the many Roman inspired paintings and architectural details.

"And that is why I'm asking you. You've solved a mystery like this before. I have every faith in you to do it again."

"If I may be so bold in correcting you, but I did not solve the mystery in its entirety, Solomon Smith did."

"That bloody pauper again. For goodness' sake, stop mentioning his name."

Catherine ignored his choleric remarks and chose to peruse the books on the shelves behind his desk. "What investigations have you undertaken since we have been on this island?"

"There is nothing obvious like underground tunnels. I have delved into the cellars and can confirm the damp walls house nothing but mould. I am an architect and have studied the walls, measured both interior and exterior, and there are no hidden rooms or priest holes or secret chambers. There just isn't unaccounted for space. I'm utterly at a loss as to where we go from here." He poured himself another drink.

"The estate is extensive but with definitive boundaries. Have you any reason to suspect the treasure is buried in the grounds?" Catherine sat back down.

"You are quite correct, but it would be an impossible task to dig up seven acres. We have only rented the place for a month."

"Could there be any underground caverns, accessible by water or by a hidden hatch?"

"I have discounted that notion. The estate shelves away so gradually to the water's edge that any boat would ground on its approach to the island. Only the jetty area is deep enough for a boat. There are no obvious caves there."

"Then that leaves the church and folly."

"My conclusion too, especially the church, this would seem an obvious place to hide a treasure but alas I am no further in my explorations."

"Leave it with me. I'll have a wander and see if I can add any further considerations."

"Thank you. I know I have been cruel and demanding recently, so please forgive me. It is the pain I endure that makes me so cantankerous."

Catherine smiled. Treasure hunting would be a great distraction from her troubles.

On seeing Catherine leave by the front door, Madame De'Ath climbed the mountainous stairs to Jeremy's suite.

"Did you manage to read her cards?" asked Jeremy.

"She's a difficult woman to pin down, always out and about, but yes, I have read Catherine's cards." Madame De'Ath waited to be invited to sit down. Jeremy pointed to the chair on the other side of his desk. She sat down and wiggled her bottom to the back of the seat for comfort. Her muscular legs dangled, her feet a few inches off the floor.

"Would you like to see my notes or shall I read them to you?"

A crooked smile formed on his face. "Read them to me." He sat back in his chair and prepared to listen.

Madame De'Ath cleared her throat. "Her first choice was the major arcana card, Wheel of Fortune. This card represents her distant past which has been about her destiny. There has been good and bad luck along the way but everything that has happened has put her on the path she was meant to follow."

"With a little shove from me at times." Jeremy used his long nails to comb at his long hair. "Go on."

"She then chose another major card, The Lovers." Madame De'Ath raised her eyesbrows. Jeremy met her gaze. "Do I need to explain this one or is it self-explanatory?" A flush of red appeared on her cheeks.

"Please explain, I value your interpretation," said Jeremy.

"The Lovers represents beauty, perfection, attraction, intimacy. Being the second card, its position represents the present or events that have only just passed. From what I gather, I know you admire honesty so I will say what is on my mind." Madame De'Ath took in a large breath in preparation for what she had to say. "From what I know, you and Catherine are not intimate, at least, not until your wedding day." She took in another deep breath. "This card is about being lovers and it is in the present. Does she possibly have another … man in her life?" She let out the rest of the breath she was holding.

"I admire your honesty, Daphne. The truth means a lot to me. Catherine has indeed taken two lovers before me, and from her first bore a bastard child. It pains me to say but she still has feelings for these men. Thankfully, one has died and the other remains in the lunatic asylum." Jeremy folded his arms and stared at Madame De'Ath, as if waiting for her response.

"I had no idea. I'm so sorry to hear this. Is the wedding still to go ahead tomorrow?" Her small hand rested on her chest.

Jeremy did not answer the question directly, "What was the third card? Her future?"

Madame De'Ath scanned her notes. "The third card was the Six of Cups. This means memories, past influences, nostalgia about things which have vanished."

"How can the past be her future?" asked Jeremy, his eyebrows knitting together.

"I'm not sure. The twins are not with me to offer further explanation. I believe you have known each other for twenty or so years. Maybe that is the answer. You are her past, present and future. And if my memory serves me well ..." she scanned her notes before continuing, "yes, you had the same card for your future. The Six of Cups. Your future is the same as hers. The key to both of your futures lies in the past."

He heaved a sigh of relief. "Thank goodness for that. Then I would say the wedding shall go ahead tomorrow, even if she does need a little persuasion."

DIARY

When in his presence I am always on edge, his unpredictable nature so contrary. How he tortures me with his cruel sneers, his rude remarks and his derogatory statements but then he smiles and all seems to be forgiven. Why do I continue with this facade? I could so easily walk away and never see him again, yet I know this would break his heart. He bears so much pain and I must admire his resolve to continue with his life's work. A lesser person would give up, admit defeat and just fade away but no, he continues to fight this cruel disease and still remains interested in the world around him. As the wedding approaches, I must remain calm, keep my dignity and feign happiness. To do the opposite would be both spiteful and demeaning and despite everything, I will continue to be by his side, for I made a promise. I know all he wants is to find happiness but seeing him suffer so, maybe health, rather than wealth is the key. But one needs wealth to be healthy. Sadly, maybe happiness can only ever be a fleeting emotion. A temporary joy. A small glimmer of light in the consuming darkness. A fond memory to alleviate the stress of existing, the repetition of chores, the trials of life, a cross we need to bear. What would make me happy? To be truly loved and adored.

PRESENT DAY

Jack repeatedly checked his phone; she should have been here by now. Snowflakes were falling and he was praying that she wouldn't cancel their appointment due to the weather. He checked his phone again, jeez, it was becoming habitual. He put another log on the fire to ensure everything felt warm and welcoming for when she arrived. He tried to remain positive. He went through to the kitchen and put the kettle on, so if she did want a cup of tea or coffee it wouldn't take long to re-boil. He checked his phone again, damn, he put it on the kitchen table with a view to leaving it there.

He walked through to the ballroom and sat on the sofa. His fingers played the piano on the sofa arm and seat as he waited. Abruptly, he stopped the incessant tapping and held his breath. What if she was ringing for directions? He jumped off the sofa and returned to the kitchen to retrieve his phone. No missed messages or phone calls.

Ten further minutes passed and he was starting to doubt her sincerity. Maybe the weather had deterred her. Maybe going to a stranger's house that was supposedly haunted was putting her off. Maybe the bus was late or she was stuck in traffic. The front doorbell chimed, then a knock. Blood started pounding in his ears. *Take your time. Don't be an idiot. Just act normal.* Feigning indifference, he strolled along the hallway as he didn't want to appear too keen; didn't want to give the impression of watching for her and then pouncing. A small shadow could be seen through the stained glass window. He turned the door handle and there she was. About five feet, petite frame, jet black hair, amazing eyes, creamy skin and rosebud lips. She was really pretty.

"Hi, I'm guessing Soo-Min," he said in a slightly higher octave than normal.

She briefly bowed her head. "Yes, you Mr Jack?"

"Yes, I am indeed." He invited her inside. The snow was laying. Her tiny footprints evident on the path.

Leading her into the ballroom, he offered her the sofa nearest the door and he sat opposite.

"What a beautiful home. Very nice."

"I love it, but my wife hates it." He wanted to mention his wife right from the beginning.

"Please, no offence, do not tell me anything about the house. I want to build that history in my mind, see if I correct with my memories."

"You work on memories?"

Soo-Min put her rucksack on the floor and took off her padded jacket. "Very warm in here. Where shall I put it?"

"Give it 'ere. I'll hang it in the hallway." He came back seconds later.

"About memories. So far, I never seen a ghost. Not that I do not believe, just that I never seen one, or interacted with one, but my mind remains open. Somehow, not sure how it works exactly, but I go into a sort of hypnotic trance then I sense things. As if I seeing pictures or a film, I get glimpse of something that has happened. As if a memory, a clip being played over and over through time."

Jack was shaking his head, lost for words. "Would you like a cup of tea?" That sounded lame after what she had just said.

"Do you have lemons?"

"Sorry, I don't. We only bought them when Millie fancied a gin and tonic." He was an idiot. He needed to shut up. It sounded like Millie was an alcoholic.

"Just hot water then, please."

Jack came back a couple of minutes later with two cups.

"My friend said you're from Korea."

Soo-Min smiled, "Yes, South Korea, from Busan."

"So how come you're in Carlisle?"

"My parents want me to perfect my English and I want to learn about criminology and forensic science. So here I am."

"Why Carlisle though? Not very exciting here."

"I love history and I love rock climbing. Carlisle very close to Lake District so perfect for me."

"Makes sense." He sipped his tea. "So, what's the plan for today? What will happen?"

"If okay with you, you show me around the house so I get my bearings. Do not tell me anything though. Then I come back here and prepare to open up my mind."

"What does that entail?"

She opened up her rucksack and brought out her phone and a small, terracotta jar. "I play music to open up my brain. Not sure how it works but pieces such as *The Aquarium* by Saint-Saëns work best."

"Never heard of it. And the jar?"

"A blend of fragrances in there. Essential oils, all organic. Geranium, jasmine, sage, sandalwood and lavender. There been research into smells and how it affect our mind. There is part of the brain called the amygdala which process our emotions. Another part of the brain, the hippocampus, is linked to memory and thoughts. For some reason, this combination of oils stimulate my brain in a way I detect people's thoughts, emotions and memories."

"Wow, that's unbelievable." Jack was genuinely interested. "Oh, I mean in a good way." He felt the need to explain, that he didn't mean she was lying or deluded, just that what she could do was amazing. He decided to move on and change the subject. "I'm so glad you can hopefully help me get to the bottom of what happened here in this house. See its memories. That must be really strange for you though, seeing those time loops."

"It is why I go into forensic science. I feel I been given a gift from God that I need to perfect. For so long I tried to hide it. Was very scary as a child."

"I can't even imagine what that was like." There was a pause as she sipped her water. "So what exactly do you do with the oils?"

"I rub it in as if I apply hand cream. I put my hands in prayer and smell the fragrance when I want to open up memories and emotions."

"Fascinating," said Jack.

After a few more minutes of general chit-chat, they finished their drinks and commenced the house tour. Not wanting to give anything away, all Jack said was the name of each room. Even though some of the rooms were obvious, like the kitchen, he continued to give Soo-Min the official title.

After completing the ground floor tour, they headed up the stairs. The house was like a show home, each room dressed to perfection, effortlessly combining old and new, traditional and modern.

The last room to view was the attic. They climbed the stairs and stood on the small landing. Jack opened the door, switched on the lights and allowed her to look inside. He had done a fair bit of work up there. He had put in more light fixtures, so everything was bright. He had cleared the attic of all the old suitcases, furniture, coffin and scary mannequin. The long term plan was to convert the attic into a massive suite to be used as their main bedroom when they had saved some money and paid off some of their debts. The room was relatively empty now, apart from Christmas decorations, suitcases and painting stuff. Jack was desperate to buy a real Christmas tree and put it in the ballroom, but Millie hated clutter and had always insisted the week before the 25th was more than sufficient.

"That's it, you've seen everything now. Any first impressions?" asked Jack, eager to know her thoughts.

"Your home is beautiful. I very jealous."

"Thank you," he said with a smile, "but sorry about the jealousy."

She laughed, "Maybe one day I build a home like this."

He wanted to ask his question again but rephrased it, so he didn't sound too pushy, "As we were walking around did you sense anything?"

"My mind deliberately closed. We head back down the stairs. I play my music, smell the fragrance and pray. I prefer to be on my own if that okay, just so I relax and open my mind. I come looking for you in the cosy room once done."

They headed down the stairs and stopped in the entrance hallway. Jack said, "Okay, so you go in there, I'll go in here and we'll see each other shortly. Good luck." She put her delicate hands together in prayer and slightly bowed. They parted ways.

Soo-Min stood at the double doors overlooking the garden. Feathers of snow were falling more frequently now and she shuddered looking at the wintery scenes outside. She didn't want to tell him she had sensed something as they were walking around. She rarely picked up on past memories without first preparing. Emotions were obviously strong here.

Heading back to the warmth of the fire, she put her wireless earphones in place and put her favourite song on repeat. She opened the terracotta jar and with the back of her index finger scooped up a little oil onto her nail and circled it on to the back of her left hand. She then put the backs of her hands together and rubbed. The oil seeped into her creamy skin as the warmth and friction aroused the fragrance.

Soo-Min put her hands together in prayer and closed her eyes. The music was soothing, she imagined exotic fish, a rainbow of colours, swimming in the various oceans and seas of the world. The sounds were melodic and haunting. She felt herself swaying with the waves of notes. Dreamy and calming, the music was flowing like a gentle stream, taking her to places she had never been before, then deeper, descending, delving into darker realms, where the dead tend to linger. Her body was heavy, yet she felt so light and free.

Struggling to breathe, she inhaled deeply, the fragrances stimulating her brain, wiring her mind to alternate realms. Her eyes painfully wide open, she was at a depth she had never dared to venture before.

CHAPTER THIRTEEN

Mr Notts announced dinner would soon be served and requested their presence. As they wandered through the hallway and into the dining room, they were saddened to see two filled crystal glasses to honour the memory of Bernard and Daniel.

Once everyone was seated, they realised there was another empty chair. "Has anyone called on Theresa?" asked Catherine.

"I called on her earlier. She seemed a little depressed in mood, but she was conversing and tolerating my company," said Sarah Silver. Her white hair was tied in an elegant bun and pinned with a row of pearls.

Vivienne Kry was only in her early twenties, pretty and dainty, like a fairy at the bottom of the garden, but she dressed so very plain. For this evening, she was wearing a shapeless, grey woollen skirt and a blue blouse with a high neckline. Her blond hair was pulled back into a severe bun. Her amber eyes were heavy and laced with dark shadows. She seemed to be aging by the hour. "I brought Theresa a tray of tea earlier. She seemed a little dull but was thankful for the gesture. She apologised profusely but stated she wanted to be alone, needing some time to come to terms with a few home truths, so I honoured her request and left. I haven't seen her since."

Cornelius Binks confirmed, "I saw her about half an hour or so ago. She had obviously been crying but I thought she was probably heading downstairs for dinner, if a little early. She nodded her head to acknowledge me when I asked her if she was well."

"Would you like me to go to her room and check on her?" offered Cliff Dacosta, his blue eyes appearing darker in the subdued candlelight.

"Mr Montgomery has gone to a lot of trouble in preparing this meal. If she cannot be bothered to attend, or send her apologies, then why should we care. Let's eat and we will check on her afterwards. Bon appetite everyone." Jeremy Fisher raised his glass and the others reluctantly reciprocated.

"Health, wealth and happiness," said Eliza Hart, then downed the concoction in her tumbler.

By nine o'clock, all the guests had been well catered for with bellies stuffed to the brim. They were reluctant to move.

"Oh, what about Theresa? We really must check on her. I feel awful for momentarily forgetting about her." Sarah placed her napkin on the table by the side of her dessert plate then pushed back her chair.

"I'll come with you," said Eliza from the other side of the dining table. "I need to move for this dress is too restrictive for what I have consumed." She tottered a little. "George, would you be so kind as to undo the ribbon at the back." She turned her back to him and he gladly loosened the pretty pink material. "So much better, thank you." A sense of relief appeared on her face.

The guests chatted amongst themselves, too idle to move, but still had a little space left to continue drinking the delicious fruity punch from the decorative bowl.

Harry Arnold was rather worse for wear, slurring his words, his eyes unable to focus for long, "I could live 'ere quite 'appily, 'aving this served to me every night, no arguing, no bloody back chat." He lit up a cigar offered to him by Mr Notts and for a few minutes after, could not suppress his cough.

"What a life, eh? Being waited on hand and foot. I could get used to this." George Jones puffed on his cigar too, with slightly more decorum.

"No grief from the missus," Harry attempted to blow a smoke ring.

George laughed, "No missus for me. Too many lovely ladies out there to settle for one, and they cost a fortune." The men laughed.

"Too bloody right, mate." Harry patted him on the shoulder. "Cheers to that." He offered up his glass and George tipped his, a pleasing resonance was heard.

"Us men … should show … us women … should show their place." Harry's eyes were circling in his head. "They're getting all mouthy now … answering us back and giving us their fuckin' opinions when we're … they're … not wanted." His movements were lacking coordination as he tried to top up his drink.

"I agree, just need a nice, quiet one, bonus if she's a beauty, but knows when to shut up. You want one that's educated, you want to be proud of her, but she just needs to know when to be quiet."

"That's the problem, mate, too bloody gobby now. Can't have … these bloody women want everything." Harry puffed on his cigar once more. Fighting to suppress the cough.

"So true, young man. So very true." They both leaned back and took a long, slow mouthful from their glasses.

In his inebriated state, Harry poured more drink down his neck than in his mouth. "Bloody 'ell."

George laughed.

Eliza hurried into the room. "She's not there."

Breathless, Sarah added, "We've looked in all the communal rooms. She's disappeared."

Harry leaned across to George and whispered, "Who's dis … ppeared?"

"Theresa," said George. "Pay attention."

"Not fuckin' likely, mate," snorted Harry.

Jeremy eyed Harry, "For goodness' sake, are there no normal people here? It seems I have invited the uncouth dregs of society." He got out of the chair and limped over to the women. "Did you search her room?"

"Everything neat and tidy. All her things still there," replied Sarah.

Catherine Fawcett added to the conversation, "This has heightened my nerves. She said she didn't want to be here anymore."

"The bloody ungrateful wench," said Jeremy.

"No, she meant life in general."

93

The women gasped. Sarah tried to remain positive, "Maybe she's gone for a walk to clear her head. Get some fresh air."

Eliza said, "I've suddenly got a chill." Goosebumps trickled down her arms.

"Women … always causing us problems." Harry sneered, "Look at yas. Like a coven of ugly witches. Well … you can go out in the bloody dark … miserable cold … and searching for who … ever. Sick of this." He got out of his chair, stumbled, and made his way up the stairs.

"What a vile man. I feel sad for his wife having to tend to that thing." Sarah shuddered. "Horrible."

"Right, ladies. Eliza, Sarah, Vivienne, Madame De'Ath, grab a lantern and we'll go in search of Theresa." Catherine checked the time, "We will gather in the hallway in ten minutes and be prepared for the bleak conditions outside. I was outside just before dinner, and I do believe snow may fall. We do not want any more dea—"

"Stop there, don't say what I think you were going to say. We do not want any more *dilemmas* this weekend," said Madame De'Ath.

CHAPTER FOURTEEN

Ignoring the men's pleas to wait until the morning, the ladies left Derwent Isle House in search of Theresa Franks. Each holding aloft a lantern, they navigated their way around the grounds. Lily accompanied them, excited by the night-time walk, sniffing every inch of ground, as if searching frantically for her best friend.

They started with the boathouse and church, then wandered through the formal gardens. The air was freezing cold but no one dared to complain even though their hands and feet felt close to dropping off in the biting conditions. Catherine suggested they head towards the folly, wondering if Theresa had already sought sanctuary there. There were only two rooms in the tower, connected by a spiral staircase. She knew there were tidy stacks of kindling there and she suggested they start a fire to warm them through for some respite from the cold - and from the men.

With the folly now in view, they approached the round tower with mixed feelings. They were thankful for shelter from the bleak conditions but worried as to what they may find.

Eliza opened the door, then hesitated.

"What is it?" Catherine enquired.

"Is she there?" asked Sarah.

Eliza did not move or speak.

"Would you like me to go first?" asked Madame De'Ath.

Finally, Eliza replied, "Sorry ladies, I just had a little wobble. I'm fine now, honestly. But if someone else wants to go first …"

Catherine led the way into the folly which was dressed like a miniature medieval castle. There was a suit of armour, a colourful tapestry on the wall, a dark dresser displaying various items and a working stove in a rustic, stone surround. At the centre was a small table with four simple chairs.

"So as not to give anyone a fright, I am about to shout for Theresa." Everyone silently acknowledged Catherine's statement with either a nod, a hand placed on their heart or their hands in prayer.

Catherine stood at the bottom of the stairs. She took a deep breath and sighed. Building up courage, she eventually asked, "Hello! Is anyone there? Theresa, we are here to help you. I'm coming up the stairs now. Please do not be afraid." She was met with silence.

"Is that wise?" asked Sarah. Her teeth chattering.

"What do you mean?" asked Catherine.

"Someone may be lurking in the shadows."

"Jeremy and I have been on the island for a while prior to your arrival. I can assure you, no one else is on this island."

"But you also said that when Daniel Watters was scaring us to death when he was knocking on the windows and door," said Eliza.

"His boat was moored though, and we quickly ascertained why he was here. We have already searched the boathouse and there was no evidence of another arrival. I think it is safe to say we are alone on this estate." Catherine tried to remain calm.

"Let's just get this over with." Vivienne dismantled the suit of armour and gave Catherine the shield. She kept the sword for herself and marched over to the stairs.

"Hold on, if Theresa is up there, seeing you brandishing a sword may push her over the edge. She was in such a fragile mood, this may unsettle her nerves unnecessarily so," said Sarah.

Despite reservations, Vivienne crept up the stairs, the sword held in front of her, anxiously expecting an attack at any moment. Catherine followed closely behind defended by the shield. Little Lily chased after Catherine. Eliza, Sarah and Madame De'Ath remained downstairs. Eliza and Sarah searched the drawers for knives and potential weapons. Madame De'Ath prepared a fire.

On landing at the top of the spiral stairs, Vivienne could see the only door ahead was closed. She braced as she turned the handle.

CHAPTER FIFTEEN

The ladies on the ground floor listened with intent. Barely wanting to breathe, their ears were attuned to the slightest sounds. Everything was silent, until they heard the scream.

"Oh, heaven help us!" said Sarah Silver, her spotted hands now in prayer.

"Do we stay here or go up there?" Eliza Hart was shaking.

"We can't leave them to face this alone," said Madame De'Ath. Nervously, she made her way over to the stairs.

"Then take this poker as a weapon." Sarah picked up the implement from the nearby stove.

"Are you not coming with me?"

Sarah shook her head.

"I'll stay here and look after Sarah," said Eliza.

Madame De'Ath tutted discreetly and made her way up the spiral stairs; the stone steps high for her short stature. Her breathing was laboured during the climb, partly due to worrying about what may greet her at the top of the stairs. There had only been one scream, but it sounded like Vivienne rather than Catherine. Her imagination was running riot: murder, kidnap, being dragged into the room, a gloved hand over the mouth, a dark solitary figure lurking in the shadows, a monster, a fiend ... She was now at the top of the stairs on a small landing area. The only door was closed. With caution, she tiptoed closer to the door, her heart beating so loudly she felt the intruder would surely hear her approach. She stopped for a moment and thought about options. One: barge through the door and charge at the assailant. The element of surprise may unbalance him. Two: open the door discreetly and peek at what was going on inside the room. Three: was there a three? Her head was so foggy she could barely think. She didn't have the time to open up to her spirit guides. She needed to remain focused. A decision had to made. She would swing open the door and burst into the room full charge.

Her left hand rested on the handle, and she pushed the door open as slowly as she could. So much for the element of surprise. Vivienne was being held by a dark figure. She was sobbing, her body twitching with the snatched cries. Madame De'Ath pushed the door a little further and saw it was Catherine holding Vivienne. She was trying to comfort her.

Catherine noticed the door moving and looked over at Madame De'Ath. Her eyes were glistening. "It's not good news," she said. "It may be best if you wait there."

Trying to be brave, Madame De'Ath stepped into the room and nearly fainted at the sight before her. Hanging from the timbered ceiling was a noose. Professionally crafted, this did not look like something Theresa could have concocted from a piece of rope she had found in an outbuilding. Theresa was still, her body limp, her face and hands a colour incompatible with signs of life.

The room was circular with a conical roof. The wooden struts resembled a large spider, with eight legs protruding from a central body. The rope had been hooked over one of the struts. Theresa's body was hanging central with the window, as if she was searching for the perfect view over Derwentwater. Her vacant, protruding eyes forever looking, but never seeing.

Catherine Fawcett was the first to speak, "I think we should head back to the main house and discuss things there."

Vivienne Kry and Madame De'Ath initially did not say anything, they remained still, frozen by the chilling scene. Eventually, Madame De'Ath spoke, "Why would she do this? Her poor children are now without their mother. She only had to wait until Sunday then she would have been rich, which was her dream. She would have wanted for nothing. She could have—"

"Madame De'Ath, let's refrain from jumping to conclusions." Catherine walked over to Madame De'Ath and held her hand.

"What do you mean?"

"I'm not sure she could do this on her own."

CHAPTER SIXTEEN

Back at the house, everyone gathered in the main sitting area. A few were drinking tea, but the majority were consuming something stronger.

"We have only been here two days and already three people have died." Cliff Dacosta was pacing the room. "Mr Fisher, Miss Fawcett, what is your response to this fact? Is this part of your sick game?"

"I invited you here for a number of reasons. To kill you is not one of them," answered Jeremy.

"Then how do you explain the deaths?" Cliff stopped pacing and stood in front of Jeremy and Catherine. He folded his arms, waiting for their response.

"I'm not psychic." Jeremy dabbed at his mouth with his handkerchief. As ever, he remained calm and sophisticated despite the subliminal accusation. "What I do know is every single one of you has a history of hurting people. Catherine and I do not need to explain ourselves for we have done nothing wrong. You all sicken me. You should turn your accusing finger around and point it at yourselves."

Cornelius Binks bounded out of his chair and mirrored Cliff's stance. "How dare you go around insulting people without any evidence. You have brought us here under false pretences. Explain yourself!"

"Do not insult me. I am no amateur host. Of course I have evidence to corroborate my claims. Notts shall bring me ten sealed envelopes. Each and every one of you will pick one and read out its contents." The right side of Jeremy's mouth could not help but rise in sickening amusement.

Sarah Silver was shaking and looked close to tears. "This is getting out of hand. Please, it's getting late. Poor Theresa, she's still hanging there in the folly. Can we not at least untie her and place her somewhere, lie her down and cover her body. Let her at least rest in peace."

"Forget it. She's dead. Won't bother her hanging on in there 'til morning," said Harry Arnold. His fisted right hand pushed into the cup of his left, and he cracked his knuckles. "I would prefer to hear the evidence. Sounds interesting."

In her seventies, Sarah was still relatively spritely, and she jumped up out of her chair. "I implore you to help poor Theresa, God bless her soul. The colour of her hands, it was as if the blood was pooling, as if gravity was ... Anyone, please?"

Eliza Hart unpinned her hair and the silky dark length cascaded down her back. With her fingers at the roots, she teased the strands to ease the tension she was experiencing. "I'm not sure I want to hear what's in those envelopes."

"Nor I," said Vivienne. Her hands were shaking.

"Am I invisible?" asked Sarah. By the reactions of the others, she was.

Cornelius and Cliff made subtle suggestions to each other and headed to the far side of the room, away from the fire. They were whispering among themselves.

Madame De'Ath waddled over to the drinks area and poured herself a glass of wine. The bottle seemed enormous relative to her size. She needed both hands to pour the contents into the glass.

George Jones could not muster a smile. "As Sarah said, it's getting late. We've had a few drinks. We're a little worse for wear. We are all a little upset by this evening's revelations. Why don't we just head to our rooms, sleep this awful day away, and resume tomorrow with positive hearts for the wedding."

Vivienne could hardly believe what she was hearing. "Is the wedding still on? Surely not. Not with everything that has happened. Three people have died. I'm convinced we have a murderer lurking among us."

"Of course the wedding is going ahead. I am not letting anyone or anything stop me. Us. You are here to bear witness to our love." Jeremy stood from the chair and gave himself a moment to straighten up.

"The two of you should be incarcerated for what you have allowed to happen on this island." Cornelius walked away from Cliff and strode over to Jeremy. "Give us our money and we all leave now. We don't not want to witness your poxy wedding. You've brought us here on a lie."

Catherine's emotions were tumbling at the unfolding accusations and threats. "Please, if we could all just settle down and be polite. We are tired, we are shocked, we are devasted by the unfortunate passing of Bernard, Daniel and Theresa. Please, we must remain strong and come together over these tragedies."

"Tragedies? Someone has killed them." Cliff marched over to the centre of the room. "Can't remember who, but one of you suggested Bernard could have been poisoned. We assumed Daniel fell into the lake or tried to swim his way off the island. But what if he was pushed? From what you have said about Theresa, she must have been assisted into hanging herself."

"Cliff, please do not stoke these flames and add fuel to your fiery accusations. Unless you can provide evidence of—" Catherine was interrupted.

"We are not imbeciles, or blind, or deaf to your pathetic games." Cliff turned his back on Catherine and Jeremy and faced the other guests. His eyes like sapphires against his dark skin. "I propose we stop playing their weird games and insist we get our money now. If our hosts refuse, I say we search the house from top to bottom and on finding the money, we vacate the island." Intending to leave the room, Cliff stormed over to the doorway but instead he stopped and listened to the hive of animated discussions: the invitation, the rules of the game, the wedding, the money, the untying of the boats, getting off the island, the deaths, the mystery.

Mr Notts coughed, which momentarily gave Cliff a shock and he moved out of the way. Notts jingled the bell on the mantlepiece and eventually everyone fell silent. With a smile on his face, he addressed the room. "Thank you for your attention. It is clear to see emotions are running high. Everyone is upset and has been affected someway by the unfolding of the weekend's tragic events, and understandably so. Residing on a beautiful island in a luxurious villa may seem idyllic, somewhere to escape, somewhere to explore and take in the breath-taking views. However, some find the remoteness of the island claustrophobic. An island may protect you from the harsh realities of life, create distance from your maddening adversaries, but can it protect you from yourself? The island is not for everyone. One cannot escape from what is inside your head." Notts straightened his already immaculate jacket. "Please be reassured that we have a delivery of food coming on Monday. Therefore, we are not imprisoned here, we are not to be held captive or forced to stay here against our will. Come Monday you will be free to leave. All I ask for is calm and civility among guests, hosts and staff. May I suggest we retire for the evening, and we will start afresh tomorrow morning, bright and early for the wedding."

"Shut up, Notts! We've already argued about that." From the doorway, Cliff walked back into the room. "Jeremy said you are holding information about us. Just bring us the envelopes and we will read them out loud. I have nothing to hide, but some of you obviously do." Cliff looked around the room. Everyone remained silent. "Anyone care to share why they wouldn't want to know what information these people hold? There may be accusations, false statements, defamation claims. I certainly want to know what they have on me."

Jeremy crossed his legs and relaxed in the armchair. With claw like nails, he combed the ends of his grey, limp ponytail as it rested over the left side of his chest. "I quite agree, Cliff. You deserve to hear the information I hold." Jeremy stood from his chair and approached the mantlepiece. He opened a decorative wooden box, removed a fat cigar and proceeded to light it from the fire. "Notts, be a good boy and bring me the envelopes detailing their misdemeanours." After a few puffs, the cigar was glowing and Jeremy blew smoke signals into the air. "I do love house parties, don't you?"

CHAPTER SEVENTEEN

The group were eerily silent as Mr Notts entered the room. He was carrying a silver tray with ten envelopes neatly bound with purple ribbon. Without being asked, as if this had already been agreed, Notts placed the tray on the table at the centre of the room and unfastened the purple ties. He shuffled the envelopes, as if he was a card dealer, and placed them back on the tray. Gracefully, he walked around the room, bowing to each individual guest and offering the silver tray. Each took an envelope. There were no names or addresses on the uniform envelopes, a watermark the only distinguishing feature. This was the whitest paper they had ever seen, pure and unblemished and so soft to touch.

Cornelius and Cliff were about to tear open their envelopes when Jeremy shouted from across the room. "Do not dare to open the envelopes yet. My house, my island, my rules. The invitation clearly warned, you have to participate in all tasks. You must obey the rules of the game."

Vivienne Kry was the last guest to take an envelope. Three remained on the silver tray.

Jeremy commanded the room. "Each of you have in your possession an envelope. Inside will be an overview of the heinous crimes or misdemeanours you have committed. By the end of this task, you will be given the courtesy to respond. I want to hear, in detail, your thoughts pertaining to the evidence presented before you."

With support of his black cane, Jeremy meandered between the guests. "One by one I will ask you to open the envelope and read out its contents so everyone can hear. Catherine, Madame De'Ath and Mr Notts will read out the remaining three since Bernard, Daniel and Theresa are no longer with us."

A few guests squirmed in their seats.

"Cliff, perhaps you will start since you were so eager to open the envelope." Jeremy stood by the warmth of the fire. His claws overhanging the silver dragon's head of his cane.

Cliff tore open the envelope and discarded the paper onto the nearby table. He placed his left hand in the pocket of his jacket and started to silently read the words.

Lacking patience, Jeremy intervened, "For goodness' sake, man, just read it out so we can all understand the contents."

Cliff cleared his throat. "I have the letter meant for Theresa Franks." His voice was shaking, a crack to the initial few words. "Theresa Franks, you have been invited here to discuss how your actions have impacted on the lives of others. On the night of 13th October 1865, you broke into someone's property and stole items of food and personal belongings. The owner of the property, Mark Templeton, a frail, old gentleman found you in his kitchen. You then stabbed the elderly gent with his own kitchen knife and left him for dead. He was found by his daughter the next morning. Barely alive, he thankfully recovered but ended up being admitted to the lunatic asylum. Scared, weak, hallucinating, he spent the rest of his days screaming out due to hideous nightmares and pus-filled wounds." Cliff turned the paper over but there were no further words.

Everyone was silent but eyes were busy and inquisitive, gauging a reaction.

Cornelius was the first to speak. "Sadly, Theresa is no longer with us to confirm or deny if this is true. According to the ladies, she is now hanging from the gallows of her own making. If I may be so bold, Jeremy, did you write this letter?"

"I personally did not write the letter but the information is true."

"How can you be so sure?" Sarah Silver was shaking.

"I am a benefactor of the Cumberland and Westmorland Lunatic Asylum. I have access to medical records, and I am on the board of governors. Please believe me when I say the information is true."

"But the words are from a confirmed mad man. You may have read or heard this information but how can you categorically confirm it is the truth?" Sarah felt brave in standing up to Jeremy.

Catherine replied, "Earlier today, I spoke with Theresa in her room. I have to admit that she confided in me about this very incident. Her response was that she was desperate to feed her children and that she had climbed through an open window to steal items of food but this elderly gent had found her in his house. He started to beat her with a stick, so she retaliated by stabbing him with a knife. The information is true." Catherine walked over to stand by Jeremy's side. He held out his hand for her to hold.

"How very convenient. The two of you could have easily concocted that story." Cliff was suspicious of everything.

Cornelius agreed, "The two of you have set up all of this. We cannot believe a word you say."

Catherine was mortified by the accusations. Her eyes were wide with fear. She gripped Jeremy's hand, unaware her nails were biting into his flesh.

With a wry smile, Jeremy responded, "Then let us open another envelope. Hopefully from someone who is still alive." He perused the room with an air of superiority. "Cornelius, your turn."

As requested, he opened his envelope. Although Jeremy had reprimanded Cliff for silently reading ahead, Cornelius could not refrain from reading the first few words to gain the advantage. "Vivienne Kry, you have been invited to this island as you instigated the admission of your partner into the lunatic asylum. You and Michelle Dupois were engaged in a secretive homosexual relationship until you requested her admission to the asylum for an increasing madness and deep depression."

Vivienne remained stone cold. Her skin remaining fair with no flush of embarrassment, although inwardly, her heart was pounding.

"What do you have to say for yourself?" asked Jeremy.

"I don't see why I should have to explain myself. You have already made up your mind that I am guilty. You are aware I desperately want to leave this island and was happy to forfeit the money. I do not need to play your games."

"Genuinely, I admit, I would like to hear your version of events. I have had numerous liaisons over the years, with men and women, orgies, theatrical performances of men dressed as women, women dressed as page boys, etcetera, so I am no prude." There were gasps from his captured audience. "I just want to hear the truth. Why was your lover really admitted to the asylum? What did you do to her?"

Vivienne remained closed, her body language still, while she considered her response. "Michelle, my lover, was in service at Mountly Hall. She had been in employment for around six months when the head of the household, Lord Greyson, took a fancy to her. Against her will, she was taken to a room, bound and gagged to a four-poster bed and then forced to engage in intimate acts. When she arrived home that evening, she was battered and bruised and distraught to the extent of wanting to take her own life. Day by day she relived the horror of that encounter. Eventually, I was forced to take her to the asylum to seek help."

Catherine and Sarah made their way over to Vivienne. They tried to comfort her, but sympathy was only making her worse. "Please, I'm fine, I would prefer no fuss."

"Is she still there?" asked Madame De'Ath. "In the asylum?"

"Two months ago she finally achieved her goal, which was to take her own life." Vivienne was trembling but pretended to be strong.

"Oh no, I'm so sorry to hear this. Please accept my condolences, you must be distraught." Catherine rested her palm on the top of Vivienne's crossed hands.

"How utterly sad. I was not aware of the incidents leading to her incarceration. Please also accept my apologies for raising this matter." Jeremy headed over to an empty armchair at the far side of the room. "See, this is why it is good to talk. Our beliefs, things we read or hear, may not necessarily be the truth. George, would you be so kind as to read the contents of your envelope."

Vivienne interrupted. "Really? After everything I have just said? After everything that has happened here, you still want to proceed?" She rose from her chair. Her fair skin now blushed with emotion. "You seem to delight in destroying people's hope. You revel in disgust and sleazy gossip. You have no decorum when it comes to respecting the dead and instead you find some sort of gruesome satisfaction in other people's misery." Vivienne walked over to the door. "I will no longer participate in this evil game."

"You never left the island. The gift is still yours if you participate ..." Jeremy raised an eyebrow.

"Don't make any hasty decisions, Vivienne. Please, reconsider this in the morning. Please don't do anything that you may regret." Sarah walked over to the door and held out her hand. Vivienne did not take the offered hand but did come back into the room.

"Money can buy almost anything," Jeremy said under his breath, and winked.

CHAPTER EIGHTEEN

George reluctantly opened his envelope. He was feigning positivity but droplets of perspiration on his forehead gave away his real feelings. "Here goes. Bernard Pratt, you have been invited to this island to discuss your involvement in the demise of your parent's health and estate. Your selfish demands were too much to bear and your father, a broken man for being unable to cater to your needs ran away with another woman, leaving your mother to fend for you alone. Barely able to move, your failed business ventures scuppered any chances of making money and your mother, now at her whit's end, admitted herself to the lunatic asylum, where sadly, she refused to eat any food and wasted away just over a week later." George puffed out his cheeks. "Poor Bernard, and he seemed such a jolly soul, even though his heart must have been broken."

"Pathetic. Bernard does not deserve your sympathy. He's been gluttonous to the point of greed and turned his family away from him." Jeremy could rarely hold back from speaking his mind.

"Well, he's not here to give his version of events but I can confirm he mentioned his mother's death to me and that he wanted to make her proud by opening a bakery or confectionery." Sarah sighed.

For most of the evening, Harry Arnold had sat quietly, sipping some wine. His earlier stupor had subsided, but he was looking rather exhausted. "He would have eaten all the profits by the sounds of it." He got up to refill his glass.

"Please do not speak ill of the dead," replied Catherine. "All we ask for is respect."

"Then let's move on. He's gone now anyway so we won't learn anything new." Jeremy looked around the room. "Go on then, Harry, your turn to read a letter."

Harry returned to his chair and flopped into the comfy folds. He was surprised to see it was his own letter. "Harold Arnold, you have been invited for the weekend to explain why your wife was admitted to the lunatic asylum. She arrived with various injuries: a cut above her eye, a sprained wrist, broken knuckles and numerous bruises. Her eyes were like black puddings and her nose out of joint. She insisted that you incarcerated her to get rid of her so you could run off with your mistress. She currently still resides in the asylum." Harry shook his head. "What a load of drivel."

"Are you saying the asylum holds incorrect information?" Jeremy shuffled forward to the edge of the armchair and leaned forward onto his thighs. "Then please do enlighten us to the truth."

"For a start, Elsie has been the one beating me up. She has broken my nose a couple of times and knocked out teeth. For some reason, she keeps accusing me of having an affair with one of our neighbours. The woman is about sixty years old for fuck's sake and I only go round there because she pays me to do odd jobs around the house as she has a bad leg and can barely walk. Then when I get home, Elsie accuses me of all sorts and hits me with the broom or thrashes the towel around as if whipping me. I've put up with it for years. She's bloody paranoid and delusional, asking where I'm going or where I've been. Then about three months ago, I came home from work one night, and yeah, I'd stopped off at the inn to have a couple of beers so I was a bit late, but she kept battering me, wouldn't stop. Accusing me of sleeping with different women. I grabbed her wrists, that was why she had bruises on her forearms. She was fighting to release my grip. When I eventually let her go, she attempted to punch me, but I moved out of the way at the last second and she hit her hand on the wall. That's how she hurt her wrist and broke her knuckles. By now she was livid, squealing like she was possessed. She screeched at the top of her voice as she lunged at me. I pushed her out of the way. She fell and hit her nose on the sideboard, which caused the black eyes and she ran out of the house, accusing me of beating her up. She ended up in the lunatic asylum with her hysterical ways, shouting, screaming, and all that kind of thing. She was so bloody angry. Life's been hell since then. Nobody believes my side of the story."

"Well, you do come across as a bit of a dick," said Cornelius. For the first time in a while, everyone sniggered. "I'm not sure you are aware, but you totally wind people up with your snide comments."

"Fair enough, I'll take it, but I've never hurt anyone. I'm all talk. I do a few dodgy deals here and there, but I swear to God, I have never physically hurt anyone other than in defence. But she drove me to it. I was only protecting myself."

"How interesting," said Jeremy. "And has this episode taught you anything?"

There was a reasonable delay before he answered, "I will never trust anyone again. I think that is why I distance myself from people. I've erected a barrier. I don't want anyone getting close."

"Sad but fair." Jeremy nodded his head. "Who's left? Sarah, who do you have?"

Her hands shaking, she opened the envelope. "Cornelius, I have yours." She took a moment to settle her nerves. "Cornelius Binks, you have been invited for the weekend so we can hear your story on achieving fame and fortune. Please tell us how you swindled your employer out of £10,000. Apparently, you embezzled a small fortune from the company you worked for, leading to the incarceration of the owner into the asylum. Too melancholy to function, he was unable to continue with the business and his family suffered by your illegal gains. Jonathan Swift continues to be imprisoned within the asylum walls, crying rivers of self-pity into his pillow each evening. His family, now living in poverty, are being hounded by investors demanding the return of their money." Sarah had tears in her eyes. "Did you really do this, Cornelius?"

"What is written there is a complete exaggeration of my involvement in this sorry saga. Through bad investments, I lost the company money, but I did not profit from my mistakes. On the contrary, my reputation and standing in the community dwindled to an all-time low. People in my village despise me, they have me hung, drawn and quartered without trial or jury. The police have no proof whatsoever as to what happened to the money. It is all speculation. I'm sorry for what happened, but I cannot take one hundred percent of the blame for the missing funds."

"What a sorry state of affairs. Jeremy, can we at least take a break from these awful revelations? We could rest for an hour then resume. My head needs some clarity by distance." Catherine walked over to the door.

Sarah, Eliza and Vivienne all stood up and agreed to the suggestion.

"Honestly, does nobody have any perseverance these days? I can see I am outnumbered. So be it. We will meet back here at midnight. God willing."

DIARY

I am exhausted by the revelations so far this evening. Jeremy has been delighted by his investigations and is enjoying the debacle. I truly cannot decide whether I can go through with this ceremony tomorrow. My nerves are shattered, my mind in turmoil and I am emotionally drained by it all.

As usual, Jeremy seems to be thriving on the negativity and attention. He loves winding people up and getting a reaction. Why he continues to be driven to understand the human psyche and insist on following weird psychological experiments is beyond me. In one sense Jeremy seems so frail, yet he is stronger than ever in his mind. Driven by this desire for entertainment, for purpose, for reason.

Alas, I will soon have to return to the sitting room and listen to the rest of the evidence. Mr Notts also gave me an envelope to read. I hope I can stay strong for everyone's sake. Jeremy is certainly challenging but, with God as my witness, I can't help but love his eccentric ways.

CHAPTER NINETEEN

Just before the stroke of midnight, everyone gathered in the sitting area, poured themselves a drink and as the clock chimed twelve, Jeremy and Catherine sauntered into the room. Little Lily remained at Catherine's heels.

"Thank you for keeping excellent time and meeting back here as instructed. By my reckoning, we have five more letters to read. These relate to Daniel - God bless his soul, George, Sarah, Cliff and Eliza. Who wants to go first?" Jeremy perused the room. "No volunteers? Then Eliza, read your letter, please."

Eliza stood from her chair as if she were about to do a speech to a receptive audience. "Cliff Dacosta, you have been invited to this party so we can hear your side of the story pertaining to criminal undertakings and rival gangs. For years, you have been involved with illegal trade: the distribution of medicines and money laundering. You have been involved in various fisticuffs with rival establishments and have now gone underground. You have left people fighting for survival after sustaining life changing head injuries where their brains have become fuddled due to the trauma you have inflicted. Three people remain in the asylum after they were savagely beaten by your own hands." Eliza took a deep breath and exhaled. "I'm truly sorry for having to read this out, Cliff."

Everyone diverted their gaze over to Cliff, waiting for his response. They expected deniability, the twist in the tale proving his innocence. But they were met with stony silence.

Jeremy stood once more. "No comeback, no pleading innocence, no explanation for your actions?"

"You wouldn't believe me anyway, so why argue." Cliff

remained calm, his only offering being open palms.

"I hear you have a reputation in Whitehaven. You are untouchable. People consider you to be king," said Jeremy.

"If that is true then it is other people's opinion, not mine."

"Have you no remorse? Three people are locked up in a lunatic asylum as a result of your actions. Do you have any regrets, any concerns, any … oh I don't know …worries about what you have done?"

"It was in defence. A me or them situation."

"Ah, now we are getting somewhere. So there is an explanation?" Jeremy waited patiently but no justification was forthcoming. "Very well. We will form our own conclusions and consider you a cold-hearted criminal." Jeremy straightened his jacket. "Vivienne, please read your letter."

"Mine is about Eliza." She lifted her eyes briefly and whispered to the dark-haired beautiful woman in front of her, "Sorry, Eliza."

Two men had been admitted to the asylum as a result of their courtship with Eliza. They had pursued her for many a month, with Eliza feigning love for her admirers. Gifts had been lavished upon her which she had professed were unnecessary but accepted them anyway. Unaware of their rival, the men had finally come across each other and battles had commenced. They were now reeling from the consequences of becoming involved with Eliza Hart.

"What do you have to say for yourself, Eliza?" Jeremy lifted his chin, peering down his nose as he waited for a response.

"They lavished gifts upon me. That was their choice. I placed no demands. You are implying lies, and theft, or taking money by underhand deeds. They loved me. I loved them. I may have omitted the full truth, but I stole nothing but their hearts."

"Do you not regret anything? Two men have been driven insane by your actions. Once they were rich, now they are paupers. Not only have they lost money but they lost their minds." Jeremy's nose wrinkled with disdain.

"The fault lies entirely with them. When they found out about each other, they plotted and schemed for many a month to seek revenge. Their games were entirely as a result of their own actions. This was how their money was squandered. I was out of the picture by then."

Jeremy's eyebrows furrowed, "But surely you were culpable to a degree. You lied to them, keeping secrets, pretending you were madly in love with each of them."

"I did love them, for different reasons, it was hard to choose. And anyway, where is your evidence that I lied? They did not ask me if I was in love with another. They presumed my love was entirely directed to them." With grace, she sauntered over to the drinks table and poured herself a whiskey. "I have done nothing wrong." All eyes were on her as she returned to her seat in the bay window. Her olive skin now a shade warmer.

"By my reckoning, we have still to hear about George, Sarah and Daniel. Please open the three remaining letters and let's hear their stories." Jeremy started coughing which did not immediately abate. Catherine came over and rubbed between his shoulder blades, helping to ease his discomfort. When able, he then took a swig of his whiskey then coughed some more.

When silence cloaked the room, Daphne De'Ath and Mr Notts read out the letters for George and Sarah respectively. George had seemingly been a bit of a romancer in his time, having frequently fallen in love and promising his intended a happy ever after. Then the next love interest came along and he fell in love once more, leaving his bride-to-be at the altar, or disappearing from the lives of his fiancées. Thankfully, in time, each had recovered to live a happy and fulfilling life, except for one. They had indeed married and she had fallen with child. They had been blessed with a healthy daughter, but George had become bored with the monotony of married life: crying, responsibility, demands, changing nappies, sleepless nights. He had soon moved on in many ways, reverting to his womanising ways and leaving his loving wife to fend for their child on her own. Susan had ended up in the asylum and the child taken to a workhouse.

He had no comeback, he admitted everything was true. The guests were not impressed. George was known for his infectious smile, no one was smiling now.

Mr Notts read Sarah's letter. She had been accused of having her husband admitted into the asylum. She had driven him mad with her obsessions. Every day she had to clean the house from top to bottom, her routines had been restrictive, her demands impossible to follow. She had to bathe every day when she would scrub herself clean to the point of her skin almost bleeding. Bert had always thought she would be the one who ended up in the asylum, but sadly, he had succumbed to the constant wearing of his patience and one day he had flipped. His memory had deteriorated to such a point that he was unable to function, even for the simplest of tasks. With Bert out of the way, Sarah was happier being able to do what she wanted to do.

"I admit this to be true," said Sarah, "but I was only wanting everything to be clean. Something happened years ago. Something that I cannot erase. That one event has forever tainted my life."

"Are you able to tell us?" asked Cliff.

Sarah squirmed in her chair. She was obviously toying with the idea of sharing her secret. "I've never told anyone this, not even Bert."

"Why are lies acceptable but the truth something to fear? Come on, just tell us," demanded Jeremy.

Sarah's eyes were glistening with tears. With her hands in prayer, she covered her mouth and nose for a moment before saying, "I bore a child out of wedlock and left it on the steps of St Mary's Church." She broke down, sobbing. The women crowded around, offering her their support. "Please, I don't deserve your sympathy."

"Bert may have short term memory issues but his long term memory remains intact. During a therapy session, he spoke of your past. He was there that morning. He saw you leave the child and run away. He picked up the child and took it to the nunnery down the road. Knowing you must be hurting, he took his time in getting to know you. He followed the child's progress, gifting money to the nuns to help pay for the child's care." Jeremy leaned back in his chair and waited for the response. He tried to suppress his smile.

"My child survived, and Bert knew?"

Jeremy replied, "Seems we all have secrets."

Sarah asked, "Do you know where my son resides?"

"I do. But I will not tell you here, not now. If you wish to find out more, then I will tell you in privacy later."

Sarah nodded.

"I thought you said your husband died years ago?" asked Eliza.

"I lied," confirmed Sarah, "and now I feel so awful for abandoning him after he has protected me and my son all those years." Tears trickled down her cheeks.

The guests started different conversations.

Jeremy insisted Catherine read out the final letter. "Daniel Watters," little Lily's ears perked up at the sound of her best friend's name, "you have been invited to Vicar Island to discuss your involvement in the admission of your mother to the lunatic asylum. An imbecile from birth, your feeble mind was too much for your mother to bear and she ended up in the depressive institution of a paupers' asylum." Catherine paused, her eyes continued reading the letter but she did not speak. "There's obviously more, but with his passing, what is the point in continuing?" She folded the letter and placed it on the nearby table.

The room was once again silent.

Cornelius was the first to speak, "What is this all about, Jeremy? You invite us here, accusing us of misdemeanours and implying we have deliberately been involved in someone's downfall. You are ill, sick in the head for concocting such devilish schemes. What pleasure can you possibly gain from our suffering?" He stood from his chair, not waiting for answers. "I'm going to bed. I will stay for your wedding, if only to fulfil the contract and be awarded the money. Goodnight, and may God bless your evil soul." He stormed out of the room.

George and Eliza glanced at each other. With flawless synchronicity, they each shrugged a shoulder and raised an eyebrow.

Sarah and Vivienne were whispering, then together they walked out of the room without saying anything to anyone.

Harry said to Cliff, "Well, that was interesting."

"Will be interesting to see what happens at the wedding tomorrow."

"You definitely going?"

"Wouldn't miss it for anything." Cliff managed a rare smile. "You going?"

"Hell, yeah."

DIARY

What an evening! I cannot believe Jeremy has taken this so far. His work with Doctor Wainwright at the asylum and his commitment to researching mental health has been interesting, but this is so ludicrously over the top, I find myself questioning his sanity and motives. What is he hoping to achieve by all of this? He has confided in me about another reason for being on this island. Apparently, German miners once lived on this island, back in the 1500s, as they searched for precious minerals, metals and jewels. They worked all day, mining the fells, but retreated here for safety to protect and hide their finds from the locals and from Queen Elizabeth's men. Jeremy does not know what happened to the Germans, but he then told me that the monks from Fountains Abbey in Yorkshire came to this island and renamed it Vicar Island. He believes there is treasure hidden here. What that is, he does not know, but he so desperately wants to find it. I know he wants to research thoughts pertaining to life, death and happiness, which is why he involves me but I swear he has taken things to extremes this evening. I was unaware he had prepared so much for this weekend's events. This obsessive nature, I worry for his sanity. I dread to think that the guests turn on him, or me for that matter. I can only pray and hope to God that everything goes smoothly tomorrow. The wedding is forever on my mind but with this evening's events, I hope everyone remains calm and that we can all leave safely on Monday when Simon the delivery boy rows over with the food. It is now two-thirty in the morning. I have tried but I cannot sleep, too many thoughts racing through my head. I will look dreadful for the wedding. I still do not know if I can go through with it. With recent revelations, I am seriously thinking Jeremy is the one who is insane.

CHAPTER TWENTY

The mood was sombre as guests gathered for breakfast. Catherine had sent her apologies as she wanted to follow the tradition, or possibly superstition, of the bride not seeing the groom on the morning of the wedding.

Very little conversation took place but by eight o'clock the guests had gathered except for Vivienne and Harry.

"Do you think we should check on them?" asked Cornelius. He seemed to have a few more speckles of grey at his temples.

"Oh dear, this brings back memories of the others." Sarah put down her knife and fork, her appetite suddenly diminished.

"I'm not that hungry anyway," said George. "I'll go and check on them."

"I'll check on Vivienne if you check on Harry." Sarah Silver had tears in her eyes.

"Deal," said George.

Eliza, Cliff and Cornelius sat in silence, drinking tea from a beautiful bone china set. In their own way, they each looked exhausted. Eliza had dark shadows under eyes. Cliff's eyes were glazed and staring into the distance. Cornelius looked unkempt with the emerging stubble on his face and his normally upright posture was slouched.

Alone for only a handful of minutes, Madame De'Ath waddled into the breakfast room. "Where is everyone?"

"I thought you were psychic, surely you should know?" Eliza continued to sip her tea with an air of superiority.

"I never said I was a psychic, I read tarot cards. They are completely different gifts."

"What a shame," said Eliza. "Maybe all this chaos could have been avoided if you were truly talented."

Madame De'Ath scowled, but Eliza was oblivious.

Ever the gentleman, George offered his arm for Sarah to ascend the stairs. He felt her shaking as they made their way to Vivienne's room. The first-floor landing was impressive, with a beautiful Persian rug running the length of the corridor. Classical statues of naked beings were placed between each door. There were stunning paintings of immense size detailing European cities: Venice, Barcelona, Paris, Prague and so on.

As they stood outside Vivienne's door, they looked at each other for a moment. "Maybe we should do this together," suggested Sarah.

"Good idea," said George. He put his ear closer to the door. "Sounds quiet in there."

"I'm not sure that is settling my nerves," said Sarah.

"Shall I knock?"

"Go on then." Sarah took a small step backwards and partially hid behind George. She clung onto his arm once more.

George knocked but there was no answer. He tried the door handle, but it was locked. "Maybe she's still asleep. It was very late when we finally got to bed last night."

"I suppose. But I've an awful feeling, what with everything else that has happened. Can you break down the door?"

"I'm sure Mr Notts has a spare key. I'll run downstairs and ask him."

"I'm not staying here on my own."

"Then go to your room. Lock the door behind you. I'll be back as soon as I can." George soon disappeared round the corner leaving Sarah on her own.

With Eliza excusing herself from breakfast to go and get ready for the wedding, Cliff Dacosta and Cornelius Binks agreed to have a walk around the grounds to get some fresh air and blow away the cobwebs after a challenging night. They headed out the front door and turned left. The northerly wind was biting, and the lake rippled in the chilling breeze.

Not wanting to venture too far, they meandered through the sunken formal gardens at the rear of the house. From here, they were offered a little more protection from the wintery winds. There was little to see as the winter beds had been cleared of all the annuals and only a few evergreen shrubs remained. However, the stunning Lakeland fells with their snow-capped peaks were delightful to see. A majestic landscape formed over millennia.

Cornelius and Cliff climbed the stone steps up to the terraced area and stopped in their tracks. Each took a sudden intake of breath. They looked at each other then ran. A body was lying on the terrace, initially hidden from view by the grey balustrading surrounding the sunken formal gardens. Their worst predictions had come true. Harry Arnold was lying face down. His right upper limb twisted into an unnatural zigzag. His head severely flexed to the side. His right lower limb was twisted so his foot turned outwards. His pallor grave. Blood pooled around his head.

Cliff and Cornelius took a while to speak, struggling to believe their own eyes. Like Harry, they could not move, frozen with the shock of seeing their fellow guest lying dead on the ground.

Cornelius scratched at his emerging beard, "Do we attempt to carry him back to the house?"

"By the look of his broken limbs, I'd say they'd drop off if we carried him by his arms and legs. Let's go back to the house and tell the others. We'll get a few sheets, like we did with Bernard, and carry him that way."

"Yes. Yes, of course. Makes sense." Cornelius puffed out his cheeks as he sighed. "Do you think the wedding will go ahead?"

"I don't give a toss about the wedding. I'm more interested in who is going around murdering people." Cliff stormed off back to the house leaving Cornelius staring at Harry's crippled body.

CHAPTER TWENTY-ONE

Little Lily stared at the bedroom door. She occasionally cocked her head side to side as if listening intently at something in the corridor. She sniffed the air wafting underneath the door, then scratched at the wood panelling.

Catherine was in her room getting ready for the wedding. "Do you need to go outside? What a good girl you are." She tickled the top of Lily's head, but the dog seemed on edge.

Suddenly, there was commotion in the hallway, panicked voices and calls for calm. Initially reluctant to engage, curiosity got the better of her and Catherine opened the door to peek at what was going on.

With the guests obviously distraught about something, she closed the door, pulled on her dressing robe, and ventured into the hallway.

On seeing Catherine standing there, Sarah ran up to her and started crying, "Vivienne and Harry are dead. I can't do this anymore, I'm losing it. The sights I have seen. I can't cope."

"Sarah. SARAH!" Catherine managed to gain eye contact. "Relax your breathing." She demonstrated a slowed respiratory rate.

Cornelius, Cliff, George, Eliza and Mr Notts were standing in the corridor outside of Vivienne's room, waiting for guidance from Sarah's conversation with Catherine. "Let us give ourselves some distance from these shocking events. Mr Notts, if you could be so kind as to escort everyone into the sitting area, offer them drinks, anything they require to help them settle their nerves. Stay together. I will talk with Jeremy about what has happened." She watched them walk down the long corridor. Sobbing, holding hands, shaking heads and holding on to each other for comfort.

As they walked around the corner and descended the stairs, Catherine let out a much-needed sigh. Her wedding day of all days, such a bad omen. What on earth was going on? Surely this was not part of Jeremy's plan, or was it? He wanted to understand happiness, to be able to create happiness and maintain this fleeting emotion. He had devised a theory, a totally whimsical idea of knowing for certain what would make someone happy: knowing their dying wishes as they lay on their death bed, waiting for angels or demons to escort them to their final resting place. This would be the key to someone's happiness.

Murder had never been on the agenda though, someone's dying wish was a hypothesis, to be used to prove or disprove his theory about happiness. Murder was never mentioned as part of his plan. He only wanted the guests to imagine the scene. What would they say? What would they ask for? What would make them happy as they passed over? To be held in the arms of their loved one? For their children to be happy? To find peace? To be free from pain? To have a sip of cool, fresh water? He just wanted to know people's thoughts, to test out his theory. So, why were people dying on the island?

Jeremy had obviously researched the guests' history and found they had each played a part in another's downfall, resulting in people being incarcerated in the lunatic asylum. Maybe they were all crazy.

Being the closest, she inspected Harry's room first, Walla Crag. The covers were strewn as if he had just got out of bed. Yesterday's clothes were piled on the chair. His shoes had seemingly been kicked off last night and had landed in different places. Nothing worrying to see. No signs of forced entry to the room or specks of blood or evidence of a fight. There were no weird smells or signs of medicinal abuse. Catherine walked over to the open sash window. The curtains were blowing in the chilling air. The opening was sufficient for a grown man to climb through. She leaned on the windowsill to steady her balance and poked her head outside. A prone, lifeless body lay on the terracing below, surrounded by congealing blood. His right arm appeared to have too many joints; his humerus obviously severed mid shaft. There were signs of blood on the grey balustrading. Harry must have hit the coping stone first, his right side taking the brunt of the fall, before he fell onto the terrace below. She shuddered. The questions were: did he jump or was he pushed?

Next, she plucked up the courage to enter Vivienne Kry's room, Castle Cragg. The room was neat and tidy, but the distinct odour of death pervaded the air. There was sufficient light penetrating through the curtains to see the young woman was lying on her side in bed, facing the window. Her blond hair was a little messy. The outline of her body under the covers was plain to see. She was in the foetal position, all curled up and looked cosy. With a racing heart, Catherine pulled back the covers to reveal a subterranean crimson lake. Vivienne had slashed her wrists, the knife remained in her right hand. Catherine had seen enough. She replaced the covers, this time covering her head. Trying to portray a sense of calm, she walked out of the room and closed the door behind her. The corridor was silent.

Jeremy's suite was on the second floor. Failing to suppress her raised respiration and heart rate, she was breathless by the time she ascended the stairs. Physically fatigued by the weekend's events, she was also mentally drained of energy, trying to formulate a plan in her head as to how to deal with the situation. As far as she knew, a delivery boy was coming on Monday with fresh produce so until then, they were marooned on the island. The wedding couldn't possibly go ahead. Fate was certainly warning of impending doom. She was now at his door, struggling to breathe. Blood was pounding through her ears, the rate and strength of her heart too loud, confusing the other sounds. There was scratching, like talons tapping against wood. She sensed movement behind her. It was Lily, wagging her tail as she made her way towards Catherine. The dog was so happy to see her that her whole body was now wagging. Catherine couldn't help but smile at her new-found friend and scratted the dog's neck and back.

Suddenly, from behind the closed door came strange noises: moans, pain, suffering. A low growl trilled in Lily's throat. Was the killer torturing Jeremy? An awful thought popped into her head. Should she walk away and leave him at the hands of the murderer? This would certainly solve her predicament of marrying him. She could walk away and go in search of Solomon Smith. How she missed his tender smile, his handsome looks, his impressive strength, his sense of humour, his - there was another cry of pain, Jeremy sounded in agony. Catherine had to do something. She could not leave Jeremy to suffer at the hands of some sadistic killer. She flung open the door to surprise them and her heart momentarily arrested.

CHAPTER TWENTY-TWO

As Catherine had predicted, Jeremy was not alone in his room. His eyes were closed and he was oblivious to her presence. He had a flushed, agonised look on his face. Sitting astride him, wearing nothing but overpowering perfume was Madame De'Ath. She continued to gyrate on top of him.

"How could you both, you disgusting pair of ... uh!" Catherine's face distorted into anger. Her fists clenched so tightly that her fingers turned white. She stomped towards them with intent but then stopped when she saw their shocked faces. Madame De'Ath grabbed the sheets to hide her exposed body.

Breathless, Jeremy soon regained his composure and started laughing. Brazenly, he lay there naked, his slim torso on show. "Dear Catherine, your frigidity towards me has left me seeking pleasure in others. You cannot expect me to be a born-again virgin for our wedding day, can you?" He slapped Madame De'Ath's left buttock and she climbed off him, sneaking under the bed covers with shame.

"I have come to expect the unexpected with you. But on our wedding day. How could you? For goodness' sake, she's a ... she's a ..."

"Dwarf? Is that what you are trying to say?" He laughed. "You have judged me numerous times, but you hold your own prejudices, just like everyone else. You are far from perfect, Miss Fawcett." He retrieved his dressing gown from the bottom of the bed and proceeded to put it on. "In my eyes Daphne is beautiful, with glowing copper hair, green eyes and fair skin. She loves me and I love her. My infliction has not revolted her, and we have regularly sought pleasure in each other's beds. Yes, she has weird little stumpy fingers, but … hmmm … I find that intriguing, seeing her hands feel the length of my—"

"Stop it there, Jeremy. You disgust me on so many levels. I am leaving now. I cannot marry you, not having seen this. I cannot bear to look upon you. The pair of you disgust me. Goodbye."

"You will marry me, Catherine. Even if it is only for my money. You know my secrets. On our marriage you will gain my fortune. You want to support Mary, your daughter, and the orphans. You want to turn your old home, Petteril Bank House, into a safe haven for children with inflictions. Those who are blind, have missing limbs, those disfigured by birth. The money I have promised you will allow you to do that. We have already agreed our relationship will not be physical. You worry about catching syphilis and becoming ill. Then spare me the pain of a lonely life. You of all people know how much intimacy means to me."

Catherine stood there, frozen, incapable of moving, devoid of comment. She looked at Madame De'Ath. "What do you have to say for yourself?"

"I'm so sorry, Catherine. I never meant to hurt you."

"But you have."

"You and Jeremy can still be together. I know he loves you. He worships the ground you walk on."

"Then he has a funny way of showing it."

"Eleven o'clock, Catherine. I will be waiting in the church for your hand in marriage." Jeremy was now sitting on the edge of the bed. "There will be severe repercussions if you are not there."

"What does that mean?"

"Do not let me down. Do not let yourself down. Do not let your daughter and the orphans down. She needs my financial support for the orphanage."

"Are you saying you will withdraw all financial support if I do not marry you."

He shrugged his shoulders and opened his palms. Catherine

stormed out of the room.

DIARY

I am utterly distraught by this morning's events. I'm devasted by what has happened. Jeremy, as usual, finds every excruciating detail amusing. Oh my, I cannot help but bow my head in shame. Making love and being naked. Jeremy saying he finds my stubby little fingers intriguing. Why do I love him so when he insults me? He pays me well. Maybe it is his money that I love. He mentioned syphilis. He never confided this to me and now I may be inflicted with this dreadful disease. He may be slowly killing me. This horrendous disease may be coursing through my body. Together we have experimented in so many ways, enjoying despicable acts and craving such sordid intimacies. And now this disease may be rotting my insides. Poor Catherine, I cannot help but feel pity for her. So pious, she is so prim and proper. I cannot for the life of me understand what he sees in her but seemingly they have this weird sort of relationship in which they need each other. All of this is way beyond me. However, I have to admit, she is clever and quite beautiful for her age. I still love him and still dread the wedding going ahead. Can I really go through with the ceremony and witness them exchanging vows with what has transpired today? There is the possibility that I am no longer invited. Jeremy has been the only man to love me. Others shy away from these unusual dimensions. I am all woman and Jeremy knows that. Smiling, I will proceed to get ready and be in the church as instructed by my true love. I shall forever love him and be there for him should he need me.

Jeremy, you have both destroyed and saved me.

Forever yours,

Daphne

CHAPTER TWENTY-THREE

Catherine stood on the jetty, taking in the snow-capped mountainous heights of Skiddaw and the chilling depths of Derwentwater. Dressed in cream silk with gold Honiton lace detailing, her wedding dress was regal. Her hair was styled to perfection and pinned with an expensive gold and diamond clip. She was a princess in all but name.

Flakes of snow were falling and starting to lay on the ground. She shivered but found comfort in the numbness of her limbs, the blood diverting away, closing down her system in an attempt to preserve body heat. She felt herself falling. She could so easily end this now. The icy water was inviting, moving as one, the ripples taunting, the sound mesmerising. She could fall and be wrapped it its cold, grey depths forever. The only thing preventing her from falling was little Lily as she wagged her tail, seeking comfort and attention. Catherine once again tickled and scratched around the back of Lily's neck and ears.

Then she noticed movement, someone readying a boat on the Keswick shoreline. A man sent from God. He could save them all, free them from this open gaol. A beautiful house, extensive gardens, stunning views, glorious mountain vistas, a glistening lake, warmth, food, a perfect setting, a heavenly façade to entice you to the depths of hell.

She waved with both arms, desperately wanting his attention. After a few seconds, he waved back. He stepped into the boat and rowed towards her. His back to her, he would occasionally look over his shoulder to get his bearings. Who was this saviour? Had someone sent him? Was he part of Jeremy's plan? This all seemed too good to be true.

As she stood on the jetty, she realised Bernard Pratt's wrapped body was no longer under the shelter of the boat house roof. She walked over to the end bay and searched in the bushes. No signs of Bernard. She wondered if someone had rolled him into the lake to dispose of the body.

Fifteen minutes later, the man from the shore was mooring the rowing boat and he locked the boathouse doors behind him.

He wore odd clothes. A black billowing dress of sorts with a peculiar hat. He touched the brim as he bowed. "Good morning, Miss Fawcett I presume. Are you well?"

"My wellness is questionable if the truth be told." Catherine was shivering, with extreme bouts of uncontrollable movements. "And you are?"

"Reverend Robinson. Not easy to say, I must admit, so please feel free to call be Bob."

"Thank you so much for rescuing us. There have been so many terrible things happening here on the island."

Reverend Robinson's head retracted and he studied Catherine for longer than he should. There was now a look of uncertainty on his face. "I'm here to conduct a wedding. Jeremy Fisher and Catherine Fawcett are the bride and groom I do believe." He searched his satchel, then pulled out a map. "Is this Vicar Island?"

Catherine nodded.

"And is there a Jeremy and Catherine who are expecting me?" He raised an eyebrow.

Catherine once again nodded.

Now uncomfortable, the vicar cleared his throat before offering, "I apologise about before. Naturally, with the way you are dressed I assumed you were the bride. I can see the church in front of me, could you possibly take me to see Jeremy, or do you know where he is?"

A nod was her only reaction.

"Well, I can see a path round to the right. I shall make my way round there and go in search of the groom. Thank you, miss?"

"Miss Fawcett, Catherine."

He smiled, "Pleased to meet—" he stopped abruptly and the smile vanished. "Would you like to accompany me to the house?"

She shook her head.

"I'll be right back."

CHAPTER TWENTY-FOUR

From the outside, the church was a simple rectangular shape with a square tower. Grey stone for the walls and grey slate for the roof. On the inside, a stunning stained-glass window provided some much-needed warmth of colour. Everything else was carved out of wood. There was no gold, no jewel encrusted treasures, no brass rails, no marble statues and no tapestried pew cushions. The wood was dark brown but expertly crafted down to the minutest detail. The bases of the various candlesticks were carved to represent pinecones, a symbol of eternal life. Wooden angels gazed down upon winged creatures and fiery beasts, depicting heaven above hell, an eternal battle. Scattered around the church, on beams and columns, were wooden butterflies signifying resurrection. There were snakes and apples, arrows and shields, flowers and bees - a menagerie of life - God and man-made creations.

Mr Notts was rushing around the church, lighting candles, tying flowers to the end of the pews and perfecting the colourful displays in the urns either side of the altar.

Reverend Robinson stood at the doorway to the church, rocking back and forward on his heels and toes. His fingers interlocked. A warm smile planted on his face, ready to welcome the wedding guests.

Guests arrived in dribs and drabs. Sarah Silver and Cornelius Binks walked arm in arm down the centre aisle and sat on the third row. Sarah was holding back tears from finding Vivienne and Harry earlier that morning. Cornelius was trying to distract himself by looking around the church.

Eliza and George were the next guests to grace the church. With little to smile about, the corners of their mouth briefly rose when greeting the vicar, then the sombre mood returned. They sat behind Sarah and Cornelius.

Daphne De'Ath and Mr Montgomery made their way to row five. They sat in silence, there were no appropriate words to describe the weird situation.

Cliff Dacosta was the last to arrive. Confidently, he walked down the aisle and chose to sit on his own in row three on the left side of the church.

Ten minutes later, Jeremy limped down the aisle, his face aglow, his smile beaming from ear to ear like a juicy melon slice. He stood on the right in the front row and waited.

Minutes ticked by in awkward silence. The vicar pulled the chord to ring the bell denoting the eleventh hour. Two figures walked the rough path. Against the pure whiteness of the falling snow, her shimmering cream and gold dress reflected a warm glow opon her face. Her teeth were chattering. Her hands trembling. Little Lily trotted alongside. Her blue coat stunning against the crisp white feathers of snow. Catherine and Lily were greeted in the doorway by the vicar.

"Are you sure about this?"

She nodded.

The vicar sighed. "You are making a vow in front of God, to love, cherish and obey this man for the rest of your life. Are you ready to make such a commitment?"

She nodded, her eyes glistening with the swell of tears.

"Would you like me to escort you down the aisle?"

She nodded, then a solitary tear trickled down her face.

With a sad smile, Reverend Robinson held out a flexed arm and Catherine linked her hand through the hook of his elbow. He made to start walking but she flinched. The movement pulling him back.

"Would you like me to fetch Jeremy?"

She shook her head.

The delay was now creating tension among the guests. The church organ was silent, creating a bizarre atmosphere for a wedding ceremony. Jeremy had been pacing up and down the aisle and was now marching towards them. He stood in front of Catherine and the vicar and asked, "Well?" He shook his head with an air of impatience. He studied their faces. Lily growled.

"Catherine, is there anything you would like to say?" The vicar placed his hand over hers. She was still shaking.

"Pull yourself together, woman, and let's get this over with. You'd think you were marrying a pauper with leprosy." He rolled his eyes, tutted, then stormed off.

Catherine stared into the distance. Reverend Robinson tried to work out what she was looking at. Her gaze veered towards the wooden depiction of Christ nailed to the cross. His head bowed, crowned by thorns.

"It's now or never," said the vicar.

Catherine stepped into the church. There was an audible sigh from the guests. Mr Notts started to play the organ and the guests stood as she walked down the aisle.

Reverend Robinson left her standing next to Jeremy but Catherine could only look ahead, staring at the crucifixion of Christ.

"We are gathered here today to witness the bringing together of …" his words were soon lost, his voice losing power, becoming a whisper on the breeze. The sounds were familiar, words forming sentences she had witnessed before, but they made no sense on this occasion.

The vicar stood there in his white vestments with gold detailing. He was holding a book. He asked her questions and waited for a reply. He was prompting her to repeat what he had said. It made no sense.

Jeremy was animated, he was smiling, his voice a siren in the storm. He made to kiss her. Their lips touching for the first time. His lips were hard, dry and cracked, not what she was expecting. A reflex action, she wiped her lips with the back of her hand.

Subdued clapping was heard in the distance. Everything was

surreal, a questionable reality.

Catherine turned and there were people, sitting there, looking at her. Someone was holding her hand. It was Jeremy, he was smiling and talking but she could not hear. His words muffled in the foggy atmosphere. He led her to a table. He made her sit by putting pressure on her shoulder. She did as she was told. A feather was placed in her hand. No, a quill. She had to sign some papers. They sang a song. The vicar spoke some more and then Jeremy led her down the aisle. He stopped at the fortified doors and once again kissed her. More lovingly this time. A longer embrace.

There was a scream. People were shouting. She turned her head to see what all the fuss was about. These strangers were crowding Jeremy. A man was pointing his finger in his face. A woman pushed him in his chest. The man in the white and gold cassock was asking for calm. Then a crack, resonating through the echo chamber of the church. Jeremy fell to the stone floor. Catherine made to run but stopped. She saw blood, a halo of red pooling around his head where he lay on the floor. His body was convulsing. Catherine heard gasps, then panicked voices.

With difficulty, she opened the door to the church and ran to the jetty. Lily followed at her heels. The vicar's boat was still there, locked inside the boathouse. She found a fallen tree branch. After three blows, the branch snapped but the lock on the boathouse door was still intact. She found a large stone. Blow after blow did not help. The boat remained secure in its temporary home. Snow was now falling heavily, an inch thick on the path.

The water was grey, mirroring the blanketed sky. Her limbs shivered at the thought but with no further ado she jumped in the icy water. Her breath was immediately on hold, momentarily frozen by the chilling temperature of the water. She grabbed the upright pillars of the wooden jetty then clung onto the rope edging. Swimming was not a pursuit she had tried before so she knew she had to keep hold of the rope for the weight of her dress was dragging her down. She had been holding her breath but now she gasped and desperately pulled herself along to the boat. Her teeth were chattering, her limbs frozen, she could barely move. Numerous times she tried to climb into the boat but the movement was nauseating and the rocking of the boat relentless. The layers of her dress were absorbing water. Now so heavy, she wanted to let go of her lifeline and settle in a grave at the bottom of the icy lake. Maybe she could finally find peace. Her tomb the water. A rickety old boat house her headstone for eternity.

As she kicked to stay afloat, her foot found leverage on a support beam or metal casing for the rising timber of the boat house. This was sufficient leverage to haul herself into the wooden vessel. Little Lily had been watching from the jetty. On seeing Catherine in the boat, she dropped to her belly and crawled under the doorway of the boat house. Her back arched but she became wedged under the door. Catherine made her way to the other end of the boat and reached across to the dog. Grabbing under the shoulders, she pulled the dog towards her and with a little jiggling, the dog slithered under the door and Catherine lifted her into the boat. Lily stood on the seat and tried to lick Catherine to death.

Having never rowed a boat in her entire life, Catherine soon sussed its workings and managed to move away from Vicar Island. Lily took up position on the bow of the boat, standing proud, her nose in the air, taking in the smells.

The snow kept falling, the sky laden with white powder. The chills were now violent, her body spasming to create warmth. Drenched through, the cold was seeping into her bones. Inch by inch the shoreline became closer. She run aground on the shallow pebble beach, and abandoned the boat, not bothered about mooring the boat properly. She walked up the hill. She knew where she wanted to go but had no idea how to get there. Faithfully, Lily followed alongside.

Catherine desperately needed to see Solomon. The last time she had laid eyes on him was on that fateful day. *They* had come for him. The faceless men had detained him. *They* had incarcerated him in the lunatic asylum and stated he was crazy. She had asked to see him, but *they* had denied her pleas.

For the last three years he had been on her mind. Hoping he was safe, praying he was sane and believing one day he would be free. She had to see him, otherwise her heart would drown in an endless sorrow of never feeling his love again.

Now in the heart of Keswick, people were frowning at her bedraggled state. Few were out and about on this Sunday afternoon, the snowy weather probably deterring them from venturing outside.

She had to keep moving, to stagnate would mean freezing to death. Her options were walk to Carlisle, but it would take her most of the day and night to get there, and in this weather she did not know if she would survive the ordeal. Maybe she could hide in a barn. Remove her wet attire and give herself some time to dry off, stealing warmth from the hay and the animals nearby. Could she knock on a door perhaps, and ask for clean clothes? Her previous experiences were that people were reluctant to engage with those in need. Turning up their noses at the dirty, the desperate, the deranged. She had no money, but she wondered if maybe someone would be so kind as to give her fare for the train. She wasn't even sure if trains ran on a Sunday.

Thinking back to the day of Solomon's capture, she had tried to flag down numerous carriages and riders but the horses had been spooked by her pleas for help and the riders had shouted obscenities at her for upsetting the horses.

She was on her own, but at least she had company. With faith and the strength of God within her, she headed to the station, praying for salvation from this nightmare.

CHAPTER TWENTY-FIVE

Although she politely asked for directions to the train station, everyone recoiled away, giving her a wide berth. She could understand why. Her hands were tinged blue, the chill creating a numbness to any sensation other than pain. Her beautiful gold shoes squelched with each step and her feet were solid, like a lump of ice on the ground, making her balance precarious, her gait awkward. Her wedding dress was sodden, forming puddles on the ground if she dared to stop to ask someone for help.

Sod them, sod them all, she thought and with a strong will and sheer determination to be independent, she traipsed the bleak streets in search of the train station. A small crowd had formed by Keswick's Moot Hall to listen to a choir singing Christmas carols. Bay-fronted windows were steamy with condensation. Shopkeepers were lighting candles and stoking fires in an attempt to entice punters into the shops as snow continued to fall and the light fade. There were only a couple of weeks until Christmas and the window displays were bright and cheery with beautiful gift ideas. Catherine sighed, hoping she would survive this ordeal and make it home to spend Christmas Day with her daughter and the children.

Shivering uncontrollably, she nearly cried on seeing a sign for the station. Exhausted, she managed the last few hundred steps and just wanted to collapse in a heap on walking through the arched entrance way. Catherine gave herself a moment before approaching the ticket booth on her left. A clerk at the desk said a train was due just after two o'clock. She had an hour to find the money to purchase a ticket. Sadly, there were already too many beggars hanging around the station. Sitting on the hard ground, flat cap open to monetary offerings, filthy clothes, pitted skin, and gaunt cheeks but their stomachs swollen from prolonged hunger. She knew she could not sit amongst them. She would feel a fraud, begging for money and would feel guilty at taking away their chance to survive. Anyway, if she were to remain still she would cease, the ice forming within her bones. She had to keep moving.

"Please, sir, can you spare me some change to get to Carlisle?"

"If you would be so kind as to …"

"Sorry to bother you, but would you be able to …"

"Something awful has happened, and I was wondering if …"

Time and again she begged for money but her desperate presence revulsed people. Explanations for her appearance fell on deaf ears, justifying her bedraggled state bore no sympathy. Everyone cast her aside. Time was slipping away. Her energy depleted. Her will to survive and see Solomon once more was now a dream, a hopeless desire. She slumped to the floor and sat crossed legged. She unbuttoned her dress and untied the ribbons. She needed to remove her clothes. The weight was dragging her down. The garments were on fire. So heavy with water, her clothes were melting to her skin. She was burning up. All little Lily could do was sit by Catherine's side and lick her exposed ankles.

The platform guard saw travellers gawping at the floor. A crowd was beginning to form. Something was amiss. He summoned a couple of staff and went to investigate what was grabbing people's attention. As they pushed through the crowd, they saw an almost naked woman close to giving up the ghost. With skin like alabaster, she was about to crumble. One of the guards picked her up in his arms, carried her to a nearby waiting room and instructed everyone to leave. A blanket was wrapped around her by kind hands. The guards roused her with some smelling salts as she lay in someone's warm embrace. A hot cup of tea was placed in her hands and she was encouraged to drink the steaming fluid. Like fuzzy shadows, the guards moved around, communicating with each other, but to Catherine they were incoherent. Like angels in a hazy light, speaking an alien tongue she was at their mercy.

In time, everything came into focus and she apologised profusely for the spectacle she had created. She thanked them all individually for the care they had shown. By then, the guards had managed to pull together some items of clothing, men's garments, but at least they were dry. They gave her privacy to change and finally Catherine sighed with relief. The small pleasures in life were the best: tea, warmth and someone who cares.

Although her clothes were soaked through, the men realised her attire was of the best quality as the beautiful cream and gold dress was embellished with so many intricate details. They found a bag in which to place her wet belongings and Catherine could not thank them enough for taking care of her.

Eventually, she was well enough to walk, having also been given a pair of men's shoes but she did not care. To be dry and warm felt wonderful. The guard sorted her a ticket to Carlisle and helped her climb into a carriage. Dogs weren't allowed on the train but in the circumstances, the guard turned a blind eye. It was then she remembered the gold jewellery in her hair. She removed the pin and placed it in the guard's hands. "Thank you so much, you have saved me today." He wished her bon voyage and waved at her until the train left the station and she was no longer in sight.

There were two other passengers in the carriage, but they avoided eye contact with her. Catherine was relieved she did not have to make polite conversation.

The train pulled into Penrith station for a connecting train to Carlisle. Forty minutes later the Glasgow bound train pulled into the station, steam billowing from the funnel. A loud whistle made her jump. She looked around at her fellow passengers as they waited to board the train. They were looking at her with disdain.

Once everyone had disembarked, Catherine stepped into an empty carriage and was thankful for the peace and quiet. She instructed Lily to hide beneath the seat and was thankful when the train pulled away without incident.

The screeching noise of the wheels on the track was somehow

soporific and for the first time in many months, she truly felt relaxed and free. The rolling hills of the Eden valley gradually became industrial buildings and warehouses as the train approached Carlisle. Snow continued to fall but was failing to lay to the depths it had been in Keswick.

She got off the train and again wanted to cry. She was unsure why. Partly, she was relieved to have distanced herself from Jeremy and the island but she also felt overwhelmed at what would happen next. Why did life have to be so hard? Why did life have to be a constant struggle? She did not have the time or energy to contemplate the answers at this moment.

Determined to be independent, having been on the receiving end of so many aspersions, she walked out of the railway station and stood in Court Square. The familiar Citadel towers had defied time and stood proud in defending the city. Black cabs and their bridled horses awaited fairs, but she had no money. She refused to beg and plead for help so started walking. The men's brogues she wore were too large and uncomfortable but she was determined to make her way to Solomon. But where was he? Jeremy had said he would be in the asylum forever so she wondered if she should visit there first. However, the thought of turning up in the dark and dressed like a man would confirm her insanity and she risked the threat of being admitted.

Having considered all options, she decided to head to Wetheral and visit her daughter, Mary. From there she could bathe in warm water by the fire, change into something more suitable and then visit Solomon tomorrow.

Whilst walking, and with everything she had been through, she thought about her own happiness. Wealth had not brought happiness, but neither had poverty. Excitement initially brought happiness but then the perils of dallying with the criminally insane had led to worry and her incarceration in the lunatic asylum. Finding her daughter after so many years of believing her to be dead should have brought happiness but initially it brought an awful melancholy. To have been robbed of motherhood through her daughter's childhood years made her want to cry. She had been denied seeing her first smile. She had missed her first words. She had never witnessed those tentative steps to walking independently. She then contemplated how she had been deceived by her parents for eighteen years. Her mother and father had blatantly lied to her, saying her daughter had died at birth. Surely this ranked high on mental cruelty. Family had not brought happiness. Giving birth to her own flesh and blood, the miracle of life, that unconditional love. That was happiness. Then thinking her dead, seeing her taken away, that was soul destroying.

Seeing Solomon again, how the butterflies tickled her tummy. He would bring her happiness. She imagined his warm embrace and tender kiss. His smile, his eyes, the firmness of his body, his strength, his passion, his love. This was happiness. Why had she doubted it at the time? Jeremy had made him out to be some ragamuffin, some deluded fool, a desperate excuse of a man, making ends meet by working in a public house. Jeremy had made her question her love. Jeremy had a lot to answer for.

An hour and a half later, dragging her blistered feet in the oversized shoes, she found herself on the outskirts of the pretty village of Wetheral. Lily had been limping for a while now, her left front paw lifted off the ground. Catherine picked her up and carried her for the last mile. Lily rested her front paws over Catherine's shoulder and occasionally gave her a lick on the cheek. The dog was solid and with the bag she was carrying with her wet clothes and shoes, she was struggling to drag herself to her destination. She properly cried, having suppressed all her emotions for the last few dreadful hours. The strange people on the island. The murders. Jeremy lying on the church floor in a pool of blood. Jumping in the lake. Freezing to death. Seeing angels. She stopped herself from thinking about it. She looked at Lily who was lying across her right breast. The dog had tears in her eyes. She licked at her bleeding paw. Catherine's heart was close to breaking.

She was now standing at the heart of the village on the green. Very little had changed since her last visit six months ago. She had no idea of the time but darkness had contaminated the land. Solomon's house, the orphanage and even Oak Bank Hall were all black and lifeless.

She knew she looked a state. The baggy trousers she wore were rolled at the waist numerous times to get some form of leverage and stop them from falling down. The hems of the legs were rolled up too to prevent her from tripping over the length. She wore a jacket which was about five sizes too big and she wore no hat. Having jumped in the lake, the length of her hair was like rat's tails hanging limply over her shoulders. However, this did not deter her. She so desperately wanted to see Solomon, she did not want to put off seeing him, even for an hour to get changed. He had always been in her heart. Never a day had passed without her regretting how they had parted. He had always been so kind, thoughtful and caring. He would not mind seeing her like this. She knew he would hold out his arms and she would fall into his warm embrace. She could explain her appearance and he would reassure her that all would be well.

Unable to keep the shoes on her feet, she dragged them along the road until she stood outside his house. No light was visible through the closed curtains. Maybe he was still in the asylum. Maybe he was out, visiting family or friends. Maybe he had his old job back, working at the Wheatsheaf Inn.

With trepidation, she knocked on the door. No answer. With more force, she once again knocked on the door and waited. The front yard was orderly with only a faint sprinkling of snow. The door was clean, not a speck of dust or dirt. The windows were gleaming. Someone had to be home. Her attention was diverted back to the door as she heard noises from inside the house.

"Who is it?" Solomon's voice, a hint of paranoia.

"Hello, Solomon. It's me, Catherine."

A pause. No noise. Then a key was being inserted in the lock. The door opened slowly. The person was hiding behind the door and in the darkness it was difficult to see who it was but she knew it was Solomon.

"I'm so very sorry for everything that's happened. Can you ever forgive me?" She felt close to collapsing. Her limps were like lead, bizarrely she was freezing and burning at the same time. "I'm so happy to see you. I've longed for this day so much." She stepped forward, expecting to be let in, but the door remained still.

"Solomon, please let me in, I'm desperate. I have been forced into this bizarre situation with Jeremy and—"

"Please, just leave. I don't want to deal with this."

"If you would let me explain—"

"I don't want to hear your excuses." He made to close the door, but Catherine put her large shoe across the threshold.

"I love you, Solomon. I really do. I can't bear that we are not together."

"That was three years ago. You left me in the asylum under false pretences. You agreed to marry another man. You abandoned me and broke my heart. You didn't even say goodbye."

"That wasn't me, it was Jeremy, and Doctor Wainwright. I was forced—"

"Too late, I'm sorry. Remove your foot, otherwise it will shatter as I slam the door shut."

"Solomon, please, I beg you. If only we can talk."

"I'm happily married now and have a child on the way. Leave us in peace. I'm sorry too. I never wanted it to end this way." He closed the door as the shoe slipped away.

Her heart could quite easily break. Her lungs no longer required air. Not only was she numb from the cold, her life was now devoid of any kind of warmth. There was no reason to live. Her skin was chaffed by the rough material of the trousers. Her hands were sore from carrying Lily and the bag. Her feet were bleeding from the friction of the oversized shoes. So much pain. She needed a release from the suffering. She lowered Lily to the floor.

She dragged her feet along the road and headed downhill towards the railway. Lily trailed behind her, whimpering, limping. Suicide Point was calling.

PRESENT DAY

Soo-Min was emersed in a world full of wonder. Like the old, silent movies of the early 1900s, she saw flickers of the past and disjointed images, accompanied by the haunting notes of *The Aquarium*.

She wandered around the ballroom. There was a man. Dressed in a smart suit, he had a severe parting with his dark hair slicked to the side. A pretty face, his features were soft and rounded. He was bending over, no, he was scoliosed, his spine twisted and flexed. He pottered around the room, limping as he went, one leg shorter than the other, a built up shoe. He had kind eyes, a gentle smile, he was deciding where to put the pictures and paintings that once adorned the room. She liked him and felt calm in his presence. She assumed he was the original owner of the house.

The film in her head flickered and she saw a young woman lying on the sofa in front of a blazing fire. She was sad, confused, haunted. Soo-Min was unsure who she was or why she was there.

Opening the door to head into the hallway, she felt uneasy as she approached the cosy room. She would leave that room until last. She knocked on the door and waited for Jack to answer.

"You ready?" he asked.

"Yes, I am. We go upstairs first, if that's okay with you?"

"Did you feel anything in the ballroom?"

Soo-Min smiled, "I sensed a lovely gentleman." She described the man in the sepia images.

"If you say something, do you want me to confirm if I know it's definitely true?"

"Yes, that be good."

"Then the man you describe I reckon is the original owner of the house. His name was Samuel Thompson. We found pictures of him as we renovated the house."

"That do for now. Do not tell me anymore."

They started to climb the stairs when Soo-Min gasped. She stood still for a while, holding onto the banister for support. She faced down the stairs, as if staring into space. In her mind, the reel played images of an old woman with bony hands and white hair. A younger woman was screaming. She described the scene she was seeing, "You here too, Jack. Is the younger woman your wife?"

"Sounds like it. That was the first day we ventured into Fernleigh. Our elderly neighbour popped by to see us. Millie nearly had a heart attack when she saw the old woman. She thought she was a ghost."

"Poor Millie." They both laughed.

They headed up the stairs and Soo-Min paused for a moment on the landing. "I want to go into this room first." It was decorated as guest bedroom in shades of cream and gold. The room felt luxurious with different textures: satin, velvet, wood, metal. She stared as if in a trance for a long time, her hands together in prayer, smelling the essential oils. "Do you really want to know everything? What is the term you use, something like *ignorance is nice*?" Soo-Min's mouth distorted to the side. She knew that wasn't the saying but something along those lines.

"Ignorance is bliss. I get what you mean. Are you seeing something horrific?" Jack grimaced, unsure if he wanted to know any gory details.

"Not horrific, more like sad." She stared once again, as if watching the memory play over again and again. "Have you changed the room? The lovely gentleman, Samuel, is walking through a door here." She placed her hands on the wall.

Jack nodded; Soo-Min was good. "Yeah. There was no bathroom when we moved in, so I changed the dimensions of the rooms around a bit to fit one in. Originally, there was a door there." He took in a large breath and held it momentarily. "Go on, tell me what you're seeing."

"The room as I see it is a nursery. The lovely gentleman is sad, he carry a baby in his arms and he lay her down to sleep in a crib. The baby has died." Tears welled in her eyes.

"There was a wooden crib in here. It had a little pitched roof." He refrained from telling her the police had found the remains of a baby buried in the garden under the oak tree. He hadn't told Millie either. If she knew, she would never come back home.

"I want to go in this room next." She walked along the corridor and stood outside the main bedroom. Soo-Min placed her hands in prayer once more and inhaled the lovely fragrance of essential oils.

Jack opened the door. As every room, the place was immaculate. He would always deny having OCD, but he did like keeping a tidy home. That was probably why his joinery business received such high praise.

He was a perfectionist. When he was a child, all he could remember was the mess. The empty wine bottles lying on the floor. The discarded beer cans crushed by his dad's hand. The junk food: wrappers, pizza boxes with discarded crusts, cold kebab meat leaving greasy stains on the sofa. He couldn't remember his mam or dad ever cooking a proper meal. He shuddered.

Soo-Min was staring at the bed. "I only see one significant event. The baby was born in this room, a girl."

Jack shrugged his shoulders. "Are you sure there isn't anything else happened in here?"

"Why you ask?"

"You want me to tell you?"

"Yes. I not getting much in here. Nothing bad anyway."

Jack was so relieved to hear that. "Millie says she gets sleep paralysis and a demon lies on top of her."

Soo-Min blushed, "I never heard of this." She got the phone out of her pocket. "What you say? Sleep paralysis?"

"Yeah, and demons. Millie did mention a name. Can't think what it is." Jack got out his phone and the pair of them did a search. "Here it is. *An incubus is a male demon who torments you when you are in a state of sleep paralysis. The succubus is the female form.* Millie got to the point she could no longer sleep in this room. This demon would terrify her. She said she would often wake up and find the succubus lying on me."

Soo-Min continued to read the article on her phone. "That very scary. No wonder your wife been in psychiatric hospital and no want to come back here. Sounds awful. But I not picking up on anything like that in here."

"Do you think it *is* all in her mind?"

"I really not know. All I see is a baby was born in this room. I'm not picking up on anything else."

In agreement they left the room. Soo-Min walked along the corridor, heading towards the stairs.

"Are we not going in the attic?" asked Jack.

"No, I not getting any significant memories from there. I think it all happened in the cosy room."

"Gruesome?"

Soo-Min nodded. "Horrific."

CHAPTER TWENTY-SIX

Catherine stood at Suicide Point for what felt like ages, trying to pluck up the courage to climb over the high wrought iron railings of the railway viaduct and fall to her death one hundred feet below. Little Lily had been lying at her feet, shivering the whole time. With little energy to draw upon, Catherine collapsed in a heap on the wooden slats, just hoping the icy chill would drain her soul, a slow slipping away into oblivion. Lily crawled on her tummy and nuzzled under Catherine's arm.

Drifting in and out of sleep, Catherine was aware of a young man striding along the viaduct from the village of Great Corby on the east side of the River Eden. He stopped to stare. She huddled into a foetal position. He placed his hand on her shoulder, an insignificant but comforting warmth. She prayed he would pick her up like an old sack and discard her onto the road below but instead he offered her his hand. She remained coiled.

"I'm heading to the orphanage with these." He held aloft two rabbits tied together with string. "I'm sure they would let you stay if you're homeless or in trouble." There was no response. "What's your name, lad? I'm Ben."

In her muddled state, Catherine was unsure why he was calling her a lad, then she remembered she was dressed in men's clothing.

"I help out there when I can. The children have been performing some musical thingy at the church this evening. Not my kind of thing, so I've been to catch something for tomorrow's dinner." Still no reply. "There's other lads there. You'll fit right in. Don't worry about the Governess. She's a bit stern looking, doesn't smile much, but she really does care about the bairns. She doesn't shout but she'll protect you. She's quiet but very strong. She'll not judge if that's what you're worried about."

Catherine was now sobbing into the jacket sleeve. She wiped her nose on its rough material then started to cough. She tried to stand but her legs collapsed at each feeble attempt. As Ben caught a glimpse of her face in the flitting moonlight, all he could say was, "Oh, you're a woman."

She nodded. Her frail voice could barely be heard, "I'm so close to the light. There's a roaring fire crackling away in the hearth. It's so warm and I'm so sleepy. My loved one is there. He's no longer of this earth, but he's waiting for me. There's a magical Christmas tree, twinkling in the candlelight. There's a huge banquet, with many a tasty delight. I want to join him and be free from this pain."

Ben squatted beside her and scratched the back of Lily's neck. "The orphanage is as you describe, with glowing fires and tasty food. There's laughter and fun and giggles. The Governess has even put up a Christmas tree this year. The children have made ornaments and things to decorate its branches. It's special, well it makes my heart smile anyway. Maybe your dream is a sign. Please, let me help you. I'll gladly take you there."

"Thank you, you are most kind."

With her arm over Ben's shoulders and his arm around her waist, Catherine managed to trudge past the station master's house. Little Lily continued to limp; her sore paw held aloft. They reached the railway bridge and paused. Catherine's legs kept buckling as she tried to ascend the steps over the railway tracks. Ben was struggling to hold her up against gravity. He was only a slim lad and he was already carrying a gun and two rabbits. Ever the chatterbox, he kept talking and encouraging Catherine to stand. On her last attempt she collapsed, and he caught her in his arms.

Her body now limp, he scooped her up into his arms and attempted to carry her all the way to the spooky-looking orphanage. His legs were buckling with the strain, his back aching with the effort and his arms felt on fire with holding a static position. His muscles were burning up, his heart pounding with the burden and his lungs were struggling to take in sufficient air.

When he got to the top of Station Hill, he stopped outside of Dawson's Store and rested Catherine's weight on a low brick wall. She was out cold. He adjusted his gun and the rabbits, moved his arms a few times to improve the flow of blood and stretched his back a couple of times before proceeding once more. By the time he got to the imposing gothic house, his legs were wobbly and the final climb up to the front door required every morsel of strength he possessed.

On reaching the front door, it was evident that everyone was still at the church as the house was in darkness. Ben placed Catherine in the sheltered area of the doorway and then flexed and extended his arms a few times. His hands numb with the effort of carrying such a load for such a distance.

With some feeling returning, he tried the door handle but it was locked. He sat on the ground next to Catherine, the coldness of the stone quickly seeping through his bones. He placed his arm around her, trying to keep her warm. As they huddled together, Ben rubbed her shoulders, then her face, then her hands, trying to get her to open her eyes. "Stay with me, come on, open your eyes. Miss Montgomery will be here soon. Come on, lady. Stay with me." Lily huddled between them, her sad eyes flicking between her two new friends.

As the minutes ticked by, the burning pain in his muscles subsided, only to be replaced by a deeper more sinister sensation of a creeping chill. He shuddered, knowing he would soon have to move to relieve his discomfort and he was beginning to question whether this lady sat next to him would survive. Her breathing was now a little raspy.

Familiar sounds were faint on the subtle breeze: children's laughter. Ben got to his feet and saw the orphans making their way up the hill. "They're here now, miss. We'll soon have you by that fire and giving you something to eat. Come on. Come on." *Please*, he prayed.

As the children reached the boundary wall of their home, they saw the huddled figures up ahead. Miss Montgomery put out her arms as a protective gesture, making them stop until she weighed up the situation. She recognised Ben with what seemed to be a teenage boy wearing oversized clothes. She told the children to stay where they were. She quickened her pace and climbed the numerous steps up to the house. It was only when she was up close that she realised the teenage boy was her mother.

"Catherine, it's Mary." No response. "Let's get you inside where it'll be warmer. I'll get the fire going and make a nice pot of tea."

Ben and Mary carried Catherine into the house, along the hallway and into the back room. They placed her on the sofa and made her comfortable. Mary instructed Ben to bring the children in from outside, then get some blankets from upstairs.

The coals in the grate were still glowing, so Mary set to work on building up the fire and soon the room was cosy. With her mother settled, she went to make a tray of tea but when she returned Catherine remained in a deep sleep.

Covered by a crocheted blanket, Catherine had been sleeping on the sofa for over two hours before she showed any signs of rousing. First there were a few moans, then mumblings. Her body was twitching and then fidgeting. Her eyelids started to flutter but it took a while before her eyes remained open and focused.

With assistance, Catherine eventually managed to sit upright propped up with cushions. It was a while before she spoke or responded in any meaningful way. In the meantime, Ben had been busy in the kitchen preparing something to eat and drink. He brought through a huge tray laden with offerings. There were two doorstop slices of bread and butter on a side plate. There was freshly prepared rabbit stew in a bowl. Not knowing her preferences, he had poured a glass of milk, a glass of wine and had made another pot of tea.

With Mary encouraging her to eat and drink, Catherine managed to nibble on the bread, swallow a few spoons of stew and take a couple of sips of tea.

"Do you feel up to telling us what happened?" asked Mary.

"I'm not quite sure if I'm being honest. It all seems surreal now."

"First of all, are you able to tell us why you are dressed in men's clothes?"

"I was on an island. I wanted to escape. I jumped into the lake to get in a boat." Catherine's forehead furrowed, as if she could not quite believe what she was saying.

"Why were you on an island?"

"Unbeknown to me, Jeremy had arranged for us to marry on the island as a surprise but at the same time he was undertaking an experiment, then he said there was a treasure hidden on the island and asked for my help in locating the item. But he didn't know what the item was or where it was hidden."

Mary and Ben discreetly looked at each other and grimaced, but Catherine noticed the brief exchange.

"It sounds mad saying it out loud, but it all felt so real at the time. Maybe it's me, maybe I am mad after all. It all sounds so far-fetched." She tore off a small piece of bread and dipped it in the hot stew.

"But you sent me an invite. You were getting married at the end of December in Cheshire. You said Jeremy had arranged a rather large gathering, with over one hundred people and that I was your only guest."

"Yes, I remember writing to you. It just doesn't make sense, does it. Why then would he want to marry in relative anonymity with strangers as guests?" Catherine sighed. "And then I think he died."

"What? Are you sure?" asked Mary.

The front doorbell rang and then persistent knocking. "I'll get it," offered Ben and left the room.

Catherine's eyes lit up. "It's Solomon, I know it is. He really does love me, even with everything that has happened. I knew he wouldn't let me down. We can sort this out."

Ben walked back into the room. "Jeremy Fisher is here to see Catherine."

CHAPTER TWENTY-SEVEN

"I have been most worried about you. Are you alright?" Jeremy approached Catherine who was now standing behind the sofa. She was shivering. "You look ghastly. Whatever has happened to you? And why are you sporting men's attire?" When he received no reply, he looked at Ben and Mary. "Well, do *you* know?"

Mary spoke calmy, "She's been here for around four hours, but she's barely spoken a word. Ben found her on the viaduct, at Suicide Point, and carried her here. She slept for a couple of hours and in the past hour or two she's nibbled on some food, other than that we do not know anything." She glanced sideways at Ben.

"I've only just got here by carriage. We were in the Lake District. She just ran off, without saying anything."

"Is everything agreeable between yourselves, for you are soon to be married?" Mary did not falter even though her heart was doubling its efforts.

"Well, that's a whole story in itself." He turned his attention to Catherine. "Come with me now, over to Oak Bank Hall. I called there first but alas they had not set eyes on you. They are preparing a room for you. I then came over here. I'm so pleased I found you. I have been worried sick, wondering where you could be, hoping you were somewhere safe and warm in this bitterly cold weather." Catherine stared at him, swaddled in her own arms.

Jeremy turned his attention back to Mary. "Apologies, but could I have a word with Catherine in private, please?"

Mary gazed over to Catherine and sensed the look of horror. "Ben and I will be next door. If we hear anything untoward, we will be straight back in here." Mary stared at Jeremy. "I will not tolerate any wrongdoing in my house."

"Just remember this is *my* house, darling." Jeremy sneered at Mary, his eyes like buttonhole slits.

Alone in the living room, Jeremy sat on the sofa with his back to his intended. He patted the soft fabric, encouraging her to sit down next to him. "Tell me what happened, please. Why did you leave?"

Like being dragged through gravel, Catherine said, "They were surrounding you, shouting at you, pushing you, you fell to the floor. There was blood all over your head. Blood pooling on the church floor."

"Who's they?" He tilted his head to the side.

"Our guests. They were blaming you for everything that had happened."

"Our guests? What are you on about? Have you banged your head or sustained an injury?" He turned around and looked her up and down to see any obvious marks.

"Cornelius Binks, Sarah Silver, George Jones and all the others. They were swarming you. Cornelius kicked you as you were lying on the floor."

"I'm sorry, but I have no idea what you are on about." Jeremy patted the sofa once more. Exhausted, Catherine complied with his suggestion. He put his arm around her shoulders. "Where do you think we've been?"

"We were on Vicar Island, in Derwentwater, Keswick. You told me you were undertaking a psychological experiment, about life and death and happiness."

"Doesn't sound like the foundations for a happy story to me."

"Everyone was dying. We were in a beautiful house. You said there was treasure hidden there. The German miners, the monks from Fountains Abbey. There was biblical treasure hidden somewhere in the house or on the island."

"And did we find it?"

"No."

"You said, 'Everyone is dying'. Who specifically?"

Catherine stopped to think. This all sounded crazy. She recalled the day of Sam's hanging. The heavens had opened that day. She had been drenched by the deluge of rain. By the time she got back to Fernleigh, the chill had progressed to a fever. The fever had progressed to insanity and her confusion had resulted in her incarceration in the asylum. She dared not say anything else to confirm her delusions.

"Have you reported your findings to the police?"

Catherine remained silent but shook her head.

Relying heavily on his walking stick, Jeremy got off the sofa on his second attempt and proceeded to pace the room. "I cannot for the life of me explain how you happen to be dressed like a man, a pauper at that. You have delightful clothes over at Oak Bank Hall, so let us return there and we'll get your scruffy hair sorted with a nice warm bath. Mr Schubert can prepare everything you need." He continued to pace the room as he talked about their plans for the next few days until he was interrupted.

"I swear on my life you were bleeding. They were pushing you. You were on the floor. They were kicking you. There were splatters of blood ..."

Jeremy stood in front of her. "And as you can see with your own eyes I am in fine fettle: no cuts, no pain, no bruises, no swellings. My only concern is you."

Catherine slumped back in the chair and closed her eyes. "I'm so confused."

"There, there. We will sort you out. A good night's sleep in a comfortable bed will do you the world of good. We can call back here tomorrow morning to say goodbye to Mary before we set off on our travels."

"Where are we going?"

Jeremy tutted and sighed before saying, "Are you not listening? I told you only a minute or two ago before you rudely interrupted me. We are supposed to be heading to Cheshire to see my parent's. We are soon to be wed in St Mary's Church, Nantwich."

"I thought we were already married ..."

Jeremy was talking but Catherine could not focus sufficiently to take in what was being said. The grand house, the surrounding mountains, the rippling lake, the staff, the dead guests, the little dog. The vicar turning up in a rowing boat. Their wedding on the Sunday. Jeremy being attacked by the remaining guests. She had run away. The snow. In desperation, she had jumped in the freezing water knowing she could not swim. She had climbed in the boat and rowed to the shore. Being offered dry clothes. The train to Penrith. The train to Carlisle. Her walk to Wetheral. She wasn't crazy. Everything was so clear up to that point. But where was the dog? Lily proved everything! She had to find her.

Jeremy was encouraging her to stand. He was pulling on her arm. She sensed he was saying derogatory statements about her hair. He was poking fun at her clothes. He was adamant she was coming with him to Oak Bank. He was distant, his face was distorting with emotion, she could sense anger and frustration in his voice, but the sounds were muffled.

Her daughter, Mary, she had spent so little time with her since finding out her baby girl had survived. Over the past few years, Jeremy had kept them both so busy. She was sad that Mary could not summon the strength to call her 'mother', but time would bring them closer. Her priority was to her daughter and their special wards. The beautiful children of Eden Hill House. Jeremy was rich and required no help. He could fend for himself, whereas the little waifs and strays of Carlisle were really where her heart lay. A smile appeared on her face.

Realising his rants were falling on closed ears, Jeremy laughed out loud. "You really are insane. I cannot be part of this any longer. You can be the bearer of bad news. Tell Mary the funding to this madhouse will be withdrawn with immediate effect, unless you and Mary agree to cooperate with my demands." He marched over to the door, his limp barely visible. "I will see myself out. You either comply or die. Your choice, Catherine, *darling.*"

CHAPTER TWENTY-EIGHT

On hearing the front door slam, Mary and Ben rushed into the room and sat either side of Catherine, their arms wrapped around her shivering frame.

"What has happened?" Mary did not immediately get a response from her mother. "Please, we are worried about you." Another pause. "Tea always soothes the soul. Ben, would you mind bringing us another pot?"

"Of course, I'll be as quick as I can." He gently closed the door behind him.

"Catherine, I know we have so much to talk about our past lives and what is happening presently. But we also have so much to talk about in the future. I would love us to work together, for us to bring up these peculiar but wonderful children. They are truly a gift from God and need us in their lives. Together, we could achieve so much. You mentioned converting Petteril Bank House into a home for those children who are blind, or have deformities, or those who cannot hear. There are so many children living on the streets, struggling to exist, devoid of love." Catherine was staring into the fire. "Seeing you like this pains me. Talk to me, tell me how I can help, share your worries, let me hear your dreams. Please, help me out here." Suddenly, Mary cried out in pain. She pressed her hands to the right side of her tummy. She cried out again, catching her breath. She hauled herself up off the sofa, then supported herself on the dresser, still gripping her right side. Now breathing through pursed lips, she staggered around the room, trying to walk off the pain. Her dress was the darkest blue, with puffy sleeves and a wide base.

Catherine made her way over to her daughter. "First, let me help you."

"I cannot possibly tell you my news in your fragile state."

A rising sickness came into Catherine's mouth. Her beautiful daughter was ill and looked ever so pale. She had only just found her and now may lose her.

Jeremy had introduced them three years ago, but he always had excuses or extensive plans which, with hindsight, was possibly to keep them apart. Over the last three years, they had travelled to many exotic places, had explored remote and fascinating locations, had witnessed stunning scenery and had friended many an interesting local, but all she had yearned for was her daughter. Catherine had dreamed of spending time with her, helping her with the orphans, becoming properly acquainted, building trust, sharing every possible emotion such as joy, fear and anger, being there for each other having been denied the pleasure for eighteen years.

Mary groaned again but insisted the gentle stroll around the room was the most comforting thing to do. Catherine thought back to her time in the House of Recovery, the contagious disease hospital. She ruminated on possible conditions, tried to fit together the symptoms to form a hypothesis. If they had a working diagnosis she could help Mary.

On reaching the table, Mary placed her left hand on the polished surface for support, then stretched out her spine, trying to find a way to relieve some of the pain. As she rubbed the right side of her tummy, it became clear what was causing her pain.

"Are you with child?" Catherine asked.

Mary nodded her head.

"Is Ben the father?"

Mary shook her head, then tears welled in her eyes.

CHAPTER TWENTY-NINE

"I apologise profusely for what has transpired." Mary was now sobbing, struggling to stem the flow from her eyes and nose. Normally so composed, Catherine was shocked to see her daughter show emotion.

"You can tell me. I'm here for you as you have been for me."

Mary pulled out a dining chair and sat at the table, continuing to rub her tummy.

"Tell me in your own time," said Catherine.

Through pursed lips, Mary practised soothing breathing techniques.

A knock on the door interrupted them. In the circumstances, they had forgotten about Ben making a pot of tea. Concentrating on carrying the tray, it was only after he had placed the wooden tray on the table that he saw their faces and all he could muster was, "Oh."

"Can you give us a bit of time, Ben?" asked Catherine.

"Of course. I'll sort the children for bed. Some of them are getting a little irritable as it's way past their bedtime."

"Thank you," said Catherine, "and for the tea."

After Ben had closed the door, Catherine dared to asked, "Who's the father of your child?"

"Please do not judge me. Please have the courage and patience to listen to my explanation." Her face was blotchy and tear stained.

Dread swamped her entire body. Catherine instinctively knew

what her daughter was going to say.

"The father is Jeremy Fisher." Mary blurted out a cry.

Having had only seconds to prepare herself for the news, Catherine's stomach churned at this devastating turn of events. She waited patiently for Mary's explanations, trying desperately not to judge and place blame at this stage.

To fill the awkward silence that ensued, Catherine poured the tea, needing both hands on the pot to steady her trembling limbs. They sat there in silence, sipping their tea, until Mary summoned enough strength to continue.

"When you and Jeremy returned from Egypt six months ago, he announced that he had made plans for you to marry in December and that I had to encourage you to go through with the ceremony, as you were having doubts, as you frequently reminded him that your heart lies with Solomon." She sniffed and took a moment to breathe through her mouth as her nose was completely blocked. "He said if you did not marry him he would wipe his hands of us both and leave us to fend for ourselves. He threatened to turf us out of this house and make me and you and all the children homeless." Mary paused again as she reverted to the pursed lip breathing pattern.

Catherine wanted to respond but thought it best to first hear the full story.

"You and Jeremy visited the orphanage every day that week. Jeremy wanted to spend time with his son and daughter, as well as the other children. They were having fun and the children looked forward to his visits as he entertained them with magic tricks and kept them enthralled with his wild story telling."

Seeing her daughter shaking, Catherine put her arm around Mary's back and gently rubbed her shoulder. They sat for a few moments in silence.

"You were both so kind. If you remember, you and Jeremy went shopping in Carlisle and bought the children new clothes and shoes and toys and books and loads of lovely things. The carriage was full to the brim. The children could not believe their eyes. We were all so happy and thankful."

Catherine held Mary's hand.

"If you recall, you had a severe headache on the last evening and apologised for leaving early. You returned to Oak Bank Hall, but Jeremy said he wanted to stay a little longer, to see Angel and tell her about your next adventure. I remember him mentioning Transylvania and Vlad the Impaler." A sigh slowed her breathing. "Once the children had gone to bed, he admitted to having feelings for me. He said he had watched me grow from a miserable child to a well-educated and confident young woman. That I was a little aloof perhaps, but he liked that. He said I was 'a dark horse that needed taming'. He then concluded that my cold exterior was a front for a wild and wanton side and that he could set me free from my self-imposed restraints. As usual, I rolled my eyes and sighed at his distasteful comments. Until then, over the years he had been quite the gent with me, more like a father figure, helping me with the children and catering for their every need. He was always so generous, so kind and thoughtful, the children adore him. He then made more personal comments, such as how beautiful I was becoming. How life experiences were moulding my attraction. How my aloofness was alluring and that he so wanted to take care of me. To protect me. To love me as his own. I will refrain from divulging all the details, but with each rebuke from me he became nastier and more condescending. He started to ridicule me, cast aspersions and question my life's work. He threatened to withdraw all funding from the orphanage unless I slept with him. He said he would go to the authorities and accuse me of abusing the children in my care. When I argued the point and stated he had no evidence, and anyone with an ounce of sense would see the children are so happy and cared for, that was when he turned on you. He said he would dispose of you and that I would never see you again. He did not clarify what he meant by the statement but my mind was fraught with losing the house, losing the children and most of all losing you. I thought he would have you incarcerated once more in the lunatic asylum, like he did with Solomon or worse, that he would make you disappear forever if I refused to lay with him."

Catherine was raging. Blood was coursing through her veins. Her temples pounding with the rhythm. Her head felt ready to explode with the building tension. The sound of blood whooshing through her ears was deafening. "The man is the devil. He's pure evil. I cannot begin to think of words suitable for how I feel. I despise him, loathe him, hate him. He is despicable, he truly is a satanist. He thrives on depravity, on hurt, on pain, on control. I cannot find a way out. He has threatened me with the same. To keep Solomon locked in the asylum, to evict you out of here and make you homeless. He has threated to send the children to the workhouse. I no longer trust a word he says. He has been playing us both. No wonder he has tried to keep us apart."

"So where do we go from here?"

Catherine answered immediately, "We kill him."

"We couldn't possibly do that."

"We shall and we will."

"There must be another way."

Catherine took a moment to contemplate their situation. "You are now with child. I will do it on my own. I will find a way."

CHAPTER THIRTY

Through sheer exhaustion, Catherine had eventually fallen asleep on the sofa in the tower room of the orphanage, as far away from Jeremy as she could possibly get. Faithful as always, little Lily was lying on the floor close by, her tail wagging on seeing Catherine wake. This confirmed the island was not the imagination of a psychotic mind.

Just before midday, Jeremy turned up at the orphanage as if nothing had happened. He enquired about the children and conversed with everyone as usual. He was either aware of the atmosphere and was an extremely convincing actor or he was totally oblivious to the mood.

Demanding to be alone with Catherine, he said, "I've been thinking about what you said last night. We'll stay here in Wetheral a little longer as I can see you are still not quite yourself. I will task Schubert with tracing the staff and guests you mentioned yesterday. I would like a list of all the names, where they were from, or the jobs they did, anything to help locate them. It will be interesting to know why you came up with the names of people we supposedly met on an island. It upsets me to think of you worrying unnecessarily about strangers. I would like us to meet up, somewhere neutral, maybe Penrith, somewhere like that, and thrash out this theory you have. Above all else, I want to prove to you that all of this is, was, in your mind, and that we can hopefully avoid another long period in the asylum."

She looked down at Lily. The dog's head was lying over Catherine's slippered feet. The island must have been real. There was no other explanation as to how or why she had obtained a dog.

Under Jeremy's watchful eye, Catherine wrote an extensive list of the staff and guests on Vicar Island. Names, distinguishing features, locations, employment, what they had been accused of, and what had happened to the ones that had died. She wanted as much information documented as possible.

Jeremy said, "Thank you, Catherine. When we return to Oak Bank, Schubert will follow up on these leads. We will invite them to a party and you can see for yourself this has all been a terrible dream."

Lily was now lying on her side, stretched out in front of the fire, warming her exposed tummy. Catherine knew she hadn't imagined Vicar Island. Where else would she have acquired a blue Staffordshire Bull Terrier? Lily had been distraught at losing Daniel Watters. Since the day they had found him face down in the cold lake, the dog had been Catherine's shadow, barely letting her get out of sight. "And what if my thoughts are proven to be right?"

Jeremy laughed out loud.

"If I am correct, then it is you who is indeed insane."

He smirked, his lip rising in the corner, puckering his cheek.

"Do you really love me, Jeremy? You know my flaws. You know how I feel about Solomon. You believe my mind is unstable, that I struggle with determining what is reality and fantasy. Should we not postpone the wedding? That is, until I am well enough to proceed. I would be mortified if I was to embarrass you in front of your family and friends."

"Do not worry, my darling. I have loved you and your flaws for many a year. There is nothing you could say that would deter me from my destiny; to marry you and for us to be a family. Mary, Angel, Jonathan and the children at the orphanage. We can be one happy family."

"Then thank you for standing by me, knowing I am of rather a delicate mind and struggling to grasp life's complexities. I am most appreciative of your support."

"When Schubert has made contact with these so-called guests and staff, we can cast your worries aside and make promises of being husband and wife."

"Let's hope he makes haste, for I cannot bear to live with this uncertainty any longer. I would dearly like to clear my head of all delusions and feel content in a settled family." She smiled.

Within the month you'll be dead, and I'll take great pleasure in being the one to serve justice.

CHAPTER THIRTY-ONE

Catherine opened the curtains to a crisp blue sky and the ground blanketed in snow. The stillness in the air was comforting allowing her to hear birds chirping and the gentle flow of the River Eden below. Catherine had agreed to come back to Oak Bank Hall, rather than stay on the sofa in the orphanage which was becoming intolerable. In order to avoid staff and other guests, she had requested breakfast be delivered to her room. At five minutes past eight, she opened the door and there on the floor was a silver tray laden with a variety of food and most importantly, a pot of tea.

Carefully, she carried the tray over to the small round table by the window and gazed over the delightful countryside. The location was truly impressive. She sighed and proceeded to pour the tea. It was then she noticed the letter, neatly folded with a crisp edge, tucked away under the plate.

Dear Catherine,

In the limited time I have had, my contacts have happened upon a few of the people on your list that fit your descriptions. Lunch has been arranged for midday at the George Hotel, Devonshire Street, Penrith on Saturday 15th December:

Bernard Pratt, missing
Daniel Watters, deceased
Sarah Silver, attending
Cornelius Binks, attending
Thomas Worthington, untraceable
Luke Notts, attending
George Jones, attending

Eliza Hart, attending
Vivienne Kry, untraceable
Harold Arnold, missing
Madame De'Ath, there is a Miss Daphne De'Ath but she refutes being called
Madame
Cliff Dacosta, unable to attend
Theresa Franks, missing

Yours sincerely,

Mr Schubert

Catherine considered the list. From her recollection, Bernard Pratt was found dead in the maze, surrounded by vomit and foaming at the mouth. His faced was speckled with tiny red spiders of blood and his eyes had haemorrhaged from internal pressure. At the time, she had suspected poisoning, but others said he had been seen to overindulge on the food and drink on offer. The conclusion was he had choked to death, probably on his own vomit.

Daniel Watters was found face down in the lake. Unable to retrieve the body, it was unknown whether he had sustained any injuries. Whether he had tried to swim to shore or had been pushed in the water, no one knew for certain, so the conclusion was he had jumped into the icy waters of his own volition, to try and head for home, having struggled to integrate with so many strangers on the island. Schubert had him on the list as deceased. She wondered if the rippling water of the lake had carried his body to the shore and had been found by a passer-by. He had obviously been identified.

Sarah Silver was a petite old woman, with neat white hair and an infectious smile. In her seventies, she had always seemed so positive and spritely for her age. It was reassuring to see her name on the list and that she would be attending. She had always shown genuine concern for the other guests and had frequently been upset by the unfolding events on the island. But Sarah had lied about her husband, telling the other guests he had died when he was actually in the lunatic asylum.

Cornelius Binks was a banker. In his forties, his distinguished looks complimented his focused approach to the horrendous events on the island. When everyone was scared, he had provided protection. When everyone was manic, he had been a stabilising force. When some were missing, he had offered his services. Cornelius had been a calming influence on everyone.

Thomas Worthington was in his seventies but he did most of the manual work, bless him. He was the cook, preparing the meat, fish and vegetables and creating delicious meals. He did all the washing up and cleaning of the kitchen. He helped with general maintenance jobs on the island. Thomas also did all the rowing to and from the island. Catherine had to admit, this did seem a little far-fetched as he was so thin and bony when most cooks were well fed and carried excess weight. And why send the most elderly gentleman to row the guests to and from the island? Catherine was starting to question her recollections.

Next on the list was Luke Notts. He was the butler overseeing everything in the house. A pleasant man, he seemed to be everywhere, doing everything yet never seemed exhausted. Could that be possible?

George Jones, what a lovely chap. Always smiling and seeing the sunnier side to life. He was charming, a positive force, he always seemed happy, seeing delight in the simplest things in life. However, he wasn't as forthcoming as the other men. He was reluctant to offer his services as readily as the others. His hands had always appeared so soft. Catherine doubted he had ever toiled doing manual work. Jeremy had made him out to be a philanderer of the worst sort, abandoning his wife and child.

All the men fawned over the exotic nature of Eliza Hart. She was so beautiful and confident, as if she did not care what anyone thought of her. Catherine wished she had that confidence.

Schubert had written that Vivienne Kry was untraceable. Did this mean no one knew who she was? When the accusatory letters were read out, her partner had taken her own life. Maybe she had no one else in her life. Catherine racked her brain. Was it something Jeremy or a guest had mentioned or Madame De'Ath had found out at the tarot card reading? Something to do with Vivienne having a different name, or had changed her name. Oh, she could not think. One thing was certain, Vivienne had been found in bed, coiled into a foetal position, having slashed her own wrists.

According to the list, Harold Arnold was classed as missing. He had supposedly jumped from his bedroom window and had landed on the stone balustrading surrounding the sunken garden. There was always the possibility he had been pushed but compared to the other men, he was so strong and could have easily fought them off. Harry had always been a bit of a joker, not very funny, more like a sarcastic sense of humour, and seemed to give little care to the thoughts of others. But was this enough to want him dead?

Madame De'Ath was a dwarf with beautiful copper hair, green eyes and a sprinkling of freckles. Jeremy had insisted she read everyone's tarot cards when they first arrived on the island. On the morning of the wedding, Catherine had called into Jeremy's suite and found them in bed together. There was no way Jeremy could deny that encounter. Catherine could recall their features, the sounds, the smell, that scene had been etched on her brain, like a photographer capturing a moment in time, a negative still, an upside down world.

Catherine had to admit she had found Cliff Dacosta rather handsome. His blue eyes and speckles of grey hair contrasted against the dark tones of his skin. He was a serious man, as if trying to predict what was going to happen so that he was always prepared, always one step ahead. However, she admired his tenacity, he was his own man, could not be lead astray and she felt safe having him around. He could handle the truth when most people wanted protection from life's harsh realities. Shame he would not be attending.

The last person on the list was Theresa Franks. That poor woman, Catherine had found her hanging from the ceiling in the folly tower. She would never forget the image, another picture forever imprinted on her brain. The angle of her head, the colour of her face, the lolling tongue. Her poor family, something like six or seven children left to fend for themselves. Catherine recalled Theresa saying life was hard enough anyway and now the poor children were basically orphans.

Lily had been sitting patiently, waiting to be fed something from the delicious smelling plate. She licked her lips and starting whining for attention. Catherine lifted her eyes from the letter and saw the sad eyes looking up at her. "Sorry, Lily, there you go." She held out a sausage and the dog tenderly took the meat between her teeth. "Good girl."

So, Schubert had been able to trace most of the people on the list. The names were correct, being real people. They obviously lived in the areas she recalled. The ones who had died were confirmed dead, untraceable or missing by their loved ones. She knew she was not insane. The meeting on Saturday would confirm everything she knew to be true. However, what was Jeremy hoping to gain by making her believe she was mad? He said he loved her. On numerous occasions over many years he had pleaded with her to marry him. Something did not add up. He had an agenda and she would find out what it was. Until then, she would have to be patient and bide her time until she thought of a way to kill him and dispose of his body.

CHAPTER THIRTY-TWO

In the sanctity of darkness, all Catherine could think about was murdering Jeremy.

Watching him eat as he smacked his thin lips with pleasure at the delightful tastes was a sufficient motive. He would pass wind in front of her then laugh, even at the table as they were eating. Watching him breathe, and hearing the slight expiratory wheeze made her irritable. Her skin would crawl as she watched him go from charming to crazy if something fell below his high standards. She would shudder with disgust as he put his hand down his trousers, scratch his private parts, then sniff his fingers afterwards. She retched at the thought of his lustful indiscretions with other people and could still only surmise what he got up to with men. He would bite the skin around his long nails and spit the fragments onto the floor. Jeremy was supposedly a gentleman, whose family were acquainted with royalty. When in polite company, he pretended to be courteous, but his debauched nature would always surface given time. As the seconds ticked by, she detested him more and more.

Her mind could not rest as she considered different options as to how best to kill him and dispose of the body. There were the obvious methods such as stabbing or shooting but this could potentially require numerous slashings or shots before he died. It was not worth the risk as he could retaliate in that time. Anyway, the mess would be frightful to clean up.

A while ago, she had read a book which stated if you shoot someone in the head at close range with a small pistol, the bullet would be unlikely to penetrate through to the other side so there would be no explosion of skull or brains. If the entry wound was small enough, she could put some sort of pad over the opening, tie it in place and leave very little blood to stain floorboards or a rug.

A direct blow to the head with a heavy object would probably result in instant death but was not completely fool proof and sounded like she would need to put in effort, and she did not want to perspire during the act. She wanted to remain calm, lady-like and clean.

In the past she had read medical journals about arrows and axes piercing skulls and the victims walking around to seek treatment. For that reason, stabbings, piercings, blows to the head and shootings were crossed off her mental list. Anyway, she wanted him to suffer a slow and painful death while she watched.

Poisoning was an option. She could add a little something to his food or drink over several days and weeks so as not to arouse suspicion. He had syphilis and those close to him knew his sufferings. A slow poisoning would just expedite the gradual decline in his health. However, she discounted this idea as she could not wait that long. She would rather be re-admitted to the lunatic asylum than keep up the pretence of being his consort for another few months. She considered using a lethal dose of some poisonous substance, but that would look suspicious. And anyway, she detested the sound of retching, felt nauseous on witnessing someone vomit and smelling expelled contents made her feel queasy. Her stomach would surely spasm on cleaning up the mess. Poisoning would have to be crossed off the list.

The storm inside her head showed no signs of abating as her mind swirled with chaotic thoughts. She turned over, pluming up the feather filled pillow. A smile formed on her face as she imagined using his decapitated head as the ball in a game of croquet and would take delight in swinging the mallet.

She quickly brushed aside anything like pushing him in a river or pushing him off a cliff or bridge. If she were to misjudge the push, Jeremy could so easily grab hold of her and pull her into the devilish descent. No, that method was too unsure a kill. Even though his health was deteriorating, he remained physically so much stronger than her.

She sighed, struggling to create the most perfect of plans. How was she to kill him and dispose of the body without anyone knowing or suspecting a thing? Police were more astute these days. Post-mortems were being requested for suspicious deaths. They were cottoning on to murder and the disposal of spouses. They were searching for signs of foul play. They were noticing the smallest puncture wound for the injection of poisonous fluids. They were observant to burst blood vessels or bruising. They were methodical in examining the body for evidence of unnatural causes of death: scratches, broken nails, pressure, discolouration, unexplained trauma. Scientists were narrowing down the time, place and cause of death by considering: exposure, temperature, humidity, insects, rigor mortis, blood loss, putrefaction. Methods of detection were improving at an exponential rate. She had to outsmart Jeremy, the police and the scientists at every level.

Light was beginning to creep through the curtains and Catherine could hear birds singing. Sleep had evaded her the entire night. She would look and feel haggard for the trip down to Penrith to meet the so-called staff and guests of Vicar Island. Yesterday, Jeremy had insisted going through all her memories relating to their time on the island. He made her describe the house, the gardens, the setting, the church, the folly, and the people; all the things she had alluded to previously. She had recalled their wedding vows in front of the guests and that she distinctly remembered them signing the register. She even recalled the vicar's name: Reverend Robinson. He had said his name was difficult to pronounce so had suggested she called him Bob. She wished she had put his name on the list for Schubert to contact.

As they had walked down the aisle as man and wife, the guests had attacked Jeremy until he was unconscious on the floor of the church. Blood had pooled round his head, just like the lake around Vicar Island. Jeremy had been adamant that no such event took place and again had asked her to examine his head for signs of bruising or healing wounds. At the time she had decided not to argue with him as that would only help him confirm her delusions. He had reiterated that they were getting married on Christmas Eve at St Mary's Church, Nantwich. A hundred distinguished guests had been invited to witness their vows.

Christmas Eve, could she wait until then, marry him to ensure she would inherit his wealth, and then kill him in the January? Questions would be raised though, and his sudden death would raise suspicions. It would all look rather convenient for Catherine. Could she wait until February or March to kill him? The thought of tolerating him for another few months was unbearable. Christmas Eve and the 'official' wedding was just over a week away and that was hard enough to stomach. No, she needed to get rid of him as soon as possible and forfeit the money.

Whilst in Penrith, could she escape him for a few hours and return to the island to look around the church? If she was able to retrieve the evidence, that they married on Vicar island, she could kill him now and inherit his fortune. Accessing the island would be challenging. They had only rented the property, she would need a boat, and keys to open up the church. She had no idea which church Reverend Robinson was associated with on the mainland. In fact, she doubted he was even a real vicar. Jeremy may have directed the whole act as some sort of theatrical performance for some sick pleasure.

She could of course just mysteriously disappear, but how would she survive on her own with no family, friends or money? After eighteen long years of not even realising her daughter had survived childbirth, and was now expecting her own child, Catherine knew she could not abandon Mary again. Her parents, and to a lesser extent Jeremy, had lied about her daughter, denying her existence. They had kept Catherine busy and distracted her with other considerations. Now she knew why. They wanted to control her and keep her dependent and ignorant.

Mary was now carrying a child fathered by Jeremy, and conceived under threat of eviction and homelessness for her and the orphans in her care. Jeremy had threatened Mary that if she did not comply with his demands he would also dispose of Catherine. No wonder he kept them apart. He was playing one against the other. The man was despicable.

If her memory served her well, Jeremy had said he had bought

Petteril Bank House from her father but placed her name on the title deeds, so technically she could sell the estate and live on the proceeds. But then she remembered he had put in a clause that she could only sell it with his permission or if he failed to survive her. Which left her with only one option - to kill him.

CHAPTER THIRTY-THREE

The George Hotel, Penrith was chosen as a venue central to all of those invited. Derwent Isle House or Keswick would have been a more feasible option, but Jeremy was clear he did not want to influence Catherine's mind by taking her to what she was adamant was a familiar place.

The function room they had booked had understated elegance. Not palatial by Jeremy's incredibly high standards, but sufficiently decorative to add character and interest. The colour scheme was cream and sage green with a few gold touches.

According to Schubert's list, six people were attending. They had been promised a three-course lunch and fifty pounds to cover any expenses accrued in attending the venue.

Jeremy was on his second whiskey as they waited in the private dining room. "I can't stand people being late. Boils my blood when they can't be bothered to get here on time."

Catherine was sitting perfectly still, trying to supress the rising symptoms of her anxiety. Her heart was wild, her lungs squeezing rapidly, her mind less confident as the long hand of the clock approached the top. "It is not quite twelve. Give them time."

"I just want this over with. I should never have allowed this meeting to take place. I'm only playing to your delusions and encouraging dissent. I should have just said no from the start and —"

There was a knock on the door and in walked George Jones

with some hesitation on his face. Catherine recognised him immediately and could not help but smile. Relief poured cool water on her burning anxieties. This confirmed she was perfectly sane. By this admission, the alternative must be true: Jeremy was insane. He had sworn they had never set foot on an island in Derwentwater.

Her attention reverted to George Jones. His countenance and mannerisms were precisely as she remembered, and as usual, he was smiling. She assumed he was in his late twenties, perhaps early thirties. His flecked brown eyes were slitted by his convincing smile and the warm tones of his hair were a little wavy. He wore the same suit as he did on the first day at Vicar Island. Perfectly tailored to his slim physique, but the material was a little threadbare in places.

Jeremy offered George his hand and the men shook with gusto. They officially introduced themselves, which felt strange, and Catherine started chatting about the weekend's events.

"I'm so pleased you could make it, and I must apologise for walking away the other day without saying goodbye, but the sudden change in events had me desperate to leave."

Mr Jones' eyebrows dropped, "I'm not quite sure of your meaning but I would like to hear more. Sounds interesting."

Jeremy intervened, "Catherine believes she met you on an island in Derwentwater, in Keswick."

Mr Jones bowed in her presence, "To meet someone so beautiful would forever be etched on my brain."

"Are you denying our acquaintance?"

Mr Jones looked at Catherine, to Jeremy, and back to Catherine. "I think I may have seen Jeremy's face somewhere, in a newspaper somewhere … perhaps."

Catherine's lips pinched together. The men were obviously colluding in their mind games. They were trying to trick her into believing she was indeed insane. She would have to bide her time and play along with their preposterous joke. They would give the game away soon and would have to admit to everything.

Jeremy began listing all his endeavours with property and architecture, so Mr Jones could try and place why he looked familiar. Catherine's interest tailed off. Their plan was so boringly obvious. There was another knock on the door and in walked Luke Notts.

He wore casual clothes which were far removed from the slick butler uniform he donned on Vicar Island. His trousers were brown wool and he wore brown boots. He wore a simple white shirt underneath his black coat. As he walked into the room, he removed his flecked blue flat cap and it was then she saw the distinctive black hair slicked straight back with cream. His cool blue eyes contrasted against the redness of his skin. On the island, he had perfectly creamy skin, almost like porcelain, but Catherine surmised he had been out in the bleak wintery conditions and he was cold.

"Mr Notts, lovely to see you again." Catherine held out her hands, to which he held them, and they did air kisses left and right.

"You must be Miss Fawcett. Lovely to make your acquaintance. And I'm not sure why, but thank you for inviting me to this ..." he paused, "this luncheon event." He shrugged his shoulders.

"You do not recognise Jeremy, or George, or me?" Her eyebrows raised.

"Which one is Jeremy?" Luke Notts looked over to the two men who were chatting animatedly.

"The one with the stick is—" She stopped abruptly. "Never mind, please excuse me." She smiled politely and walked away, heading out of the rear door.

Jeremy noticed her absence, "Please excuse me, help yourself to the drinks on offer, over there," he pointed to a table. "I'll return shortly."

With his compromised gait, he marched as fast as he could to catch up with Catherine. He found her sitting on an armchair in a corridor. She had tears in her eyes.

"You've paid them to lie to me. I know your tricks, throwing money at every problem. No one will admit to knowing me. You said yourself you have offered them fifty pounds each for attending. They will play the game, of course they will. I admit. You win. The odds have always laid heavily in your favour. I was never going to be your equal. However, I have yet to fathom what pleasure you get from taunting me as you do. You lie and cheat and you sneer."

"Catherine, Catherine, Catherine. I have never lied to you. Haven't you always said I am the most honest person you know?" He looked down on her with his striking eyes. "You heard Doctor Wainwright say my honesty was going to be my downfall. I have told you about my indiscretions of the past, the illegal things I have done. I even admitted to having an interest in satanism and yet you still stand by me. We may be totally different, but I love you, Catherine. You are my world, and I truly hope I am yours. I want you to be well. Seeing you like this upsets me gravely. I am not playing games. I have not set this up. All this farce, this scheming you accuse me of, surely you can see this would be too much to manage, requiring so many people to be in on the act, and what on earth could I gain from all of this? Please, just come through to the room. Chat with these people and put your mind at rest. We do not know these people. I thought this would have helped. All you need to do is accept you were wrong, that I was right, and we can finally be married and live happily ever after."

"I'm sorry for all of this. I was so convinced—"

"Stop there, let's not go over this again. Come through, have a little tipple, settle your nerves and enjoy some delightful food. An hour or two max. I don't have the time or energy to be indulging in frivolities with nobodies for no gain."

"Fine, I'm sorry. Maybe I just need to rest. I didn't sleep last night."

"Not that I have seen one in the flesh, but you do resemble a panda today." He drew air circles around his eyes then winked at her. "But in my eyes, you are still the most beautiful girl in the world." She managed a slight smile.

As they walked into the room, they could see all the guests had now arrived. Catherine remained quiet, playing the doting fiancée, standing at Jeremy's side and only speaking when spoken to. Yet all the guests were familiar.

Eliza Hart was chatting with George Jones and Cornelius Binks. Her exotic skin tone, the elongated hazel eyes, the perfect curves, the flirtatious ease ... Catherine could not have made this up.

George Jones continued to smile.

Luke Notts' hair was precise, not one strand out of place. His mannerisms were those of a butler. He even offered to get everyone drinks and he was so fluid in handling the bottles and glasses. Her memories had to be true.

In her seventies, Sarah Silver's petite frame was dressed in a simple outfit, practical and warm. Her hair was as white as the snow that was falling outside the large window. She occasionally looked over at Catherine and smiled.

Cornelius Binks towered over the other guests as they conversed. His handsome looks, strong jaw, wide shoulders and speckled grey hair were heightened by his crisp suit and polished shoes. He was charming, confident and engaging, mingling with ease. Like actors on a stage, they all played their parts to perfection. They asked each other questions: where are you from, what do you do for a living, do you have any children, how do you know Catherine and Jeremy, do you know why we've been invited here today? It was laughable.

However, there was one person who looked rather nervous and out of place. Their protruding green eyes were ringed in white compared to their flushed face. Blotchy, red patches extended down their neck and on to their chest. Their chubby little hands were holding the wine glass. Madame De'Ath's copper waves of hair were level with everyone else's waist. Her eyes darted around the room, looking up at the guests and engaging in conversation, bar one. The woman could not bring herself to look Catherine in the eye.

CHAPTER THIRTY-FOUR

The waiting-on staff quietly and expertly served the food and cleared away the plates with little fuss. All three courses were delicious, and Jeremy asked the head waiter to compliment the chef. Everyone was now a little giddy with the numerous alcoholic beverages on offer and their bellies were stuffed to the brim. The conversation started to wane.

Jeremy grabbed everyone's dwindling attention. "Thank you for coming here today. I appreciate the letter you received was rather vague, so thank you once again for putting your trust in me and coming here at such short notice."

Everyone sat in silence, wondering what was about to happen. The lull predicted an upcoming storm.

"Sadly, my soon to be wife has difficulty working out the difference between reality and fantasy."

Catherine had no control, her jaw dropped open in complete shock at the words coming out of Jeremy's mouth.

"She spent many a year incarcerated in a shuttered room at home and in a pauper's ward at the Cumberland and Westmorland Lunatic Asylum. She believes each of you are acquainted. To be fair, from the list of names she provided we found you, so in a sense you do exist and not merely a figment of her imagination. However, how she knows you remains a mystery. She insists you bore witness to a series of murders." Jeremy paused on hearing shocked intakes of breath. He allowed the guests to settle before continuing. "The supposed murders apparently took place on an island in the middle of Derwentwater, Vicar Island to be precise, and she will not let this lie. She insists you and I were there and somehow instrumental in the orchestration of the weekend's events." He paused once again to down a couple of mouthfuls of whiskey. The guests were looking at each other with a mixture of expressions.

"To humour my fiancée, I have invited you here today to try and reason with the love of my life that she is merely confused. That she is nonsensical in her notions of brutality. That these gruesome deaths were all in her imagination, a play, all theatre, a nightmare that her fragile mind has created. I plead for your help in telling her the truth." Jeremy perused the room for support.

For a moment, everyone was completely silent, only the ticking of a clock on the mantlepiece could be heard. George Jones coughed, and someone's stomach rumbled.

"Mr Jones, are you well enough to speak? Please introduce yourself and reassure Catherine that her thoughts are purely the ramblings of an unstable mind."

"Thank you, Mr Fisher. I'm not sure what to say." He cleared his throat and then took a sip of wine. "I live in Carlisle. I work in an architect's office, helping out with the financial side of things, ledgers, orders, quantities, that sort of thing. I have only been to Keswick once before but that was years ago and I've no idea where Vicar Island is." He coughed once again and took another sip from his glass. "To be honest, when I first saw Mr Fisher I recognised him from somewhere but wasn't sure where. It was only when he mentioned he was an architect that I realised why I'd heard of him. I've never heard of his misses though. Mr Fisher, you're quite well known around the Carlisle area, you've been involved with quite a few building projects, I admire your work, sir."

"Thank you, Mr Jones. I appreciate your honesty. But to confirm, you have not witnessed any deaths, or been involved in any murders or seen people commit suicide."

Sarah Silver covered her mouth with her aged hand, her wrinkled eyes darting to the faces around the room.

"No, I've no idea what you are on about. I've been in Carlisle for years, never left the place, until today that is."

"Once again thank you, Mr Jones."

Catherine was flushed, her face burning with the humiliation of proceedings. They were blatantly lying their faces off. She could see it in their eyes, the lack of eye contact with her. The muted body language, the silence. The standard terms, vague responses, nothing of substance.

"Miss Hart, perhaps you would confirm who you are and whether you were on this island." Jeremy nodded towards the dark-haired beauty.

"I'm not too sure what to say. My father is from Bombay and my mother is from Glasgow but I was born in Cockermouth. As a family we have lived there for the last twenty years, since the day I was born. I have travelled quite extensively, in this country and further afield. I frequently visit Keswick and am aware of Vicar Island, it's the largest of all the islands in Derwentwater, but I've never been there. I have never heard of you or your fiancée, have never read anything in the papers about you, have never seen anyone dead or dying. Until I received the letter inviting me here, I was oblivious to your existence."

Jeremy painstakingly asked each guest to confirm their identity and asked them questions about the island, on whether they recognised Catherine or had witnessed any murders. They denied everything. The last guest to be questioned was Daphne De'Ath.

"Just the same as all the other replies. I've never seen any of you before."

"Your name is most unusual," said Jeremy.

With an awkward laugh she responded, "Ha, yes, I'm unusual in many ways I guess."

"I hope you don't mind me stating the obvious but we can see you're a dwarf. What do you do for a living?" asked Jeremy.

"I work on the train, sorting the letters. My father is a train driver, he pleaded with his boss to give me a job. I think they took pity on me."

"Catherine believes you read tarot cards for a living and that you are some sort of gypsy traveller of international renown."

Daphne giggled, "I'm special in many ways, but I have no talents for divination or anything mystical like that. Although I do get to travel quite a bit on the train."

"Thank you, Daphne." Jeremy stood at the head of the table and raised his glass. "My sincere thanks go out to each of you for attending this rather bizarre meeting. Hopefully, this afternoon's gathering will placate my dear Catherine's concerns and that we shall soon be married and be at peace. I have adored Catherine for over twenty years. She is beautiful, knowledgeable, feisty, and ... different. She is unlike any other woman I have ever met and for this reason, I wish to take her as my wife. I promise to look after her to ensure her health and wellbeing. She is truly selfless, looking after others in their time of need. In the past she has volunteered in a fever hospital, putting her own life at risk to nurse the sick back to health. She then worked in a funeral parlour, taking care of the deceased as well as their grieving relatives, again putting her own life at risk when dealing with the causes of death. She has then offered her services in a children's orphanage, not just any old workhouse with any old child, but an orphanage for children who are different. Each child is unique, overcoming physical and mental differences. My Catherine is truly special and she deserves to be taken care of by me. With God as my witness I will ensure this woman is blessed in so many ways. Cheers everyone."

The mood visibly lifted among the guests as they raised their glasses and toasted health, wealth and happiness to the soon to be bride and groom. Everyone except for Daphne De'Ath whose face was on fire, a ferocious red, yet her hands were white and shaking with intensity. In two torturous hours, she had never once made eye contact with Catherine.

Their words were irrelevant, their lies a side show, nothing more than freaks and clowns in a carnival. Jeremy was the ringmaster, whipping his minions into compliance. Catherine was the lioness willing to risk it all to protect her daughter and unborn grandchild. Jeremy had to die.

CHAPTER THIRTY-FIVE

"I swear, I will take great pleasure in killing Jeremy Fisher."
Catherine paced the floor.

"Please be calm. I have only just found you. Please refrain from doing anything you may regret. I would be mortified if you were then to be incarcerated in gaol for many a year, or worse, hang for your crime. You told me about my father, Samuel Thompson, how he was wrongly accused of murdering numerous people. How he was arrested and placed in gaol. How he was hanged in public for crimes he never committed. Please do not let history repeat itself. I cannot bear to have both my mother and father tried in a court of law and found guilty of murder." Mary Montgomery was as serene as a swan but would fight aggressively to protect her blood family as well as her adopted wards.

"But Jeremy has been blatantly lying to me, to us. He is playing with my mind. He is deliberately playing games with me and basking in my ensuing madness. He is finding pleasure in my discomfort. He is glowing with pride at how clever he is, thinking he has me completely fooled."

"And you are letting him win. Please maintain your dignity. Hold your head up high. You know you are right. You know you are not insane."

Catherine sighed, "Unfortunately, I am starting to doubt myself. On the island, on our wedding day, Jeremy was covered in blood. They were kicking him while he lay on the floor of the church, yet he has no blemish to speak of anywhere." She sat on the sofa next to her daughter. A pitter patter of tiny paws was heard coming down the corridor and Lily made an appearance.

"Maybe you just need some rest and recuperation. You've been travelling for many a month. You said yourself, you were exhausted. Maybe there is a little confusion there." Mary placed her hand over her mother's hand.

"Maybe I do have it all wrong. But Daphne De'Ath avoided any conversation with me. Why did she fail to look at me even once? Why was she shaking? Why was she so flushed?"

"The wine, perhaps? Maybe she was anxious about attending an event with strangers. Maybe that is her normal colour. Maybe —"

Catherine ignored Mary's explanations, following her own train of thought. "Jeremy has paid them well. They were all lying. I just know it."

"How can you prove it though?"

"They were exactly how I remembered them. I knew where they lived. Their mannerisms were familiar. Their clothes, their style, just as I recall on the island. I know I'm definitely not mad. For some reason, Jeremy is trying to make me out to be insane."

"I can well believe it. Sadly, I can now bear witness to his cruel and manipulative side. If you remember, he has deceived me too, forcing me to lie with him and bear his child."

"My dearest daughter, how could I forget." Tears welled in Catherine's eyes.

"Why would he do this though? What could he possibly get out of doing this to us?"

"It's simple, he's evil, he thrives on chaos and bathes in drama. He'll be revelling in seeing us squirm and playing with our minds." She took a moment to think. "Ultimately, I guess it is to gain complete control. For us to be at his beck and call. For him to totally dominate us. He'll get some sick, perverted pleasure from us being mother and daughter. I don't know. He's the one who should be locked away in the asylum."

Mary and Catherine sat in silence for a few minutes.

"I've made up my mind. I'm going to kill him. He is destroying us. Every life he touches he infests with a disease which festers, slowly killing the host. He is like a parasite that we need to eliminate from our lives, before he leeches every last drop of hope from our being."

"Mother, you can't kill him. We have already been through this before. I cannot lose you now."

Catherine smiled at her daughter. It was lovely to hear her say mother. "I can and I will kill Jeremy."

"But how? And where? And how would you dispose of the body? And how would you get away with it?"

"Don't worry about trivial things like that. Leave it to me. And anyway, I've done it before."

Mary nearly choked on her tea.

PRESENT DAY

Soo-Min played the haunting melody of *The Aquarium* whilst sniffing the essential oils on the back of her hands. Her mind drifted to a historical time and place, a completely different realm of reality. The speed of the present day slowed to a sepia form of life: devoid of colour, silent, looped.

"You call this the cosy room?" she said with an accent.

Jack replied with a crack to his voice, "We did … until we lived here."

Soo-Min walked around the room. "I see the nice man again, hunched back, small stature, pretty face, he sitting at the round table. Here." She moved to the chair nearest the fire and placed her hands on the horizontal back support. "A beautiful woman stand behind him. She wraps her arms around his body. They sad. Both have tears in their eyes. He turns, then stands. They embrace, they kiss."

"Is it his wife?" asked Jack.

"Hard to say, I don't know. They adore one another. I feel the connection." Soo-Min walks over to the door and her face distorts.

"Have you sensed something else?" Jack pulled out one of the dining chairs near the kitchen door and sat down.

"Another woman. She walk through the front door. She stand here, in the doorway. She see them kissing. She angry. Very angry. She wearing a blouse with a high neckline and a full skirt. Her clothes are stained. I think it's blood but hard to see, the colours are … what's the word … muted."

"So who is this woman, his wife or mistress?" Jack sat forward and placed his elbows on the table.

"Hard to say. But they arguing. They are … I not sure." Soo-Min placed her hands in prayer and inhaled deeply. The essential oils lubricating her mind.

Jack refrained from giving away too much information. Over the last few weeks, he had undertaken some research at the library in the Lanes Shopping Centre and Lady Gillford's House, Carlisle's Archive Centre, formally known as Petteril Bank House. He had information, but Soo-Min had reiterated a few times not to feed her thoughts until she asked.

"They argue. They now fighting. The taller woman, with the blood stains on her clothes, she pounces. She has a knife. She mad. Very, very angry. She slashing the man and the woman. Oh, it not good."

Soo-Min seems to wobble. Her face drains of colour and she steadies herself on the doorframe. Jack leaps from the chair and offers his arm for support. She sits down on the dining chair.

"The smaller, prettier woman who kissed the man, she now by the fire. She picks up the poker. Oh no!"

"What? What do you see?" Jack's heart was racing. He knew someone had died, for her body had been dumped in his pond and had been allowed to rot for over a century. But who was she? What had she done? The police had literally dug up his entire garden for answers.

"The prettier lady stabbed the taller lady with the poker. Her energy is draining. I see a bloom of blood. The stain is spreading. Her white blouse now dark. She has slumped to the floor."

Jack remained silent. This was obviously the body he had found in his pond. He dared to ask, "Have you any more details?"

Soo-Min placed her hands in prayer and did three exaggerated inhales. "The lady die here." Soo-Min walked over to the door and stopped. She pointed to the floor with outstretched hands. "They killed her."

"Can you see what happened next?"

Minutes passed before Soo-Min spoke, "They wrap her up then carry her out the house. They dump her in the pond."

Jack shuddered, an involuntary reflex, as if someone had walked over his grave. The police had confirmed there was a body in the pond, a woman, wrapped up, but hearing those words, confirming someone had been murdered in the house, his blood ran cold. Named the cosy room, it did not feel so cosy now, no wonder it always felt cold in there. Maybe Millie was sane. Maybe she was seeing ghosts, remnants of past lives ... and deaths.

"I sorry I not able to get names or be more specific. Does any of this make sense?"

Jack nodded his head. "It makes perfect sense. Thank you so much for clarifying things. Do you want to know what I know?"

Soo-Min nodded her head.

Jack recalled the day the police turned up at his house and started dredging the pond for evidence. He described the event, gloriously hot day, the smell of cut grass, the sounds of late summer. The police had uncovered the skeletal remains of a young woman. They did not know her name or how she had happened to be in the pond. They determined she was relatively young, probably in her late twenties, and had lain there for over a century. There were still some remaining skin and fragments of clothing, due to the peat and conditions, her body had been preserved more than usual.

"They couldn't give me a name or anything more concrete. There was evidence of bone trauma, so they concluded she had been murdered, suffering some traumatic event, and her body dumped in the pond. They knew she had been murdered, rather than falling into the pond as her body had been wrapped up." Jack knew more but he didn't want to say. Soo-Min had made it clear not to feed her information.

"The man and woman who killed her. They no live happy ever after. They sitting here and the man is arrested by the police. He innocent. I sense it. His energy too nice, I feel only love from him." Soo-Min eyes turned black. She looked exhausted.

"Millie and I found a newspaper from 1845. The headline was a Samuel Thompson had murdered multiple people, listing their names. But you are saying he was innocent of all these crimes?" Jack puffed out his cheeks.

"So very sad. He do nothing wrong. He a nice man. A gentleman. The woman try to kill him. He only protect his loved one."

Jack tried to hide his face as tears coated his eyes. "And the pretty woman? What happened to her?" He paused for a moment. Millie kept having episodes of sleep paralysis. She kept describing an evil man pinning her to the bed, drooling all over her. He was evil, corrupt, slimy, cruel. She detested him. Millie could not escape his sadistic advances. This didn't sound like Samuel Thompson.

"The woman who died, the woman in pond, she evil, she attacked them. But the pretty woman she ..."

"What, what do you see?"

Soo-Min shivered. Goosebumps trickled down her arms. "Oh no!"

"What? Tell me!"

"Something unimaginable!"

Jack's blood ran cold.

CHAPTER THIRTY-SIX

"Jeremy, I've been thinking about our wedded future and, well, I need to address a few issues from my past in order to move on. As you probably know, Sam left me his house in his will, and it has stood empty for many a year since his untimely passing. I am aware we have never discussed this, and perhaps Doctor Wainwright has divulged this information, but I had to visit the house before he would discharge me from the asylum. He said I had demons to exorcise."

Jeremy glanced sideways at her as he drank whiskey from his tumbler. He crossed his right leg over his left. "Go on."

"It must be well over twenty years since Fernleigh has been habited. The last time I visited, about three years ago, the house was in a sorry state of repair, and with your expert eye, I was thinking I may be allowed to renovate the property, with your permission of course, and use some of your labourers to help me spruce it up and put it on the market for sale. An end of an era for me and a fresh start for us. It would also mean I would have some money of my own, so I was not always relying on your kindness."

"You have everything you could possibly want, my darling. You only have to ask if there is anything you need."

"So, would it be acceptable for me to plan for the renovations? It would keep me busy and occupy my mind. Distract me from my thoughts. But I would really value your expertise and wondered if we may go there tomorrow?"

"But I have plans for tomorrow." Jeremy picked up the Financial Times.

"Please, indulge me, I have escorted you across oceans and seas and walked many a mile following your dreams."

"Our dreams."

She persisted, "If not tomorrow, then the day after. I would really appreciate closing this area of my past and moving on. I want us to marry knowing that everything is as perfect as it can be."

"Patrick can accompany you." He turned the large page and folded it in half for ease of reading.

"Your architect acquaintance or the carriage driver?" She received no reply. "Please, Jeremy, I want your knowledge, your experience, you have such a beautiful eye for design and your taste is impeccable when it comes to—"

"For goodness' sake, Catherine, I'm trying to read the newspaper."

"Please, just this one thing. You know I rarely ask you for anything. I'll be the dutiful wife after that. I will keep my distance when you are busy, but I shall be there for you whenever you need me. All you have to do is—"

Jeremy slammed the paper on his thighs. "Just shut up. Honestly, you do my head in at times. Fine. We shall go to this shabby run-down shack of yours, not tomorrow but the day after, and I will give you my honest opinion."

"Thank you so much! I truly am grateful. And please be reassured you do not have to arrange anything. I will liaise with Patrick about the carriage etcetera."

"Then leave me be. Please!" He picked up his paper, shook it straight, then hid behind the pages.

Catherine smiled. This time she would take pleasure in killing someone and imagined the headline news: Prominent architect missing!

CHAPTER THIRTY-SEVEN

The crisp blue morning was fresh with a sprinkling of ice on roof tops and gardens; a perfect day for murder. She detested Jeremy, despised him, hated him. He had tricked her only daughter into laying with him and now bore his child. For many a year, Jeremy had played with their emotions, had lied to them, had kept the truth from them. He had watched them from afar, but close enough to interfere with their lives. He was a madman, a control freak, and he would stop at nothing in his callous mind games. He craved the thrill, took pleasure in seeing them squirm. He fantasised about being a satanist and Catherine was convinced this is what he practised, revelling in the chaos and secrets he created.

However, there was an itch, something niggling her thoughts, a reason missed as to why he went to extremes to torment them. She needed to know why, needed to know his motivations, needed to understand his depraved ways. Closure was the only way she could recovery her sanity and free her mind from his clutches.

There were waves of excitement: nervousness, nausea, dizziness, exhilaration, fear. Her emotions were riding the stormy seas and her vessel was close to capsizing. Deep breaths calmed the undulating waters, the inhaled air helping her to stay afloat.

Three years had passed since she laid her eyes upon the decaying façade of Fernleigh. Sam's home, his dream, a beautiful fortress from the outside world. Her heart pained with the thought of Jeremy stepping over the threshold. Him being inside the house would feel like sacrilege, staining Sam's precious memory, inviting evil inside a once precious home. A house of quietus with bones buried in the garden. Maybe this was fitting. Sam had always protected her, provided for her, had died for her, and this house would forever hide her secrets.

Looking out of her bedroom window at Oak Bank Hall, she saw Frank Butterworth preparing Jeremy's carriage. Polished to perfection, the wood and metal mirrored the surroundings on this bright winter's day. The two horses were also groomed to perfection, clouds of exhaled air billowing from flared nostrils on this fresh morning. Muscular contours oozing strength, yet these beasts of burden were ready to submit to commands from a physically weaker species.

Catherine's mind was in a frenzy. She had told Jeremy she would arrange transport. She didn't want anyone knowing where they were going. Had he gone behind her back and liaised with Frank and Patrick anyway? An excuse was required to abandon the carriage and make their way to Fernleigh undetected. If escorted there, Patrick would wait outside, ready to transport them home. Alternatively, he may leave and return at a specified time, and then come looking for his master when no one appeared as agreed.

Jeremy could barely walk these days. He relied heavy on his stick to take the weight off his atrophied leg. A hike was not an option, the house too far for his infirmity. She would have to think of something soon. They were leaving in less than an hour.

Doubts crept into her mind. She still wasn't sure how she was going to kill him. She needed time and space. She was sure an opportunity would present itself once there. She sighed.

Her mind drifted to Solomon Smith. What would he do in these circumstances? Happy memories of him stealing the Dawson's horse from the field and them riding bareback into Carlisle. She had felt so alive, the wind rushing through her hair, so much air yet barely able to breathe as muscles rippled beneath her spread legs. Motions, driving forward, rotations, the rise and fall of the beast's back, working in synchronisation, three of them, as one.

That was her only option, to tell Frank Butterworth and Patrick Sims the carriage was no longer required, that they were instead only going for a walk around Wetheral and that they would be back soon. She hoped to God that Jeremy had not disclosed their intended destination.

Having spoken with Frank and Patrick, she was confident that they knew nothing about the morning jaunt to Scotby. They were preparing the carriage to pick up a guest from the railway station.

With a spring now in her step, she made her way over to the fields of Dawson's farm. On the way, she thought of available items she could use as murder weapons in Fernleigh. There were knives, the poker, scissors, blunt instruments such as pans and plant pots, something that could daze him and give her time to plan his death. Jeremy's health may be failing but he was still wiry, and his strength still surpassed her own. She had to be quick and effective, no second chances.

For the last few nights, she had dreamt of tying him up and torturing him, to make him admit to all his crimes, all the games he had played and why he had kept her from her own daughter for eighteen years. His cruelty knew no bounds. Then to force Mary to sleep with ... oh ... she didn't want to go over that again. No point in ruminating, the deed had been done and Mary would bear his child.

As far as she knew, Jeremy had two other children: Jonathan and Angel. Jonathan was mentally challenged while Angel was physically challenged. Catherine prayed for everyone's health, a safe delivery and healthy baby was all any mother or grandmother hoped for. Grandmother, she took a short, sharp intake of air. She had completely missed Mary's childhood, had been denied the pleasure of watching her daughter growing up. All that time, Jeremy knew her baby had survived but preferred to keep them apart. Oh, she was going to have to stop going over the same things, she was driving herself crazy. At least God had given her another chance in bringing up her grandchild. She had to be thankful for the small mercies.

She had no idea of time. It had taken her longer to catch the Dawson's horse than she had expected, and even longer to mount its back. She had to hurry, otherwise Jeremy would be complaining and could possibly change his mind. As she approached Oak Bank, he was waiting on the front steps of the hall.

He tutted as she turned the horse around. "All of this is for you, and you don't even have the decency to be on time."

"My apologies, please forgive my thoughtlessness." She imagined the poker passing through his heart, just as it had with Vicky, Sam's wife.

"I thought you wanted me to view the house and give you my opinion? My expertise is highly desired and expensive, yet you throw it back in my face to look like a harlot with your skirts raised and legs spread over a damned smelly farm horse." His nose wrinkled with displeasure. "A lady should be side-saddle."

"I desire your expertise. I'm grateful, truly I am. Just give me your thoughts on the house. Do we sell it in its current state of disrepair? Or would it be preferable to decorate, freshen up the interior with the help of some of your designers? Or do we—"

"You can stop there, I get the drift." He brushed his coat with the back of hand.

"Why are you so carnaptious?"

"Because you do my head in." He spread his middle finger and thumb to rub his temples.

"The whiskey or wine or beer or whatever it was you were drinking last night did your head in." Catherine lifted her nose in the air.

"Whatever." His nostrils flared. "So, what's with the horse?"

"It is for you. I recall how you loved to ride. You were so masterful and graceful, especially when bareback and the horse would always submit to your every command. I thought we could have some fun on the way."

"But why the old hag? We have perfectly groomed horses in the stables."

"Humour me, I want us to have fun. I stole the horse. I thought you would be proud. A little chaos here and there. Go on, be a devil. Ride with me."

"I would rather eat my own vomit than ride that filthy animal."

His lips descended into a scowl.

She sighed, "Do you really think we should marry? I would go so far as to say you find me annoying, like the scabs around your mouth. Always weeping, needing attention, you force a smile and they crack, making them bleed. A vicious circle of events."

She glanced at Jeremy. She could see she was goading him. His mouth was puckering, his top lip creasing with each writhing movement. She was just about to say something else but then refrained. She did not want anyone witnessing animosity between then.

"Please, I know you are a very busy man and to do this for me, well, I just want to let you know that I truly do appreciate your opinion on this matter. I want us to be close. We've never ridden together. I thought you'd like the surprise, the thrill of a ride." Praise would work. She knew he thrived on flattery.

With his teeth digging deeply into his bottom lip he managed to say, "Fine."

He limped over to the mounting steps and Catherine encouraged the horse to step forward to align with the top stone. Despite his physical limitations, he mounted with ease. As always, Jeremy took the lead and they headed towards Scotby.

As they trotted through the village, Jeremy noticed the small store. "Would you be so kind as to get me something from the shop?"

"When you were busy with your meetings yesterday, I bought quite a few items in preparation for our trip today: cleaning products, milk, tea." *And other things.* "They are already at Fernleigh."

"Did you buy any whiskey?"

"Jeremy, it's the middle of the morning."

"For goodness' sake, I'm a grown man, I do not need you to tell me the time of day." He demanded she go into the store and buy his requested items.

Minutes later, the door opened and she re-appeared having purchased a new wicker basket to carry the items.

"Some gentleman you are, leaving me to carry all of this."

"I'm not your servant."

"And I am not your maid, I'm soon to be your wife, Jeremy. Please show me some respect."

With a struggle she mounted the horse and within a couple of minutes, they were pulling up outside Fernleigh. The garden was overgrown. The once beautiful house was forlorn and neglected. Her heart fluttered as she remembered Sam's gentle ways, his tender heart and his mental resilience. He would have done anything for her. Tears formed in her eyes. He gave his own life to protect her from the gallows.

As they walked down the weed obscured path, Catherine tried to stem the flow of tears. She did not want Jeremy seeing her cry but the salty droplets reflected her sadness at his presence tainting Sam's home.

Ideally, she had wanted to arrive at Fernleigh around three o'clock, giving her time to do things and then with the fading winter light, she would have had time to dispose of the body under the cloak of darkness. But Jeremy had insisted ten in the morning was the only time. She had to concoct a plan.

As they stood outside the front door, Catherine searched for the key. Her eyes unable to focus for the salty pools that dwelled there and her hands were shaking so much she could not locate the cool metal.

Jeremy rolled his eyes and sighed. He stepped back from the front façade to take in the structure of the building. The sky was bright blue and the sun blinding, he shielded his eyes to properly take in the brickwork.

"I've found it," she said with animation in her voice as she held aloft the key. The noise and sudden movement spooked the horse and the old mare cantered off.

"You imbecile. Why didn't you tether it to a post?"

"Why didn't *you* tether it to a post? I'm carrying the basket. And anyway, the horse was unbridled. What would we have used?"

Jeremy tutted then sighed again. "Anyway, the structure of the house looks sound enough. There are no cracks, no evidence of subsidence. The roof is intact for now but the trees and greenery are starting to take over on that right hand side. You may want to consider cutting that back. The branches can start to damage the pointing, cause dampness, water ingress through the brickwork."

Catherine placed the key in the lock and surprisingly, the mechanism turned with ease. She opened the door to Jeremy's final resting place.

CHAPTER THIRTY-EIGHT

Catherine gave Jeremy a tour of the downstairs accommodation of Fernleigh. He was complimentary about the entrance and the beautiful oak staircase. He admired the colour and the pattern of the tiled hallway floor. He heaped praise on what had affectionately become known as the ballroom. The dimensions were pleasing. The orientation of the double doors onto the garden allowed rays of dust filled light to penetrate the windows. The herringbone pattern of the wooden floor added warm texture, the marble fireplace provided cool elegance and the furniture was pleasing to the eye.

As they crossed the hall, Catherine opened the door to the living room, where her life had changed forever. Suppressed memories of the body on the floor, the dark stains on the rug. The trail of blood as they dragged the body into the garden. Jeremy was talking but she was not listening. His tone had changed. She got the impression he did not like this room. Neither did she. She heard an occasional word, '... dark ... miserable ... cold ... depressing ..."

They headed through into the kitchen. "What a ghastly place. It's miniscule. How on earth can you hold a party here? Where would the cooks prepare the delicacies? Where would you store the plates, the glasses, the food, the drinks?" He opened each cupboard. "We should extend out into the garden." He had said 'we', he was planning for their future, up until now it had been her house, her project. He was seeing the potential. Pity he would not be around to see it come to fruition.

He spotted the key in the back door and went outside. The garden was a mess, but the white frostings added some interest to the overgrown greenery. He stood there, smiling, admiring the view beyond. "Not exactly an estate, but a fairly decent sized garden. The views over the fields are acceptable and the mature oak tree at the bottom of the garden is an excellent structural feature. Overall, I think it is a sound investment." He turned to look at the back of the house. "Pretty good structurally by the look of things. Just needs a spruce up, a thorough clean and some fresh décor. I'd say you'll get a fair price for the house."

They headed inside out of the blinding light and chilling air. Catherine feigned positivity. "I visited yesterday and in preparation for our visit I've brought a few things. The house has lain empty for over twenty years, so I brought fresh water, towels and brushes to freshen things up. So sit yourself down at the table and I'll pour you that whiskey. Then we can sit and discuss things." Had he sussed her intention? Her heart was betraying her, trying to give the game away.

"I'm not ruining my suit by sitting on those mouldy old chairs." Jeremy's nose puckered at the thought.

"There are dining chairs in the ballroom. I'll bring them through. I brought clean cloths, so I'll wipe the chairs down. Or I can fold a towel for you to sit on. Please, let me spend just a little more time here. Remember, Doctor Wainwright said I need to exorcise those demons."

"The place is damp, it's cold, it smells musty, let's just go." He continued to absorb his surroundings, a look of disgust on his face.

"Just a few moments, I implore you. I'll get the chairs and your whiskey."

Before he could answer, Catherine hurried to the ballroom and picked up two chairs, one under each arm. Chair first, she went through the door sideways with the second chair following. She dipped the clean cloth into the bowl of water and twisted the material. She then wiped the chairs over and dried them with a towel. "See, as good as new." She sat down and prompted Jeremy to sit on the chair next to her by tapping it three times. With his nostrils flared, he lowered himself slowly onto the wooden chair. He looked side to side. "Were these chairs swiped from a public house?"

Catherine refrained from a retort, "I'll get your whiskey then we can make a toast to our new life together, in holy matrimony."

She hurried into the kitchen and busied herself with the glasses. Jeremy detested fluff or smears on his glass. She held it up to the light and inspected it for imperfections. All good, it was sparkling.

From the wicker basket, she lifted out the whiskey bottle and opened it. After many a year entombed in the bottle, the fluid was allowed to breathe. She poured a substantial amount of the amber water into the crystal tumbler then hurried through to the living room. Jeremy gulped at the contents, the warming liquid disappearing down his throat. His face contorted.

"This is brandy, not whiskey." He stuck out his tongue and scrunched up his eyes.

"Oh, I didn't know. Sorry. I just bought the most expensive bottle in the store." She placed the bottle on the table next to his glass. Damn, how could she be so foolish as to buy the wrong thing. He was now in a foul mood, swearing under his breath. "I'll search the cupboards, maybe Sam left an unopened bottle somewhere. Give me two ticks." Scurrying back to the kitchen, her heart was trying to escape from its cage. It was now or never. She had to do something. He was threatening to leave. She had tried her best to make him stay but he remained restless. She had to be quick, otherwise he would be out of the chair and moving around. This was her only chance.

From the kitchen, she could see he was still sitting at the table with his back to her. With an insatiable thirst, he glugged the remains from his glass. He lifted the bottle and poured another measure. So much for detesting the taste.

Humming a tune to mask any noise, she checked the cupboards to find the heaviest pan. With a reinforced base, tall sides and long handle, she needed both hands to hold the metal object. Her vocal cords spasmed, her mouth and throat suddenly devoid of moisture. She was perspiring, her body on fire yet her breath condensed in the icy air. He was the shifting sands of the desert: hard to bear, insufferable, a void, unable to sustain life. She craved water but she did not have the time, not even a second to spare. He was her oasis. The mirage in the sands. She would drink from his passing and be satisfied from the fruits of her labour. She tiptoed from the kitchen and emerged into the cold, dark, damp room. Surely the beating of her heart would give her away. The pan was now raised above her right shoulder. She took in a deep breath. With as much force as she could muster, she struck him sideways on his right temple.

CHAPTER THIRTY-NINE

Jeremy felt as rough as a badger in a snare. The pain: his head, his neck, his arms. So stiff, so numb. What had he been drinking? Whiskey? No, he remembered talking about whiskey but couldn't recall its warming delights. Brandy, that was it. His head was pounding.

He tried to move but he was groggy. His limbs heavy and limp. The room was swirling. It had been years since he had experienced this sensation. Where was he? He couldn't even recall his location. It must have been a good session. He tried to move again but his body was disassociated from his mind. His limbs would not do what he wanted.

An angel's voice: distant, sweet, alluring. "Jeremyyyy."

He tried to open his eyes, but the lids were heavy.

"Jeremyyyy." In the darkness, the voice of a faerie: fluttering, teasing, genteel, magical. "Open your eyes, Jeremy."

"Am I in heaven or hell?" His eyes opened by a sliver. There was an orange glow on the left, possibly a fire, confirming he was in hell. His master beckoned. His eyes started to focus. Yes, a fire but he felt so cold. There was a pile of vaguely familiar clothes in the hearth.

"Tell me your secrets, Jeremy. I need to know everything." A whisper on the breeze.

"Who is this? What do you want?"

"I'm your nemesis, and I want you. Every. Last. Drop."

The voice was drifting from behind. He tried to turn his head but everything was so bloody stiff and sore. He winced with a spasm of pain.

"Have you realised what is happening yet? Do you see what you have driven me to do?"

"Put me out of my misery. Just tell me." Jeremy tried to move his arms. His eyes now sharp, he realised he was dressed in only his undergarments and tethered to the dining chair by ropes. "You've restrained me!"

"For safety. I will release you once you have told me everything, for there is something I need you to do for me." The angel's voice was getting closer. He could hear gentle footsteps approaching. A swish and rustle of skirts. The angel sighed in his ear. Despite the pain, the subtle warmth tickled his senses and he shivered with pleasure as her warm breath whispered in his ear. "Tell me everything."

"Fine, what do you want to know?"

Ghostly in the candlelight, Catherine glided past him and sat on the chair opposite. "Vicar Island. Why did you lie to me about what went on there?"

"I swear, I didn't lie."

"Bernard Pratt, Daniel Watters, Theresa Franks ... to name a few. Who murdered them?"

"No one murdered anyone. I told you. You aren't well in the head. It's all in your mind."

"Madame De'Ath, the little bitch. I saw you both in bed, she was riding you, on our wedding day of all days."

"You are seriously crazy. We are to be married later this month. Or we were. You'll be back in the asylum once I'm free from your pathetic attempts to imprison me." The ropes grazed his skin and he fought against his shackles.

"Bernard Pratt. He was in the maze. He had vomited. He had been foaming at the mouth. Did he die naturally or was he poisoned?" Catherine sauntered over to the hearth. She picked up the poker from its stand and placed it in the flames. "Tell me how he died!"

"Fine, he probably ate too much." His pupils dilated as he saw the poker glowing in the heat from the fire.

Catherine turned towards him. "Ah, so you admit we were on that island?"

"If you say so. I am trying to placate you."

She glided towards him; the poker held aloft like a magic wand. Catherine was smiling as she questioned him further.

"Daniel Watters. What happened to him?"

"Genuinely, I don't know. I've never heard of him." Jeremy was trying to retreat further into the chair, but he had nowhere to go.

Catherine laughed, "You always enjoyed experiencing new sensations."

Jeremy's eyes followed the poker as Catherine placed it on his exposed thigh, just above his knee. He cried out in pain as the heat seared his flesh, burning the dark hairs poking through the skin.

"Jeremy, this is going to be a long and painful night. And no one will hear your screams. Just tell me the truth."

"I really don't know anything. Catherine, please, just untie me, we can talk about this properly, back at Oak Bank."

"Daniel Watters, how did he die?"

"Fine, we were there. It was all an experiment. Just as we agreed with Doctor Wainwright. We were trying to learn about life and death and what makes us happy."

Coldly exaggerating every word, she asked again, "How. Did. Daniel. Die?"

Jeremy lowered his head. "I don't know. I wasn't there. He probably fell in the water."

Catherine sighed. "You bastard." She placed the poker an inch further up his thigh. The metal still hot enough to inflict pain and create the smell of singeing hair and flesh. She walked back over to the fire.

"You really are mad."

"Was he pushed, was it an accident or did he try to swim away to safety?"

"I don't know!" Jeremy was now sweating. His situation was not good. He was going to have to divulge everything, but this would leave him vulnerable. He would have to relinquish control. She was deranged. He could see it in her eyes. She was enjoying this charade. He had never seen her so animated.

"I'll warn you now, the poker is red hot." She sauntered back over to Jeremy before he shrieked.

"Please, wait, I will tell you the truth. I only lied to protect you. You killed them all, Catherine. You murdered each and every one of them. I have lied for you in order to protect you. Think about it. You felt sorry for Bernard as everyone was laughing at his weight and he was stuffing his face like a pig. You were the last person to check on him that night. Same with Daniel Watters. You protected him, you felt sorry for him. He was struggling with all the people. You befriended him and his ugly mutt. You were the last person to see him alive. You were seen wandering late at night with him, through the grounds, he wanted to escape the noise. He hated the noise. Remember how he would place his hands over his ears and keep his eyes tightly shut. He so desperately wanted to block everything out." Tears now poured from Jeremy's eyes. "I love you, Catherine. Please believe me, I would do anything to protect you. Everything I've lied about was to protect you."

Silence ensued. The tears tickled his face but he was unable to wipe the streams away.

He continued, "Same with Theresa Franks and Vivienne Kry. You consoled them. You talked with them. You drove them to their death. I'm not sure if you killed them directly or helped them commit suicide after talking with you about life's cruel inequalities and injustices."

Catherine allowed the poker to drop from her hand. "I murdered those people?"

Jeremy heaved a sigh of relief as he watched her slump to the floor. "I'm so sorry, my darling. I was trying to protect you. I'd rather you were in the asylum than hanged from the gallows for mass murder."

"I murdered those people?" she repeated.

Jeremy nodded. He lowered his voice, "Dear Catherine, I love you and always will. We can still marry. No one need ever know. That meeting in Penrith at the George Hotel. I have paid them well. They will never divulge what you did that weekend. We can move away. Start a new life elsewhere. A little medieval village in France or a fascinating city like Barcelona. Whatever works for you, my darling."

"But I can't remember any of it."

"We know you are not well, it's part of your condition. We know you teeter on the edge of sanity. Let us say the guests on the island committed suicide. We'll deny you were there. Yes, you were seen by the other guests walking with Daniel through the grounds of the estate, but we'll say you left him as he requested peace and quiet. Daniel then threw himself in the lake, but the icy water took his breath away. For Theresa, we know she would have needed help to hang herself from the rafters of the folly. We'll just have to say her death, her suicide, was inexplicable, and that if you are so desperate to take your own life, one will find a way. I'll describe how traumatised you were on being the one to find her."

Catherine was now sobbing. Her entire body shaking on hearing the truth.

Jeremy continued, "Focus, Catherine, we need to get our facts straight. Listen to me. Look at me." He waited for her to make eye contact. Her eyes were hollow, shadows of death circling the sockets like carrion birds. "I really do believe that Vivienne slashed her own wrists as she had a fragile mind and that Harold jumped out of the window, traumatised on finding Vivienne dead in her bed. We must believe this is the truth. We must sound convincing in case the police ever question us. Please be reassured, I will lie for you until my dying day." He regretted saying the last three words, in case they were perceived as a subtle prompt.

"But I have no recollection at all. I remember chatting with them but not killing them. I truly must be insane."

Jeremy knew he had to act fast. He couldn't keep bluffing his way out of the situation. She would continue to ask questions until everything made sense. His statements would not stand up to scrutiny and he did not want to lie with the threat of the hot poker. "Untie me, Catherine, please, I can see you desperately need a hug. I will take you in my arms and we can head home. Schubert will prepare a lovely hot bath for you, in front of a lovely glowing fire. You know I adore you and want to take care of you."

"No, I need to think about this. You've lied to me too many times, Jeremy Fisher. I cannot trust you."

She pulled herself up on the table and straightened her skirt. She wiped the tears from her cheeks and wiped her nose on her sleeve. "One thing is for certain. Vivienne Kry did not slash her own wrists." She placed the poker back in the flames.

"How can you be so sure? We all saw her. She was in the foetal position in bed. For goodness' sake, she still had the bloody knife in her hand."

"And that is why I know she did not slash her own wrists. The left wrist was almost completely severed. I examined her myself. The blade had passed through the tendons and blood vessels. Her wrist was almost hanging off."

"And your point is?"

"The right wrist was the same."

Jeremy squirmed beneath his roped bindings. "Maybe she wanted to make sure she would die. No half-hearted attempts."

Catherine laughed. She mimicked Jeremy's expressions of saying her name three times when he was in a condescending mood. "Jeremy, Jeremy, Jeremy. So clever yet so foolish."

"What, what are you on about? You're bloody insane." He wriggled his limbs, trying to escape the ties.

"Both wrists were almost severed through. The tendons completely cut. She would have been able to cut one wrist but not the other. It would be impossible to hold the knife with severed tendons, never mind slash her other wrist so deeply. Someone had staged her death. Placing the knife in her hand."

Jeremy blew out his cheeks. "Sounds plausible, I guess." She may be mad but she was clever.

Catherine examined the poker with which she had been stoking the fire. "Madame De'Ath, the dwarf. Did you sleep with her?"

Jeremy hesitated. He was damned either way. If he said no, she wouldn't believe him anyway. If he said yes, then the poker would burn his flesh once again. The pause was too long. He had to say something. "Don't be absurd, of course not. I love you."

"Lies are exhausting, aren't they?" Catherine strode over to Jeremy and pressed the poker an inch further up his thigh. She held it there until he screamed no more. The shock had momentarily silenced him as he was close to passing out. "I need the truth, Jeremy."

"She is a Madame in a different way. Daphne De'Ath and I became acquainted through a brothel. We have been seeing each other for years. She will do everything I say. Along with some of the other guests, she helped stage the deaths. The invite had warned them about taking part in tasks in order to receive the gift of one thousand pounds. I demanded some of the guests take part in a murder. Keep them on their toes, not knowing if they may be next. Everyone can be bought, for the right price. I enjoyed bartering with them. They feign shock, then horror, but if the money is tempting, they soon change their mind and come running back. By implicating everyone, it makes them keep their silence. They have been well paid. I gave them the gift as promised. One thousand pounds to start a new life elsewhere. They will not bother us again."

Catherine sat on the chair opposite Jeremy. She adjusted her skirts so they draped beautifully down to the floor. "Did anyone refuse to cooperate?"

"Vivienne Kry could not be bought, that was why she had to die. She would have exposed everything. I even tried offering the money if she stayed silent about my propostion. Sarah Silver was given the task of killing her and making it look like a suicide. Unbelievably, Harold Arnold could not be bought either. When I confronted him, he dived on top of me and was just about to punch me in the face. Luckily, Cornelius Binks was strong enough to stop him. They tousled for a while before we managed to throw Harry out of his bedroom window."

"So you assisted in his murder?"

Jeremy nodded.

"What about Cliff Dacosta?"

"A genuinely decent man. In his past he has been involved in some unscrupulous deals and participated in violence but has turned his life around. I was too scared to approach him. I respect his views."

Armed with this new information, she asked again, "So who killed Bernard?"

"Eliza Hart."

"And Daniel Watters?"

"A sad accident, I'm assuming he tried to swim to shore. There were no immediate plans for his death."

"Theresa Franks?"

"Luke Notts."

A gasp escaped her mouth, "So he was part of the plan too?" Jeremy nodded. "And Thomas Worthington?"

"Completely innocent."

Catherine threw some of Jeremy's cut clothing on the fire to feed the flames as well as four thin sticks of kindling. "The vicar, Reverend Robinson, was he part of this?"

A low, slow shake of his head.

"Why keep up the pretence of wanting to marry me? In fact, are we already married? We said our vows in the church, didn't we?"

Jeremy nodded his head. "I suppose we are legally married, although we have yet to consummate that bond. We could do that now, if you'd like?" He laughed. He had nothing to lose. He could feel the strength draining from him. A delirium was progressing.

"Mary, my daughter, said you forced her to sleep with you. Is that true?" Catherine stood by the roaring fire and held the poker in the angry flames.

"I did not force her. I merely suggested that if she did not comply I would leave you both penniless and homeless. She gladly opened her legs for me."

Catherine felt sick, with waves of nausea threatening to surface. "Do you know she bears your child?"

Jeremy could not hide his surprise. He had been laying with Daphne De'Ath for years and she had never fallen pregnant. He thought the syphilis had made him barren. "And I'm definitely the father?"

Catherine raged. She ran towards him, screaming into his face. She grabbed his hair and shouted, "How dare you demean by daughter. You have defiled everything. Everything you touch turns putrid. I despise every bone in your body. You will pay for this."

She inched further up his thigh with the poker, leaving wheals of burnt tissue in uniform lines until the heat dissipated from the rounded metal. She dropped it on the floor then stormed out of the room. She came back a few minutes later, carrying a basket laden with what looked like medical equipment.

Jeremy tried to shift the chair as Catherine was fiddling with the equipment. Squirming and wriggling were no good, she had bound him too tightly. He was now doing small jumps, trying to edge towards the kitchen door. His eyes were bulging with fear. He dared not think about what she was going to do with him. What would a surgeon do? Gouge out his eyes with a scalpel? Sew up his eyelids or mouth? His screams would be silent. Would she pull off his nails? Would she chop off his fingers one by one? His mind exploded at the thought of her chopping off his manhood. She was totally crazy, he knew she could do it, especially after he admitted to sleeping with her daughter. Christ, funny how he turned to God after all these years of fantasising about being a satanist. If there truly was a God, he needed to be forgiven of all his sins and ask for protection.

Catherine started humming a sweet song. A hymn, or some sort of child's lullaby. She was mental, proper crazy, but he could not blame her. He regretted everything. How he had treated everyone. His parents, how he had embarrassed them with his sexual deviancies instead of finding a wife and settling down. The mothers of his children, how he had used them for his sick pleasures, then got rid of them once they bore his child. The people he had used: for pleasure, for humiliation, for fun, for progress, a means to an end. He was a vile person. He hated himself. He knew he was the devil incarnate but now he had met someone stronger, more evil and more perverse than he had ever been. His flesh was tarnished, he had sold his soul to the devil many years ago with his hedonistic lifestyle and debauched nature. The pleasure had been slowly killing him over the years. The syphilis was eating away at his body. He needed forgiveness, to make amends in front of God and hang his head in shame.

He opened his eyes as he sensed Catherine approach him. She was carrying long, flexible tubing, a rather large needle and a bucket. She knelt at his feet and busied herself with her implements.

"What are your intentions?" He asked the question, but wasn't sure he wanted an answer.

"I am going to slowly drain you of blood, so as not to make a mess in the house, then chop you up into little pieces to make the disposal of your body easier. But first there is something I need you to do."

Lord, if you are listening, please help me.

CHAPTER FORTY

Catherine watched the colour drain from Jeremy's body. The blood flowing from a needle in the back of his hand, then along the flexible tube into the metal bucket. With all the excitement, his face had been quite scarlet, but he was slowly going through stages of pink to off-white.

Wishing to maintain a modicum of life, she clamped the flexible tube, hoping Jeremy would reveal the truth in his dream-like daze. Her eyes lowered to the metal bucket; she estimated a couple of pints of blood. Easier to carry this way, less chance of spilling the fluid contents.

His anger, the obscenities, the rage, all subsided as he faded into a mellow acceptance of his fate. He mumbled something about forgiveness, his love for Catherine and Mary, and his children.

"I demand to know the truth, Jeremy. Why did you lay with Mary? Why did you persist in your quest to marry me? You obviously detest me, so why go to all this trouble? Why go to these elaborate lengths to play with my mind and pay strangers to lie to me. I need to know."

He stirred. Life clinging by a frayed thread. "I needed to marry you," his voice a whisper.

Her eyebrows raised in shock. She was not expecting that answer. "Because you love me?" Maybe she was insane. Maybe she was completely wrong about his feelings for her.

A silent laugh, his smile and twitching abdomen the only signs of his amusement. "I needed to marry you for my inheritance."

"All of this was for money?" She paced the room, allowing

herself time to think. "You lied to me to inherit your parents' fortune when you are already so unbelievably rich through your own endeavours?" Her voice raised in question.

A subtle nod, "I also had to produce an heir to continue the family name, otherwise I would be disowned." His eyes struggled to remain open, his life draining.

"But you have Jonathan and Angel?"

"Useless bastards in the eyes of the law. My parents do not credit their existence. They refuse to believe I am the father, claiming the women who bore my children were whores. Tricking me into paying for their illegitimate bastards."

Catherine pondered on his words. "Why marry me though? You knew our relationship would never be intimate." A shocked inhale as she realised his agenda. "You marry me, then my daughter bears you a child which you pretend to be ours."

A weak nod.

"But you were handsome, wealthy, extravagant, masterful and exciting. Women were throwing themselves at you. You could have had anyone. So why me? Why all the pretence on the island: the strangers, the lies, the games, the money you have thrown at this charade?"

"At first you were a challenge. You are the only one who has never succumbed to my advances and that kept my interest. Women on the whole are either too demanding, or subservient, or dependent, or depressed etcetera. Then, for many a year you were classed as insane. The events on the island were to make you question your sanity. Within months of our wedding, I planned to have you admitted to the lunatic asylum and keep you imprisoned in solitary confinement forever, leaving me free to inherit my father's vast fortune in peace without being lumbered by you. Don't take it personally, I never wanted to be lumbered with anyone." His head seemed too heavy, lolling on his shoulders. The cadence of his voice slowing to a crawl. "Then six months later a baby would appear, and Mary would mysteriously disappear."

"I hate you!" She had planned to torture him, but sadly found herself being tortured by his words. Even so close to death and tethered to a chair he could hurt her. She did not doubt his words as this was the only motive that made any sense. For once, he had been totally honest and for that she had to be thankful, even though it hurt.

"I thought you a gullible fool … and I so nearly succeeded in my plan."

"You may consider me a fool, but you still begged me for help."

"When did I ever beg?" A hint of defiance in his voice.

"You alluded to treasure hidden somewhere on the island. You were oblivious as to what or where."

Devoid of strength, he managed to raise an eyebrow, "You found it?"

Catherine nodded, a smile forming at the right side of her face.

"Tell me what you have found." Catherine retrieved a piece of paper from her basket and proceeded to read out the words.

A Hunter's moon
Gone too soon
The crimson glow
The ebb and flow
On hallowed ground
A constant sound
Swords white
Armoured knight
A cavern deep
Chambers, no sleep
Sacred and pure
Broken, unsure
A precious stone
Of which to atone
Hidden there
A lifetime to bear
A labyrinth sure
Love the cure

"Where did you find this? What does it mean?" His voice was demanding but the strength required to enforce answers eluded him.

"Silly me. Stupid and gullible old me. A lunatic. Labelled insane. How could I possibly know the answers to your questions?"

He sighed, resigned to the fact he had lost his dominance over her. "Please, I did love you once. You know I did."

"What colour is a Hunter's moon?"

"I've no idea." The urge to drift into a peaceful sleep was strong but he fought to stay awake.

"Red, signifying the bated blood of the hunted or the thrill of the chase for the hunter. They bate bulls with bull dogs to enhance the taste of the meat." Catherine thought of little Lily and hoped the dog wasn't pining for her back at the orphanage.

Jeremy was struggling to concentrate, his life force ebbing away. "Do please hurry. I may be dead by the time you finish this story." He smirked. "I beg you to make haste."

He may be cantankerous but at times he was amusing. She shifted in her chair to sit upright. "The crimson glow is the Hunter's moon briefly illuminating the ebb and flow of Derwentwater. Hallowed ground: I assumed this could generally mean Vicar Island, or more specifically the church. At this point, I failed to understand the constant sound reference." She stood from the chair, seemingly unable to stay still. "Swords white and armoured knight perplexed me. There was nothing in the house, or folly, or church even remotely white. However, there are two suits of armour. One in the house on the first-floor landing and one in the folly. There were no white swords though, and when I searched the armour, I found nothing. No clues, no treasure, just dust.

"The poem then mentions a cavern, chambers and a labyrinth. When we thought we were stuck on the island when the boats were missing, or that possibly a murderer was hiding in the house or grounds somewhere, some of the guests discussed the possibility of a hidden cave, or underground tunnels, but the island is too shallow, the water lapping at the grounds depending on the weather. Again, I would have to work out the meaning of the cavern."

Jeremy was struggling to breathe, his ribs desperately trying to inhale air. Catherine poked him in the middle of his forehead. He responded with, "What did you do that for?"

"Concentrate! Your eyes were closed. Do you want to hear about the treasure or not?" Catherine stood in front of him, her arms folded.

"My eyes do not need to be open for me to hear you. Idiot." He tutted. Mustering as much strength as he could, he sneered. "Please do continue."

Looking down her nose at him, she slowly turned away to face the fire, repulsed by the pathetic creature he had become. "Sacred and broken. My mind asked what could be both sacred and broken at the same time. This was the crux to solving the clues. The only answer I could fathom was a heart. Something you would never experience or know."

He sighed with contempt.

"Working with the hypothesis of a heart, all the other lines of the poem started making sense. The crimson glow, blood red of the moon, the ebb and flow, the heart pumping the life force round the body. The heart at our core, a cavern deep, with chambers not meant for sleep. Chambers of our heart. Four of them. A lifetime to bear, a labyrinth, our blood vessels, arteries and veins, our circulation.

"If my memory serves me well, the bible quotes Jesus as saying something like, 'I am the way, the truth and the life', or maybe the light, something like that." Catherine shook her head and shrugged her shoulders. "Jesus is the cure; love is the cure. He heals the sick. Good always overcomes evil in the end. It all made sense."

"The white swords and armoured knight. What were they? Ivory, mother of pearl, something precious?"

"Precious indeed. The sternum, the ribs, the bony spikes of the spine, a cage to protect the sacred heart."

"How very clever of you, but I'm dying here, so get to the point. What is the treasure. Where did you find it? Time is precious."

"Tick tock tick tock." Briefly, she left the room to retrieve her black cape from the hallway. She flung the heavy fabric over her shoulders and proceeded to tie the black ribbon around her neck.

Lined with red silk, she retrieved an item from a deep, internal pocket in the cape. "In the church, where we married, so legally I am your wife and will inherit everything you own, I found a wooden statue of our Lord Jesus Christ, pointing to the sacred heart. As you know, the church on Vicar Island is very simple, with little colour to speak of. The only details are the textures of the beautifully carved, muted tones of wood. My attention was drawn to a distinctive splash of colour. The painted, blood-red heart of Christ. I examined the sacred heart and found a barely visible outline that revealed the hiding place for a precious stone to which you should atone."

"Just bloody tell me!" He gathered sufficient strength to hold his head at an awkward angle so he could see what she was doing.

Supinating her forearm, her hand held something small. Slowly, she opened her flexed fingers to reveal a blood-red ruby in the shape of a heart. "Isn't it beautiful?" Her eyes sparkled with delight.

He gasped, "It truly is divine. A sight to behold." A weak smile formed on his thin lips. His parched tongue tried to moisten the cracked sores. "And it could have been mine, if I had more time."

"When evil covets the divine, it is time for them to die."

Placing the gemstone safely in her pocket, she pootled along the hallway, checked the front door was locked then headed back to the living room. Jeremy was snoring, a weird sound to his breathing. His chin was on his chest. His colour putrid.

Disappointed that she had little time to torture him and see him suffer, she decided to put him out of his misery. With the needle still inserted in his hand, she removed the clamp from the tube and watched with satisfaction as his blood drained into the bucket. She was always surprised by how much blood the body held. As the flow ceased, she removed the needle, heated the poker in the flames, and cauterised the wound, just for fun. Jeremy was silent.

Feeling quite empowered, she daintily climbed the stairs to retrieve some bedsheets which were a little damp and mouldy having been stored in an upstairs drawer for twenty years. It did not matter though. It was only to protect the floorboards from blood stains.

She headed back to the room and threw the last of Jeremy's cut clothing on the fire, then added a couple more logs to keep the flames burning high. Every scrap of evidence needed to be eradicated.

With precision, she laid the bedsheets on the floor. She kicked Jeremy's shin but got no response. He was lily white; she knew he was dead, but it felt good to give him a little dig.

A completely pointless gesture, the first thing she did was chop off his limp ponytail which was tied low at the base of his neck. The scissors chewed at the grey strands. It took a few attempts to hack off the offending mess. How he used to stroke it with his long, pointy nails. Urgh … she had to stop thinking about the past. He was dead to her now, in more ways than one. A shiver ran down her spine at the hatred she felt for this beast.

Although singing wasn't her forte, she took pleasure in performing a few upbeat tunes to lighten the mood as she untethered Jeremy. She had tied his feet together, and then tied them to the front legs of the chair, to stop him from kicking or running away. His thighs had been tied down to the chair, to prevent him standing up. Rope had also been tied around his waist, to keep him firmly in the back of the chair and to stop him from sliding from his gaol. Finally, she had tied his hands to the arms of the chair, leaving him uncomfortable and limited. Learning how to tie nautical knots had served its purpose well. Her mother had never understood her desire to read books and progress her mind. This was an excellent example as to how reading broadened the mind and aided survival.

With the ropes removed, Catherine held onto his ankles and pulled. Other than the effort required to initiate the movement, his body flopped, offering no resistance as it slithered down the chair. Gravity assisted as his head bumped over the top bar and then hit the contoured seat base. Finally, his head hit the floor with minimal grace. Catherine thought she heard his skull fracturing with the force.

With a spring in her step, she headed outside to the garden and rummaged through the outhouse looking for a saw or axe in which to chop Jeremy into tiny pieces. Dampness was invasive, all the tools were rusty having been exposed to the elements for many a year. Jeremy was probably thankful he was dead. Momentarily, she froze when her eyes fell upon the saw, the one Sam had used to cut down the branch from the oak tree. The branch they had used to push her first murder victim into the depths of the pond that fateful night in 1845.

With the saw in her hand and a small axe wedged between her elbow and waist, she headed back towards the house. As her hand rested on the handle of the back door, her heart skipped a beat. Had Jeremy somehow feigned death? Had he really died in the chair? Stupidly, she had failed to check his pulse, assuming his ghostly skin tone was a sign of his passing. Maybe he was clinging to the flimsiest twig from the tree of life. How foolish she had been, leaving him alone and untethered.

She had drained his blood whilst he was sitting. Maybe this technique did not drain the blood from his legs and that life still clung to his being.

Trying not to make a sound, she closed the back door with stealth-like precision. Holding the saw in her left hand and the axe in her right, she stopped breathing so she could listen intently, but all was silent except for the occasional cracks from the fire. Creeping across the kitchen floor, she poked her head round the door frame, expecting to be ambushed by a furious fiancé. For the first time in his life, Jeremy was obedient. He hadn't moved an inch from his spreadeagled position on the floor. His pallor remained ghostly and his limbs leaden. Thank goodness.

Placing the rusty garden tools on the round table, she searched her bag for a scalpel and slashed his cheek with the glistening blade. No response, minimal seepage of blood, he was definitely dead. She sighed with relief and a smile appeared on her face.

Too heavy to carry his lifeless body outside on her own, she planned on chopping him up into little pieces to make the task easier to undertake. Memories of Sam flooded her brain. His handsome face. His calm manner. His gentlemanly ways. How he had protected her that evening. How he would have done anything for her, including taking the blame for Vicky's murder and hanging from the gallows.

Sam had been the one to suggest chopping Vicky into pieces, making the disposal of her body easier. With hindsight, after dragging the body from the house into the garden and then the struggle to throw her in the pond, she wished they had indeed dismembered his wife.

With her stomach feeling a little peculiar, Catherine focused her mind on the task in front of her: disposing of Jeremy's body. She intended chopping off his index finger as an appetiser. She prepared the scene, separating his fingers as wide as she could. She looked down on his exposed, supine body, imagining the blade of the axe whooshing through the air and landing with precision, a guillotine slicing through flesh. An image flashed in her mind, the floorboards sliced by the axe's blade, leaving evidence of foul play. She hurried to the kitchen to retrieve a wooden chopping board. This would protect the floorboards. She smiled at her foresight and ingenuity. She knew she was no fool. Throughout her life, everyone had dismissed her as some silly girl and had underestimated her abilities. Given time, she had proved them all wrong. She was strong, determined, wilful and focused. Tonight, she would once again succeed. There was no other choice. If she failed, the gallows once again beckoned. There was no Sam this time, no Solomon, and certainly no Jeremy to protect her. The responsibility was hers, and hers alone.

Repeatedly, she imagined the stroke, she would raise her hands in the air, take a deep breath and the blade would fall, severing his index finger. She had perfected the technique in her mind. It was time.

With her hands shaking, she lifted the axe into the air and inhaled deeply. She closed her eyes and allowed the blade to fall, slicing through the air with ease until the metal hit resistance and a sickening noise filled the air. The sound and sensation caused her teeth to ache, like a fork scratching a plate. She dared to open her eyes. Her aim had been a little off. She had accidentally chopped off his middle finger too, leaving two stubby mounds, but the axe had sliced through the bones with relative ease.

Reassured that she could do this, she moved the wooden

chopping board and placed it under his straightened elbow. She raised the axe above her head. The blade swooped and sheared across the joint line. Once. Twice. Thrice. The task was harder than she had imagined. With each blow, the reverberations jarred her arms, creating twinges of pain. Even in death he had the ability to cause her suffering. Perspiration was starting to form on her forehead and under her eyes. With hindsight, putting more fuel on the fire had been a bad idea. At the time she had felt a little shivery, probably nerves, the shock of what had happened. Never mind, she felt alive. Tingling, power, excitement, domination, she had never experienced these sensations in her life. Jeremy had opened her eyes to his sadistic world. A world of pleasure, with freedom of expression, with little moral thought for others. This was pure ecstasy, sheer intensity, a world of debauchery, the only limitations being the confines of imagination. A world without boundaries, or rules, or guilt or embarrassment. Bliss.

Having succeeded in chopping off his right forearm with the rusty old axe, she wanted to experience the sensation of sawing off his left forearm, although this sounded an arduous task.

Over the years, she had studied anatomy books and she knew joints had a space to keep the bones apart. As before, she placed the chopping board under his elbow and turned his palm upwards. Studying the soft fleshy part of Jeremy's left elbow, she noticed the line was on a slight angle. She closed her eyes and once again imagined herself undertaking the task, following the creased joint line as an indicator for the serrated blade.

The teeth on the saw were orangey-brown and not very sharp. She placed the jagged edges on the soft flesh and commenced the required forward and backward movements with pressure. She thought severing through the joint space would have been easier. The noise and textures grated her teeth as the saw's rusty protrusions ground through bone and gristle. She pulled longitudinally on Jeremy's wrist to try and create as much joint space at the elbow as possible. Damn, this was hard work. Catherine put down the saw and retrieved the axe. Five times she raised the blade before the forearm detached from the body. Exhaustion overwhelmed her. Physically and mentally, she felt drained. This wasn't as much fun as she thought it would be. Persevering, she alternated between the axe and the saw to severe his arms from the shoulder joints. Jeremy looked weird. Thin and … armless. Harmless. She laughed. Macabre but amusing.

To give her some respite before tackling his lower limbs and head, she decided to carry his body parts out into the garden and dispose of them in the pond. Surprisingly, the dismembered parts on their own were still a fair weight. With her right hand, she picked up Jeremy's left limb at the wrist, then curtsied to pick up the right limb with her left hand. How sweet, they were holding hands.

Catherine headed through to the kitchen and realised her hands were full, but she needed to open the back door. She placed Jeremy's severed limb under her left arm and his cupped hand rested on her breast. *Oh my goodness*, she thought, even in death he cannot waste an opportunity. She opened the door and headed outside.

The sky was clear, and stars twinkled in the darkness of the night. Her breath condensed in the freezing air as she exhaled. Everywhere was frosted white. Swinging her upper limbs with purpose, as if she was strolling through a meadow on a summer's day, she stopped abruptly at the bottom end of the pond, wanting to keep Vicky and Jeremy apart. Swinging her arms once more, right, then left, she threw his lecherous hands into the murky depths of the water, except the pond had frozen over. The limbs bounced rather than splashed. The freezing temperatures had solidified the unhallowed ground.

"For goodness' sake, give me a break!" she shouted, confident that nobody would be around at this time of night. Under the cloak of darkness, she searched the garden for a fallen branch and beat the frozen surface until the ice cracked. A dark pool loomed, a deadly grave. She turned the branch around, now holding onto the woody stem, so she could utilise the bare, spindly fingers to encourage Jeremy's discarded forearms to plop into the dark hole. This was going to be a long night.

CHAPTER FORTY-ONE

"Where have you been?" Mary hugged her mother as she stood on the doorstep to the orphanage. "After what you said, I was so scared something had happened to you."

Catherine was standing there, no reaction evident in her body. Almost catatonic, the only indication of emotion was a single tear which ran along the side of her nose.

"Please, talk to me."

Mary took hold of her mother's hands, and walking backwards, guided her through the hallway and into the sitting room. Mary positioned her by a chair, but Catherine was unable to sit. Mary gently placed her hands on her mother's shoulders and guided her down onto the armchair.

Jenny, one of the older girls at the orphanage came into the room and sensed the atmosphere. With eyes as round as saucers, she looked at the adults.

"Please do not worry, Jenny. Everything is fine. Can you be so kind as to make us a pot of tea? Ben is around, can you find him, please? He will help you make the tea." Jenny nodded and scarpered.

Mary let out a sigh. "Tell me what has happened."

They sat in silence. All Mary could do was hold her mother's hands and circled the back of them with her thumbs. Catherine initially did not move but then started to rock to and fro. Ben brought through a tray of tea and could not hide his shock when he saw Catherine rocking and staring into infinity, oblivious to his presence.

Mary poured the tea and gently spoke to her mother, telling

her about each of the children and what they had been doing the last couple of days. She could not help but notice the state of her mother's clothes, the raggedness of her hair and the filth under her nails.

Catherine did not touch her tea which was now cold. Her voice was so dry when she finally managed to say, "He's dead."

"Jeremy?"

Catherine nodded.

Mary sighed through pursed lips. She took a moment to prepare a response. "Where is he?

"In little pieces." The pounding was too strong: in her neck, her ears, her temples. Palpitations affected her breathing, an erratic fight for air. Bile was rising from her stomach.

"Where abouts? Did anyone see you?"

"You don't need to know the details. In fact, I need to forget the details." A metronomic rock back and forth.

"Were you injured during the …" Finding appropriate words was challenging. "Did he hurt you?"

Catherine shook her head. "I'm just so sore. My limbs ache, my head hurts. I feel exhausted, but he did not hurt me. Not physically anyway." She hesitated. "I don't want to talk about it."

"I respect that. But just one more thing, how are we going to explain things to Jeremy's family, Schubert, the people over at Oak Bank, the police, if they come asking questions?"

"Please do not worry. That has already been sorted."

Mary's mouth dropped open, "How? What? When?"

"Before I killed him, I made him write a suicide note. His handwriting may have been a little jittery but in the circumstances more believable. His words, his apologies. He clearly stated he would be jumping from Suicide Point into the River Eden a hundred feet below to be free from his pain and the syphilis that was cursing his body."

"Oh my goodness." Mary covered her open mouth with her hand.

"Before coming here, I visited Oak Bank Hall and gave Schubert the letter."

"If I may be so bold as to ask what else he put in the letter?

I understand completely if you would rather not speak of its contents."

Catherine sighed, "Jeremy wanted to explore the correlation between life and death. He hypothesised that a dying wish could be the key to a happier and more fulfilling life."

"And did he come to any conclusions?"

"To put it in simple terms, if someone was happy in life, their dying wish was for their spouse and children to also find happiness. That happiness can be found in caring for others, and that a dying wish was selfless, not selfish. They have righted wrongs, have lived their life to the best of their ability and made others happy. They found a balance in life which served them well."

"And if they were sad?" asked Mary.

"Then their wishes were selfish and contrary to the life they lived. If poorly they wished for health. If cruel they wished they had been kinder. If stressed, anxious or depressed, they wished they had been stronger. If lazy, they wished they had done more with their life. Regrets for doing something, regrets for not doing something, whichever it was, they wished for the opposite."

Mary gulped, "And did Jeremy tell you his dying wish?"

Catherine nodded, "He wished he had more time. Time to do the things he always imagined doing. Time to make amends to those he had wronged. Time to love and find patience for others and not think only of himself. Time to spend with his children, Jonathan, Angel and the one on the way."

A gasp escaped Mary's mouth, "You told him about the baby?"

"Let us leave it there for my mouth is so dry." She tried to run her tongue round her mouth but she was parched.

"I'll ask Ben to bring a fresh pot of tea."

She was only gone a few minutes but when she returned, her mother was asleep on the sofa. Mary picked up a throw from one of the armchairs, covered her mother to her shoulders then headed back to the kitchen.

"She's asleep, and maybe that's for the best."

"What's happened?" asked Ben. "She looks like the walking dead."

"I dare not say, but you are right. She looks dreadful."

"Is there anything I can help you with?"

"No, just being here and helping with the children is more than I can ask for." They smiled sadly at each other.

"You get yourself back through there for your mother. I'll sort the kids for bed."

"Thank you. I really couldn't manage without you."

"I'm sure you would, but thanks anyway."

Mary made her way back along the corridor and opened the door as quietly as she could so as not to disturb her mother.

For two hours, Catherine failed to move. On occasions Mary had to approach her mother to check she was alive, so shallow were her breaths. Then she started murmuring, a bad dream, as if she was trying to scream but a paralysis prevented the sound and movements.

The clock chimed and Catherine momentarily stirred. Briefly, she opened her eyes and fell asleep again. It was nearing midnight by the time she was sufficiently awake to sit up. She seemed in a daze, confused, not focusing on her surroundings.

"Hello, it's Mary. You're in the orphanage, you're safe."

"I've had an awful nightmare."

"I gathered." Mary moved closer to her mother and waited for permission before sitting next to her on the sofa. "You have two visitors."

Catherine's head twisted round like an owl sensing fear. "The police?"

"No, no-one like that."

"Then whom?"

Mary held her mother's hand. "Lily is desperate to see you."

"Little Lily, oh dear, I'd forgotten about her. Is she well?"

"She's loving playing with the children but pining for you."

"Oh bless her. And the second visitor?"

"Solomon Smith."

Catherine caught her breath, as if frozen. "Solomon Smith is here? Why?"

"I'm not entirely sure but he insisted he was staying until he saw you."

"How do I look?"

Mary tried not to show pity, "Take your time. He's in the kitchen with Ben if you want to freshen up. You can use my room. Take anything you like. I'll bring Lily up to greet you."

"Thank you."

Feeling so weak, as if her limbs were devoid of bones, she wobbled up the stairs to Mary's bedroom in the tower. The room was square and cosy with flowery dark tones of green and purple. There was a cream bird cage in the corner. The door was open, the cage empty.

Suddenly, there were strange sounds coming up the stairs. A scurrying, with nails scratching on the floorboards. The pitter patter of excited paws. Mary knocked on the bedroom door and waited to be called inside. Little Lily raced over to Catherine and smothered her with love. Wagging her tail and bending in two with excitement. The dog dropped to the floor and put her legs up in the air. Catherine tickled her tummy. "Oh, I've truly missed you." She looked up and smiled at her daughter. "I also mean you. I love you, Mary."

Mary hesitated, not one for emotions. "I love you too, mother." Tears made her eyes glisten. Now feeling awkward, Mary said, "I'll leave you to get dressed. Is there anything else I can get you before I go?"

"I'm happy now. I have everything I could wish for. Thank you."

Twenty minutes later, Catherine was at least presentable and felt a little steadier on her feet. She had washed off all the dog saliva and had cleared her nails of goodness knows what.

Why was Solomon visiting the orphanage at this time of night? He had said he was married with a baby on the way. He needed to keep his distance. She had to distance herself from him. The last thing he needed was to be acquainted with a murderer.

Mary was standing at the bottom of the stairs as her mother and Lily descended. She whispered, "He's in there." She opened the door and stepped aside, allowing her mother and Lily to walk into the room. There he was, perhaps a little pale, although it was winter and he was leaner than she remembered, but the warm golden tones to his hair, the smile and his love for her was still evident in his eyes.

"I'm so sorry," he offered, lowering his eyes to the floor.

"For what?" asked Catherine.

"For lying to you."

CHAPTER FORTY-TWO

Solomon was as bad as Jeremy. He was a liar. Had everything been a lie? Her eyes bulged at the thought of Solomon and Jeremy being in cahoots. Had Jeremy paid him off too? Had Jeremy paid Solomon to go along with the deceit, the mind games, making her appear insane to bring about her downfall? She felt faint. She felt sick. Could she trust no one?

"You lied to me? Why?" She sat down on the sofa, as far away from Solomon as possible. Lily sat down and rested by her feet.

"You caught me off guard. I wasn't expecting you at my front door the other night. You were in men's clothes. Your appearance confused me for a moment. It was dark."

"Is that all you care about? How I look? My clothes?"

"No, not at all. I hadn't seen you in three years. You left me locked in an asylum. You knew I was sane. You left me to rot in that rat-infested prison."

"I had no choice. It was Jeremy and Doctor Wainwright's plan. I had no say. They incarcerated you there. Not me."

"You married *him* after your hand was promised to me, and with no explanation." His eyes glazed with tears.

"They forced me into it. I wanted to explain to you. I asked to see you, but they denied my requests. They said if I agreed to their plans, they would discharge you and your father."

"I was in there for two and a half years. They experimented on me. They drained by blood. Used leeches on me. They deprived me, kept me in positions of torture, hoping to break my will and my soul. They tested new medications on me, I was sane and came out insane all whilst under their care."

"Solomon, I am so sorry, I had no idea."

"Didn't you even try and visit me?"

"I can only apologise for not trying harder. They promised me you'd be released immediately and foolishly I believed them. I didn't think you'd want to see me with what had transpired. I thought I was doing the right thing by protecting you."

They both sighed and sat for a while, contemplating what had been said.

"Are you well now?" asked Catherine.

"I can't sleep, but I'm as well as can be expected in the circumstances. You?"

"The same."

They sat in silence once more. "Would you like some tea? Tea always helps to settle the nerves." Catherine stood and Solomon reciprocated. He watched her walk out of the room and return a couple of minutes later. Lily was now by the fire, toasting her tummy.

"My heart was close to breaking when you left. When you turned up at my door that other evening, you were in such a sorry state, and now, you appear close to tears. Are you sure you are well? I'm worried about you, Catherine."

How her heart rejoiced at his caring tones. Hearing him say her name was a simple joy, something she had lacked in recent times.

"I have suffered so much and feel there is no happy ending for me. I seem to attract problems, challenges and grief. My time with you is truly one of the most special moments in my life. I miss your kind heart, your strength, your arms around me, your humour, your generosity, your support, your—"

He rushed towards her and held her in his arms so adoringly.

"But you're married. This cannot happen."

He kissed her so tenderly, taking her breath away by the softness of his lips. "I lied."

"About what?"

"I said I was married as a response when you turned up at my door. I was so sad when you left me to marry another. You abandoned me after everything we had been through. You left me in the asylum. There were moments when I hated you. Times when I wished I'd never met you. I swore if I was ever to see you again, I would completely ignore you, or stare at you menacingly, or—"

"Sadly, I get the gist."

"But when I saw you, all the sadness, the disappointment, the madness, the hatred all went away. I love you and always have. There has never been a day where I did not miss you or think about you, even though I pretended to hate you."

"And I feel the same about you. You have been in my thoughts every day, every night, imagining our life together and what may have been. I am so sorry for hurting you. Hurting us."

"Can we try again? Can we be together and get through all of this and put the past behind?"

A knock on the door. Ben appeared with the tray of tea.

CHAPTER FORTY-THREE

The morning of Christmas Eve, and a thick white blanket brightened the landscape. The rented terraced property overlooked St Michael's Church in Stanwix. Catherine closed the curtains, "Might as well stay in bed, it looks cold out there."

"It's warm in here though." Solomon held out his arms.

"I love being in your arms. Makes me feel so loved and safe. I cannot image life without you, Mr Smith."

"How about you open a present? It isn't much, with being in the asylum I have had little chance to earn a shilling. But what I have I give to you."

Catherine smiled, knowing she would soon inherit Jeremy's fortune. For months, she had been squirreling away Jeremy's money in preparation for her ever having to run away and hibernate for a while. For now, the sacred heart ruby remained safe in her pocket in a lovely velvet pouch. They would be financially secure for the rest of their lives. She would tell him about it soon. "Go on then, I love presents."

Solomon got out of bed and shivered. "It is bloody cold." He tiptoed over to his coat which was hanging over the chair where he had discarded it late last night. "An early Christmas present, for I cannot wait to give you this."

Totally excited, Catherine sat up in bed and rested against the headboard. She straightened the covers and prepared to open the small box. She released the red ribbon and rolled it neatly, placing it on the bedside table. The box was wrapped in a gold-coloured material. She lifted the lid. Her first response was to recoil in horror. Her second response was to cry. The third response was to rejoice at finding true love. Inside the wrapped box was the ring he had given Catherine three years ago.

"I know I have asked you this before, but will you marry me?"

She had to think quickly. She did not want her answer to linger, for the delay to appear like an uncertainty. The last time she had accepted his proposal, she had made a promise to herself to be honest with Solomon and admit she was a murderer. Would she have the courage to admit her crimes? Tell him her true nature, that she had now killed two people?

The first was in self-defence but the second was a cold and calculated kill. Pre-meditated, planned, perfect. No one suspected a thing.

She had to make a decision. Admit to Solomon she had already married Jeremy to inherit his fortune and had subsequently killed him or she had to take her secrets to the grave.

Solomon was a pauper, he had no money, living off the last little bit of savings he had put aside. The ring he had given her was tiny and tarnished. Oh no, she was sounding like Jeremy. The delay was too long. She could see Solomon was waiting for an answer. His eyebrows were raised, his forehead lined, waiting to find out his destiny. She had the heart-shaped ruby, she had Petteril Bank House, she had Fernleigh. They would survive, even without Jeremy's fortune.

"My answer is yes. I would love to marry you, Solomon."

They kissed lovingly and then Solomon got out of bed and danced a jig around the room.

"You've made me the happiest man alive." He jumped back into bed and held her in his arms. They kissed, the touches leading to an intense passion. He climbed on top of her and his lips started to kiss all the sensitive areas of her body.

She felt so happy, finding true love with a man who would love her for eternity. He adored her and would do anything for her. She just hoped he didn't do anything to make her mad or betray her trust ... Heaven forbid if he ever lied to her again ... the consequences of what she would do were unthinkable.

.

PRESENT DAY

Jack was astounded by the information Soo-Min was privy too. How on earth could she see reels of images from centuries ago? This was way beyond his level of comprehension. Fair enough, she couldn't see everything, it was not like Netflix or YouTube where she could just tune in and watch a clip of a movie whenever she wanted. Soo-Min saw images, a scene, sometimes just a still, a fleeting memory. She could not pick or choose what she saw. She couldn't ask questions or ask for names. It was what it was. Fascinating though, what a gift. She will be a fabulous crime scene investigator.

Soo-Min returned from the bathroom. She had washed her hands to remove the smell of the essential oils. "So now I told you everything I see. This man, he tied to the chair in this room. Then this woman, she torture him. Chop him into pieces and dump his remains in the pond. Why, I'm not sure. They seem as bad as each other. Not sure who good, who evil. I sorry I not more precise, but does it make sense? Do the images fit with what you and your wife know?"

"First of all, I would just like to say thank you from the bottom of my heart. Millie and I have been struggling for a while now. Not knowing what went on here. At least you have answered some of our questions." His hands were shaking with the revelations.

"So, I right?"

Jack nodded. "Back in the summer, I'd finished decorating the house and started work on the garden. I'd hired an excavator, to help me clear the garden as it was basically a wilderness. There were trees, shrubs, bushes, weeds. It was a real mess. I started digging out the pond. The bucket was bringing up all kinds of stuff, years of debris and decay. To cut a long story short, we basically found a body in the pond. Or that's as much as Millie knows."

"What you mean?" asked Soo-Min.

"When we found the body, Millie was there, in the garden so she knows about that. When we unwrapped the body, and realised what we had unearthed, we immediately called the police. They did an investigation, did an autopsy or whatever it is they do, and found out she was a young woman, probably in her twenties and that she had been murdered."

"That was the woman I sense in the cosy room."

Jack nodded, "What Millie doesn't know, is that when the police dredged the rest of the pond and other parts of the garden they found two more bodies."

"The baby and this man who been hacked to death?"

"Precisely." Jack puffed out his cheeks. "Do I tell Millie everything? Can you see into the future and tell me what to do?"

Soo-Min appeared sad, "I wish I could, but sadly I cannot see what to come."

"With what you have told me today, it all makes perfect sense. Millie has been in hospital, and everyone thinks she's mad. To be honest, I thought she was mad, but I know she isn't. She can really see these things. The woman walking the hallways. The sleep paralysis, this man fawning over Millie. She said he was evil. And she even said she could hear a baby crying."

"It all true." Soo-Min looked at her phone. "So sorry to rush off but my bus come in twenty minutes. I leave now in case it slippery outside. Snow still falling."

"How much do I owe you?" asked Jack.

"I no charge. My gift to you. I hope everything works out for you and your wife."

"Thank you, but how about a donation to your student trust fund?"

She placed her hands together and bowed. "Donations always very kind, thank you."

Jack checked his wallet and found two twenty pound notes.

"Buses are expensive nowadays."

They laughed.

"Thank you," she said.

He walked her to the door and watched her walk down the garden path and close the front gate. They waved and he shut the door.

Placing more logs on the fire in the ballroom, he sat on the sofa and shivered. What an experience. How a young woman from South Korea knew what had happened over a hundred years ago in Carlisle. Unbelievable. She was studying criminology and forensic science at university. Wow, she'll be solving crimes within no time. How amazing.

He took off his shoes and put his feet up on the couch. Poor Millie, what she must have been through seeing these sights. No wonder she felt the place was haunted. Maybe it was. He checked his phone. He had planned to visit her at her parents' house after tea. He felt awful that he had doubted her mental health but she was right all along. There had been ghosts roaming the house. Maybe Millie had a gift similar to Soo-Min. Maybe he should tell her what he had found out today. That three bodies had been found in the garden. A baby girl, a woman and a man who had been hacked to death. His body was in twelve pieces. His head, his torso, two arms, two forearms, two thighs, two legs and two fingers. Would knowing this help or hinder Millie's mental health?

Years from now he pictured the scene. They would have two kids, a boy and a girl. They would be camping in some remote woods. The kids would ask him to tell them a scary story. He would light up his torch and place it under his chin.

"I'll tell you the story of how your mam came to believe in ghosts ..."

That would never happen, Millie was barely speaking to him at the moment and refused to come back to the house. There was only one thing to do.

He did a search on his phone and pressed the call number.

"Hello, Simmonds Estate Agents." A cheerful voice.

"Oh, hi there, yes, I'd like to put my house up for sale ..."

EPILOGUE

Rain lashed at the spooky-looking orphanage set high on the hill overlooking Wetheral's village green. As lightning brightened the night sky, the girls cowered under their bed sheets, waiting for the expected rumble of thunder.

Along the corridor, in the boys' dormitory, Mark heard the girls screaming at the deep booming sounds. The world seemed destined to end. "Come on lads, let's scare the girls even more." His freckled nose wrinkled with impish glee.

"Any suggestions?" asked Willy, his wild red hair standing to attention.

"The ghost story of the armless man, that Miss Fawcett, I mean Mrs Smith told us about. Take ya arms out ya sleeves and put them down ya sides. Then twist ya body like this." He rotated his trunk left and right and the empty pyjama sleeves limply swung about.

The boys laughed. "Brilliant idea," said Seamus. His pale skin ghostly in the shadows.

Within seconds, all the boys were standing in bare feet on the cold floorboards, swinging empty pyjama sleeves.

Lightning once again filled the stormy sky, followed immediately by devilish thunder. The girls screamed again.

"Come on lads. Let's do it," reiterated Mark.

One by one they tiptoed down the corridor and stood outside the girls' dormitory. The girls were chatting, but the boys couldn't quite make out the specifics of the conversation.

Suddenly, there was a moan, followed by a scream. "What was that?" asked Willy, his eyes wide with fear.

"It's the ghost of the armless man!" cried Seamus. "Run for

your life!" Louder than the girls, the boys screamed and sprinted down the corridor, empty sleeves flapping as they returned to their room.

"That was freaky," said Mark.

"You're telling me," said George, his round face flushed from running.

Moans and groans then another scream. The boys clambered into bed and hid under the sheets.

Willy popped his head out from the covers, "The scary noises, they're coming from the tower. Maybe the armless man is murdering Miss Montgomery?"

The boys squealed in terror, their worst nightmare had come true.

Mary Montgomery had been in labour for more than seven hours. She didn't want to scare the children or cause them distress, so had silently suffered pains of childbirth, until now. The thunder and lightning seemed somewhat appropriate for the situation. The baby was now eager to make an appearance. Mary once again felt the urge to push and she grabbed hold of her mother's hand as a petrifying scream escaped her body.

Catherine mopped her daughter's brow, "The contractions are coming regularly now. The baby will soon be here."

Another desperate scream, Mary was obviously in pain and looked exhausted. They had read many books on delivering babies in the last few months. For something as natural as childbirth, there were so many complications to consider: breech, haemorrhage, cord strangulation, ruptures, the baby getting stuck. Catherine tried to put those thoughts out of her mind.

Rain pelted the windows of the tower, as if angels and demons were clawing for an advantage point to witness the birth of a special child.

Finally, after another forty minutes of pushing and screaming, a baby boy was born at midnight. Catherine wrapped the baby in a blanket and placed him on Mary's breast. The baby had a mass of thick black hair and was covered in blood, then Catherine noticed his nails. Long and pointed. There was no mistaking that Jeremy was the father ...

ACKNOWLEDGEMENTS

Thank you so much to everyone who has supported me throughout this amazing journey. As always, top of the list is my family, Stephen, Ethan and Orlissa. They make the long hours of writing, researching, editing and formating worthwhile.

To my family in heaven, Kenny, Ruth, Richard and Deborah. I hope you are with me every step of the way.

Mel Wright, my editor, has given me so much support and I thank her from the bottom of my heart for her input.

To my extended family, friends and colleagues within the NHS, you have been so kind with your encouragement.

And finally, to those who have read my books, sent me lovely messages, emailed me their thoughts, completed reviews and shared posts on social media, I could not have done this without you.

Printed in Great Britain
by Amazon

33618534R00139